"Is this some scam you run on the tourists? Tell them you're artsy just to score a date?"

"What? No," he said, but he looked guilty, and she seized on it.

"How long did you think you could keep it up? Did you assume I wouldn't talk to anyone in town about you?"

His face clouded over. "I'm sure you will. But as for being an artist, I am one," he said. "I just didn't mention that it's a hobby. I meant to, but we got to talking about other things and it slipped my mind."

She let out a skeptical huff, and he arched one brow.

"What?" she said.

"Just that I could say the same for you. Are you an artist, or a caterer?"

"Both," she said, hands on her hips. "I'm a food stylist, and I'm opening a catering business."

"A woman of many talents," he repeated his comment from earlier, with the same playful tone, but this time it registered as mocking. Or maybe that was just her own insecurities. "Look, I won't judge you for not telling me about your—" he paused "—art. We didn't exactly get into details last night."

Dear Reader,

Grab a picnic blanket because it's springtime in Orchard Harbor, a beachside town on the sandy shores of Lake Michigan. *The Fix-Up Feud* is the start of a brand-new series, and Maddie Briar has just arrived in town. She's focused on a fresh start with the launch of her own catering business and never expects sparks to fly with a handsome local, Jake Winn.

What started as a kiss gets a whole lot more complicated the next day when she finds out there's no such thing as strangers in Orchard Harbor. Maddie is learning how to chase her dreams and Jake wants the town to see he's a changed man, but neither of them is prepared for inconvenient attraction to turn their plans upside down. Good thing Maddie's two best friends, Celeste and Tasha, are by her side to support her as she makes waves in her new hometown.

I adore writing stories filled with laughter, hope and the transformative power of love. Discover more on my website, chandrablumberg.com, and connect with me on social media, where I share book updates and photos of my baking projects.

Here's to lake breezes and shoreline sunsets!

Chandra

THE FIX-UP FEUD

CHANDRA BLUMBERG

MIX
Paper | Supporting responsible forestry
FSC® C021394

Recycling programs for this product may not exist in your area.

ISBN-13: 978-1-335-18039-1

The Fix-Up Feud

For questions and comments about the quality of this book, please contact us at CustomerService@Harlequin.com.

Harlequin Enterprises ULC
22 Adelaide St. West, 41st Floor
Toronto, Ontario M5H 4E3, Canada
www.Harlequin.com

HarperCollins Publishers
Macken House, 39/40 Mayor Street Upper,
Dublin 1, D01 C9W8, Ireland
www.HarperCollins.com

Printed in Lithuania

Chandra Blumberg writes funny, heartwarming love stories about characters who feel real and relatable. Born and raised in Michigan, Chandra moved to the Chicago area after majoring in English at Michigan State University. When she's not writing, she enjoys lifting heavy barbells at the gym, making a mess of the kitchen while baking alongside her four kids and traveling with her family.

Books by Chandra Blumberg

Canary Street Press

Second Tide's the Charm
Love is an Open Book

Visit the Author Profile page at Harlequin.com.

For the friends who've supported me in big leaps and small moments and everything in between.

Chapter One

Springtime brings new beginnings, and Maddie was ready to celebrate a fresh start of her own in Orchard Harbor. When her friends invited her to their favorite local winery, she ditched her original plan to stay home in the quaint apartment she'd rented. She'd moved to this beautiful town on the shores of Lake Michigan to open herself up to new experiences and become part of the community. Unpacking could wait.

Tonight was the perfect opportunity to turn over a new leaf, despite an early spring rain shower that made her regret forgetting which moving box contained her umbrella. But the tasting room was packed, and she found herself wishing she could disappear in her friend Tasha's shadow as yet another person came over to say hello.

Under her breath, Maddie asked, "Do you know everyone here?"

Tasha laughed. "They all know *me*," she said with a flick of her wrist that sent her long twists over her shoulder. She hadn't changed much since high school, when she'd noticed Maddie moping on the beach with her parents during a summer break trip and dragged her into a game of volleyball. Over ten years had passed, but she was still outgoing and bighearted, with a way of making sure Maddie didn't stay hidden in her shell.

Celeste, the third member of the best friend trio, gave Tasha a playful nudge. "Hardly." She linked her slender arm through

Maddie's, the dainty gold-and-diamond bracelet on her wrist catching the light, and guided her through the crowded room to an open high-top table.

While Maddie was reserved, Celeste's powerhouse personality shone through in her career, where she negotiated deals for prime real estate, and onstage, in local theater productions. She'd always been the anchor of the group, ready with a well-timed word of advice and support.

"A lot of these people are just passing through," Celeste said. "Tourists. But if Tasha has her way, they'll all make a stop at her salon before they do."

"Says the queen of networking herself." Tasha set down their flight of seasonal wines and took a seat, her golden-brown eyes sending a knowing glance Celeste's way. "How many business cards have you passed out tonight?"

Celeste tsked. "We just got here." But with a glint in her eye, she added, "Not my fault the sommelier said her mom is looking to downsize." She didn't indulge in a hair flip, but for poised Celeste, the coy grin she gave them was as triumphant as a fist pump.

"Guess I'll have to learn your ways." Maddie climbed onto a high-backed stool and slipped her rain-soaked jacket off, glad she'd worn a sweater. The spring weather hadn't quite shed the chill of winter. "I've never had to go looking for customers." She did freelance work as a food stylist but had decided to take her years of experience in catering and open her own company, which meant getting comfortable with marketing.

"Clients, not customers." Tasha adjusted the wide collar of her brightly patterned shirtdress. Her move from Chicago last year and successful transition to self-employment after nearly a decade of working in a salon in the city were part of what encouraged Maddie to make the leap in her own career.

Now for the first time, all three best friends would all be calling Orchard Harbor home.

"Don't think of it as selling," Tasha continued. "Think of it as making connections." She was all about networking and knew almost everyone after growing up in town.

Celeste nodded. "In Orchard Harbor, there's nothing we love more than supporting our neighbors. And the out-of-towners come here for a unique experience." Her family had moved to town in junior high, so she was a local just like Tasha.

"Like your upscale picnics and charcuterie boards," Tasha chimed in.

Maddie hoped her friend was right. She'd dreamed of making this beautiful beach town her home ever since the first time she visited. Now here she was, moved into a first-floor apartment in a historic home a few blocks from the beach, with her name on the lease of coveted retail space downtown.

A toast was clearly in order, and for once she didn't regret putting aside her to-do list to get dressed up for a night out to commemorate the start of a new adventure. Once they'd each raised a glass of their chosen wine—dry, fruity rosé for Celeste, a bold, earthy red for Tasha and a chilled, bubbly prosecco for Maddie—Tasha opened Maddie's website and read aloud from her phone.

"'Here's to gathering with friends and family,'" she said, quoting the text from the homepage, "'enjoying a delectable arrangement of fine quality foods at the beach, orchard, vineyard, woodland trail, your own dining room or wherever your heart takes you.'"

Maddie made a swipe for her friend's phone, but Tasha held it easily out of reach, using her height to her advantage. Cheeks hot, Maddie clinked glasses and took a sip, savoring the sweet fizz of carbonation on her tongue.

She should be proud of the marketing copy she'd written, but with so many people around to overhear, the last thing she wanted was to be the center of attention. She wanted to fit in like any other local enjoying a night out.

Ever since the summer break trip to Orchard Harbor when she'd met Celeste and Tasha, she'd dreamed of moving to the freshwater coast. She'd grown up in a nice-enough suburb a few hours inland, but she craved the slower tempo and friendly camaraderie of small-town life. Not to mention being only a short walk away from her best friends in the world, instead of a long drive. But they'd warned her there wasn't room for anonymity here, and she'd need to get used to putting herself out there if she wanted to get her business off the ground.

Celeste was already using her network as a real estate agent to spread the word about Maddie's catering business, even though the property she'd rented still needed to undergo a full renovation. In between finalizing the menus, food suppliers and equipment, she'd need to keep an eye on the remodel to make sure things went according to plan. The thought of juggling everything made her head spin, or maybe that was the wine hitting her empty stomach.

A chorus of "Cheers!" pulled her back into the moment, and she smiled at her friends. "To new beginnings."

They all took a sip of their drinks, but then Tasha's phone let out a rapid series of chimes. "I swear, my family chat is no joke. I should mute it, but I'm always scared to miss something important." She glanced at the screen and let out a shriek.

"What is it?" Maddie was instantly on alert for bad news. In her experience, good moments didn't last.

"My sister's water broke." Her fingers, tipped with electric blue nail polish, flew over the screen as she typed out a response. "They're heading to the hospital."

"Isn't this a few weeks early?" Concerned, Maddie set down her drink.

Tasha nodded. The middle child in a family of five, she was an auntie already. "Izzy and Ben's first baby was a week late, so they didn't even have their bags packed." She shot Celeste an apologetic look. "I wouldn't have let you drive if I knew I might have to leave early."

"It's all good. No one can predict these things." Celeste was already putting her trench coat on, glass of wine untouched save for the sip from the toast. "But I hate to cut your celebration short, Maddie."

"No worries. You'll just have to come over and help me unpack to make up for it," Maddie teased. Maybe the night ending early was for the best. If she went home, she could wash off her makeup, change into comfy clothes and finish setting up the kitchen before bed.

A woman came up to the table, glass of wine in hand. "Not to intrude, but it looks like you're on your way out?"

"We are." Celeste slipped her purse over her shoulder.

"Awesome," the new arrival said. "A few of my friends are meeting me, and there are no open tables left. Mind if we sit here?"

"Have at it," Tasha said.

Maddie glanced around the bustling room, then back at the full glasses. Did she really want to head home early when tonight was supposed to be about new experiences? Not to mention sampling wines to serve at the parties she would cater.

"Actually," she said, summoning her courage. "I think I'm going to stay and finish my drink."

Both friends gaped at her. "You're staying?" Tasha asked, clearly surprised.

Maddie understood, considering she almost hadn't come in the first place, but she wanted to get out of her comfort zone.

What better way than this? "I'd like to finish tasting these wines." Turning to the woman, she said, "You're welcome to the extra seats."

"Thank you." She set down her drink. "I'm going to go tell my friends, if that's cool with you?" At Maddie's nod, she threaded her way through the crowd.

With the other woman out of earshot, Celeste looked at Maddie with concern. "How will you get home?"

"A rideshare. There are always plenty around."

"During the summer." Celeste tucked a strand of her long, black hair behind her ear. "This is still the off-season. You'll be waiting twenty minutes."

"That's fine. I'll request it ahead of time."

Her friends shared another quick look that had her bristling. She was perfectly capable of enjoying a night out on her own. "I got all dressed up, and besides, I'm a local now." She smiled, hoping she looked more confident than she felt. "You'd better get going. Let me know how things go with Izzy."

Tasha grabbed her clear umbrella. "That's my girl. Go all out tonight."

"Responsibly," Celeste added, and Tasha elbowed her.

"As if we need to tell Maddie to be responsible. She's the one always checking in on us, filling us in on the latest scams and fraud headlines."

Maddie bit her lip. She knew she was often over-the-top when it came to worrying about devious people, but she had good reason. It had been years since she'd lost her identity to a scammer, though, and she was here to start fresh.

Celeste gave Maddie a one-armed squeeze. "Remember to text when you get home."

"Always," Maddie promised, even though thinking of the apartment as home still felt weird. She hadn't met the other tenant in the house yet and wasn't even sure there was one, given the amount of sawdust on the stairs and hammering she'd heard coming from the second floor. Her landlord had mentioned ongoing construction, but the location and price had been impossible to pass up.

Tasha pulled her in for a hug, the herbal scent of her high-end hair products comfortingly familiar. "If you can't find a ride, let me know, and I'll send someone." It wasn't an empty promise. Between parents and siblings, cousins, aunts, uncles and grandparents, Tasha had at least a dozen family members she could reach out to in town to help.

"I'm sure it will be fine. Keep me updated about the baby situation."

"Trust me, there will be pics aplenty once the little guy makes his debut," she said.

Celeste gave Maddie one last concerned glance, but Tasha tugged her away, leaving Maddie alone at the table.

She took a moment to ground herself. She'd done it. Moved to Orchard Harbor. Started her own business. Made the decision to stay out tonight on her own, without the protective shield of her best friends. She raised her glass of prosecco in silent toast, smiling to herself, and caught the eye of a man across the room.

He was sitting on a wrought-iron stool at the gleaming wooden bar, his scuffed boots, worn jeans and faded flannel shirt a stark contrast with the elegant surroundings. A good contrast, like a sip of hot, strong coffee on a cold morning. He seemed about her own age, late twenties. Tall and long-limbed, he made the barstool look small in comparison to his large frame.

When their gazes locked, his eyes sparked with interest, and he raised his glass in salute before lifting it to his lips. Taking a drink, his face pulled into a grimace, nose wrinkled, dark blond brows pinched together.

She chuckled at the transformation, and he gave her a self-deprecating grin, as if he'd caught her laughing and didn't mind.

The guy working behind the bar said something to him, and he turned, revealing a broad back and muscular shoulders. Maddie was glad her friends had already left, otherwise they would have definitely called her out for staring. She had more important things to think about than handsome strangers, especially when no one in Orchard Harbor was ever really a stranger.

Maybe in a few years she'd have time for romance. Tonight was for celebrating being brave enough to finally make this move. For herself and her future.

Jake wasn't a fan of wine. The taste wasn't his favorite, but it was more than that. There was a whole fussy ritual for drinking it. First you had to find a corkscrew. Those couldn't be carried around on keychains like a bottle opener. Then you had to use a glass. And not just any glass; it had to be the right shape to match the wine.

And don't get him started on the temperature. He'd once put a date's red wine to chill in the fridge, and she'd declared the evening over then and there. Beer was simple. Pop the top, drink it cold from the bottle. The perfect no-fuss way to end a workday.

But he wasn't here for the wine; he was here to support his older brother, Andy. The Winn brothers had both endured their share of hardship, but Jake felt responsible for how his bad choices had made life harder for Andy. His brother had been a senior when the bottom fell out of their family, and Andy had gone from oldest son to surrogate father. His straight-A grades plummeted with the extra work of caring for Jake, and he'd lost the valedictorian spot. Instead of going to school out-of-state like he'd planned, he opted for a less expensive community college close to home, where he could keep an eye on Jake. Not that it helped much, back then.

Jake had been angry and rebelled against any attempts to set him on the right path. But he'd turned his life around, thanks to Andy, their mom, Donna, and all the other people in town who never gave up on him. Even in his darker days, he'd never once considered leaving. Orchard Harbor was home, no matter what. People here had stuck by him, and he was doing his best to live up to their faith in him.

He took another tentative drink and bit back a grimace when his brother caught his eye. Andy laughed, seeing through his bullshit. He tried to recall what he was supposed to be tasting. Oak? More suitable for flooring than a drink. All he tasted was sour grapes. His mouth puckered as he forced down the swallow.

He glanced guiltily over his shoulder, wondering if he'd been caught again by the beautiful woman sitting by herself in the corner. She was still there, but she wasn't alone anymore. A group of people had gathered around her.

Friends of hers, he guessed. But when he chanced another look a few minutes later, unable to resist catching another glimpse of those adorable dimples he'd noticed when she smiled at him earlier, he realized the others were talking loudly with each other but ignoring her. Several of them even had their backs to her, crowding her space. All it took was a quick glance around at the full room to figure out what was going on. The place was so crowded that strangers had taken over her table.

The guy sitting next to her gestured wildly, bumping her arm. Wine sloshed out of her glass, and she let out a yelp.

That was enough. Without thinking things through, Jake leaned over the bar and grabbed a rag.

His brother frowned. "Hey, that's my job."

"I've got it," Jake said, already on the way to where the woman sat. By the time he reached the table, she was blotting the spill with tissues from a to-go pack. She clearly didn't need his help, but he hated that she'd been muscled out of her spot. She deserved the chance to have a drink in peace.

"Here, let me." He picked up the soggy tissues and wiped the table. As he did so, someone behind him knocked into his arm, and he gritted his teeth, annoyed. "You didn't have to let them take over. You were here first."

"It's okay," she said. "My friends left, so I didn't need the seats."

"Neither did they. There's a whole other room, and unless there's a private event, I bet there are at least a few tables open."

"I'll keep that in mind for next time," she said. "Do you work here, or…?" Her gaze drifted between the dishcloth and his abandoned wineglass at the bar.

"I wasn't drinking on the job, if that's what you're asking." He grinned and lifted his chin toward where Andy stood pouring wine. "My brother is the new sommelier." His tongue tripped over the unfamiliar word, but she didn't seem to notice.

"Ah, I see." Her eyes flicked toward Andy, probably noticing the similarities. Both of them were tall, with shaggy dark blond hair, but his brother was wiry, slender like their mom. Jake had a stockier build thanks to his dad's side of the family and years of construction work.

"Well, thank you." She gave him a small smile and slid down from the stool. The moment she did, the person standing next to her pulled it over and sat down without bothering to ask. She met his eyes with a grimace. "I think that's my cue to leave."

"Tourists." He couldn't help muttering the word.

"What?" She looked up at him with concern, like she might've said something wrong, and it caught at his chest.

He leaned closer. "Would you like another drink? On the house," he added, when she looked uncertain.

Her lips tipped up in a shy smile. "I thought you didn't work here."

"My brother owes me one," he said. Even though he'd given Andy his share of gray hairs over the years, he'd also recently helped him convert his unfinished basement into two bedrooms and a bathroom, free of charge.

"Okay. I'll have the blackberry wine. That's the one I didn't get to try," she said with a regretful glance at the table where her drink had been spilled.

"Blackberry, got it." He carried the rag back to the bar, and she took a seat next to him.

Under the watchful eye of the sommelier who'd trained him for the job, Andy finished serving a group of people and stepped over with a smile. "Hey, didn't I see you here earlier with Tasha and Celeste?"

"Yeah," she said. "They left because Tasha's sister is in labor."

"I thought Izzy's baby wasn't due for another month," Jake said.

The woman glanced between him and Andy. "You guys know her?"

His brother chuckled. "Everyone knows the Grant family."

"We grew up hanging out with Anton and Miles. Tasha, too, when she felt like putting up with her brothers," he added with a grin.

"Everyone seems to know everyone here," the woman said wistfully.

Andy raised his brows, pretending to size her up. "We don't know you yet."

Jake shot his brother a look. His brother was teasing, but the woman might not catch on, and now was not the time to make her feel unwelcome. She'd been booted from her table, and he didn't want her to think Andy was insinuating she didn't belong. But before Jake could say anything, she stuck out her hand, reaching over the bar.

"Let's fix that. I'm Maddie. New to town, but I've been coming here on vacation since I was a kid."

"Nice to meet you." He shook her hand. "I'm Andy, and that's my baby brother, Jake."

"Baby brother, huh?" She turned to Jake, her eyes sweeping over his body in a quick appraisal, like she was taking in his size.

He held back from sending Andy a glare, just barely. "I'm only a couple years younger. He's just jealous because he's got more wrinkles than me."

"You try not having wrinkles when you're a father," Andy joked back, then turned to Maddie. "Don't let his tough guy act fool you. Jake has an artist's soul."

He wanted to throw the towel at his brother for talking him up. "In my spare time I build pieces using found objects and make collages, one-of-a-kind furniture, that sort of thing." He rubbed his neck, feeling the same shyness that came over him whenever he talked about his hobby.

"How cool," she said, sounding like she meant it, and his tension eased. "Do you find stuff on the beach?"

"Yeah, and flea markets, garage sales. There are tons of antique malls around here." He waited for her to smirk; a lot of people seemed to find the idea of a young guy visiting the local antique shops funny, but she beamed at him.

"I'd love to see your art sometime."

Was she implying she'd like to see him again or just being

polite? Before he did something outrageous and asked her out after only knowing her for five minutes, he said, "Anytime."

"Seems like the perfect place to be an artist." She fiddled with the copper bracelet on her wrist, and the metalwork caught his eye. "There are so many galleries around here."

The subject of art galleries was a sore spot right now, but not because his work wasn't in any. "I mostly sell pieces through word of mouth." Too late, he realized that might make him sound like an artist by trade, which he most definitely was not. Taking commissions had shown him that he'd rather keep art separate from his income.

But before he could clarify, Andy slid their drinks onto the bar. "He's vice president of the local art guild. Did he mention that?"

Jake groaned. He'd have to remember never to bring a date to the winery when Andy was working. This was worse than when his brother made him pose for a million prom pictures before letting Jake borrow his car to drive his date to the dance.

"Enough about me," he said, giving Andy a warning look. He didn't need his brother's help to impress a girl. "What brings you to Orchard Harbor?" he asked. "We get a lot of tourists, but not many people come to stay."

"I've wanted to move here for ages to be by the lake and closer to friends, and I finally took the plunge. Moved in yesterday."

Jake lifted his glass. "Cheers to that," he said, and they shared a toast. He took a big gulp of his drink, and son of a— "Andy, you've got to be kidding me."

His brother was grinning. "Not a fan of our smoky cabernet?"

With Maddie right there, Jake stopped himself from saying what he really thought of the drink. Scowling, he said, "I'm starting to think you're serving me the worst ones."

"All of our wines are excellent," Andy said. "But I have served you the ones with the most intense flavors." Laughing, he took Jake's glass, which he now noticed had barely been filled—a clue that his brother didn't expect him to drink it and didn't want any to go to waste—and replaced it with a pint glass.

"Citrus IPA," Andy said. "We have a partnership with the brewery."

Realizing Maddie had been watching them, Jake said, "To be honest, I'm more of a beer guy."

"Never would've have guessed." Her lips curved into a teasing smile. "You're kind of in the wrong place, then."

"Wanted to support my brother. He just got a promotion."

"Sounds like congratulations are in order," she said, turning to the spot where Andy had been standing behind the bar, but he was gone.

Jake gestured toward a two-top table in the corner that had just opened up. "Let's go, before my brother says something else embarrassing."

She grinned at him. "I dunno, he's a pretty great wingman." She slid off her stool and weaved through the tables, sending him an inviting smile over her shoulder, and he decided he couldn't be mad at Andy's meddling since it had led to more time spent getting to know this gorgeous newcomer.

Chapter Two

"Guess again," Jake said. Seated across the small table from her, his eyes sparkled like rays of light filtering through whiskey over ice, an effect Maddie had recently helped capture while styling a photo shoot for a distillery's website. His irises were a clear amber, an echo of his wavy hair, which was on the long side, falling over his forehead.

"Three questions left," he said.

She tapped her chin, thinking, then dropped her hands, embarrassed by the habit, and clasped her fingers in her lap to keep them still. Leaning sideways to peer around him—he was even bigger up close—she pointed at the array of bottles stacked on shelves. "The wine labels?"

They were playing a game of twenty questions, and she was losing this round. Not that she minded. Between arranging the move, working out countless logistical and legal details for her new business and keeping up with her job as a food stylist, she hadn't had time for fun in months. Years, even.

He didn't bother to look, just shook his head. "Two questions."

Though she'd been the one to suggest the game, it was hard to concentrate with all his attention on her. When they'd finished their drinks and he'd treated her to a flatbread after finding out she hadn't eaten dinner, he'd suggested a round of beanbag toss on the covered patio. But she'd countered with a round of twenty questions as an alternative, not keen on embarrassing herself with a game that required athletic ability.

To her delight, he'd agreed. She'd never seen the appeal of talking with a stranger in a bar, but hanging out with Jake felt effortless, and she wasn't ready for the night to end.

"You're not cheating, are you?" She grinned, still surprised at how easy conversation flowed.

At her teasing accusation, his expression turned serious. "I'm a lot of things, but a cheat isn't one of them." Then he cracked a smile. "Though maybe cheating wouldn't be the worst idea, considering how bad I'm losing."

She'd won the first two rounds but readily agreed to a third when he asked for the chance to win back some pride. "Even if you win, I'm still the champion," she said.

"For tonight, sure." His flannel-clad shoulders rose in a shrug. "But you're a local now. Plenty of chances to ask for another shot."

Was he saying he wanted to go out with her again? The idea of meeting a potential boyfriend on her first night in town seemed outrageous. After she'd been betrayed by a coworker she'd thought was becoming a close friend, she'd lost her ability to trust for a long time, and that went for dating as well. She'd never given her number to a stranger, let alone gone out for drinks with any man until they'd talked enough for her to make sure he was who he said he was. She didn't even know what this man did for a living.

But the appeal of spending more time with Jake overrode her usual reservations. She swiveled in her chair, taking in the scene around them. Wrought-iron chandeliers hung from the vaulted ceiling. The polished concrete floor gleamed. The staff clearly took pride in the place.

"You said it's not a plant, so it can't be the wall of greenery," she mused, wondering if he was trying something sneaky, like thinking of an individual leaf versus the whole wall of plants, but he took a sip of beer, his face giving nothing away.

"Not the red aprons the staff are wearing. But you did say it was a bright color."

He nodded. "Sneaky question, though."

"You allowed it."

"Hard to deny a beautiful woman what she wants," he said, and the words halted her survey of the room. Spoken so calmly, like he was giving her the time of day, yet with a playful edge that sent a thrill down her spine.

"Are you flirting with me?" She'd been in denial that this was anything more than a friendly game.

"Guess I've been doing it wrong if you're just now realizing," he said with a grin.

Her heart gave a flutter. "And here I thought you were just a fan of guessing games." It occurred to her that she was flirting right back.

He chuckled. "Can't say it was in my plans for tonight, but then again, neither was meeting you."

"I was kind of surprised you wanted to spend time with me. I've heard some locals don't take kindly to newcomers." Tasha and Celeste had warned her she might get the cold shoulder from some residents who were slow to trust anyone from out of town. And Jake had complained about the tourists who'd taken over her table.

"Some folks have been burned by people who only care about their bottom line and not investing in the community." Jake set his beer down, spinning it on the coaster. Her attention snagged on his strong arms and big hands, knuckles showing scrapes and healed scars, maybe from using tools in his creations.

"But finding out you're a new addition to our town was the best news I've heard in a long time." His gaze dropped for a moment, and Maddie could've sworn he was looking at her lips. Was he thinking about kissing her?

Her own eyes traced the angular curve of his stubbled jaw, taking in his wide mouth and prominent Adam's apple. His throat bobbed in a long swallow, and he spoke again, snapping her attention to his honey-colored eyes. "Two questions, Maddie."

Right then, the only question that came to mind was: *Do you feel this, too?* But since she had one last win to earn, she took a sip of her wine, composing herself, then asked, "Is what you're thinking of on the table?"

"Sort of." The question seemed to throw him off. "Near it, at least."

She nudged his arm playfully, trying not to notice the solid ridge of muscle her fingertips encountered. "Hey, you're only supposed to answer yes or no. Don't give me the win. I want to earn it."

He looked down to where her fingers were still pressed into the soft, worn fabric of his shirt, and she pulled her hand away, embarrassed, but he smiled at her. "We don't know each other well. Yet," he added with a smile that filled her with longing at the prospect of seeing him again. "But you can trust that I'd never let you win on purpose."

"Chivalry is dead, then?" she said with a teasing grin.

He slung an arm over the back of the chair. "Not at all. It's a matter of integrity."

"So, you're a guy with values?"

"Always have been," he said. "But lately I've been making extra sure my actions match them."

That caught her attention. Made her rethink trusting him. She'd been burned before.

But she was determined not to let fear of making the wrong move hold her back any longer. She always encouraged her friends to take brave leaps, while she'd never left home, too scared to trust her own judgment.

She must've been silent for too long, because Jake cleared his throat. "All I'm saying is I'd never patronize you by letting you win. Truth is, I suck at this," he said, cheeks turning a charming shade of pink.

Maddie laughed. "You're not bad at it. I've just had a lot of practice. I'm an only child, and it was our family's go-to game at restaurants."

"Well," he said, some of his alluring self-assurance returning, "all that practice seems to be failing you now, because unless I've lost count, you're down to one question."

Dang it. While she tried to think of what she hadn't guessed yet, his gaze dropped again, and this time, she realized he wasn't looking at her lips. Her chest? She might be offended if he'd been ogling her all night, but one quick peek was hardly anything to complain about. Besides, she'd done her fair share of checking him out.

But this time, she realized he was focused on something lower. *Near the table*, he'd said.

She glanced down and…aha! There was her answer. "It's my bracelet," she said, triumphant.

His mouth dropped open. "How'd you know?"

"You kept sneaking glances at it. Dead giveaway." She didn't tell him the embarrassing truth of what she'd assumed he'd been looking at.

"Hard not to," he said. "It's such a unique piece."

She slid the bracelet off her wrist and passed it to him so he could take a closer look. Hammered copper was welded around a Petoskey stone. The earthy elements of ore and rock were a reminder to stay grounded, not that she needed a reminder anymore. She'd been cautious for so long that it had become her default. "Do you ever work with metal in your compositions?"

"All the time. I like to incorporate different elements like wood, metal, pottery and plastic into the same piece." His finger traced the curve of the bracelet. "What caught my eye was how the artist wove the flow of water into the design."

"I never saw it that way, but you're right." She'd been focused on the solidity of the piece, a reminder to keep her feet firmly planted, but now that he mentioned it, the bracelet had fluidity, from the curve of the copper to the polished disc of the stone.

He handed it back to her. "Do you know the artist?"

"Not personally. I bought it at the farmers market in town last year. She said she found the stone up north, since those aren't common around here."

"I bet it was Tara," he said. "She's in the artist group I'm a part of. Been making jewelry for longer than I've been alive."

Maddie was pleased to discover his connection to the craftswoman. "I love the variance in textures," she said, skating her thumb over the hammered copper. "It's something I like to bring to my own work."

His eyes darted up. "You're an artist, too?"

"I like to think so. It isn't the type of work people tend to associate with art, like painting or pottery. But I don't think artistic expression belongs in a box."

"Me, either," he said. "But it took me a long time to think of myself as an artist. When people asked about my collages, I would brush it off as something to pass the time."

"What made you decide to take the plunge into calling yourself an artist?"

"I didn't, really. Other people did. My friends pushed me to join the art guild. And then it kind of hit me that I was an artist, whether I believed it or not."

"Even though I haven't seen your work, I'm sure that's true."

"Same for you."

At this point she would normally joke about how her art

was edible, mostly. But she didn't want to ruin the moment by finding out he was an art snob. "Thanks. Maybe I'll show you sometime."

He put a hand to his heart. "All I get is a *maybe*?"

She didn't bother to hold back a smile. Jake was quickly getting past all her defenses. Nervous of blurting out how much she'd like to see him again, she focused on putting the bracelet back on, but fumbled with the clasp.

He got down and came over to her side of the table. Even from her perch on the tall stool, he towered over her, but instead of being intimidated, she felt shielded by his presence from the bustle around them. "May I?"

He smelled like fresh pine and sawdust, an enticing combination. She nodded, and he wrapped his long fingers around her wrist. She sucked in a quick gulp of air at the brush of his calloused palm against her skin.

The unruly strands of his golden hair gleamed under the lights nestled in the tall ceiling, the angular lines of his jaw rough with stubble. The contrast in textures brought to mind a bite of creamy brie studded with pistachios, and she realized her fingers were curling with the desire to palm his cheek and run her fingers up through the soft-looking strands of his hair as she pulled him down for a kiss.

She couldn't remember ever having this strong of a reaction to a man, and a total stranger, no less. The bracelet warmed her skin as he finished fastening the clasp.

"All good." He let go, and she turned to thank him, but he was closer than she thought. Their mouths nearly collided, and she pulled back, startled that she'd almost accidentally manifested her desire to kiss him.

"I'd better head out," she said. She'd been aiming for brave tonight, not reckless.

He moved away, his eyes dark with concern. “Sorry, I didn’t mean to overstep.”

“No, that was helpful, thank you. It’s just…” She took a deep breath, gathering her courage. “I think I like you.”

“And that’s a bad thing?”

“Not at all,” she said. “But I don’t even usually talk to guys when I’m out or anyone except my friends, really. I guess I’m just new to this.”

“Flirting?” A hint of his earlier grin peeked through.

Once again, he pulled a reluctant smile out of Maddie with that charm. “Hitting it off with a stranger.”

Jake’s expression relaxed. “Me, either. To be honest, I haven’t approached a woman in…” He scratched his head. “Well, it’s been a long time. But I was drawn to you the moment I saw you. Didn’t hurt that you’re friends with Tash. She’s great, and if you’re her friend, you must be good people.”

She’d thought the same thing after discovering he and his brother grew up hanging out with the Grant siblings. But she couldn’t believe a charming guy like Jake would ever have trouble approaching women. “You expect me to believe a hot guy like you is shy?”

“I never said I was shy.” He smiled wide. “But hot, I’ll take.”

Maddie ducked her head, just now realizing what she’d admitted. “Well, *I* am.”

“Didn’t have to tell me.” His smile stretched wider. “I’ve got eyes.”

She realized he was insinuating she was hot and dutifully rolled her eyes at his brazenness, though her stomach flipped at the compliment. “I meant I’m shy. That’s why I don’t normally go out like this.” The winery was no nightclub, but by 8:00 p.m. she was usually in pajamas, curled up with a snack and a book on entrepreneurship or the latest episode of one of the countless cooking shows she loved.

"I do from time to time," Jake said, putting his hands in his pockets. His jeans were splattered with flecks of paint. She wondered again what his compositions involved. "Tonight I was supposed to meet some buddies of mine to celebrate Andy's new job, but they canceled last minute."

"Seems like everyone's an old friend here." Maddie couldn't wait to get to know more people in town. "It's one reason I moved."

"And the other?"

"The lake," she said frankly. The water had always lured her, as had the promise of lazy days relaxing on the beach and evenings spent strolling the shore. "I grew up visiting Lake Michigan on vacation, and Tasha and Celeste convinced me moving here could be a reality." A reality that would involve a lot of work, starting with her morning appointment with the contractor for a walk-through of the retail space she'd leased.

Reluctantly, she said, "I better order a rideshare. My friends said it could take forever this time of year."

Jake nodded. "Might take a bit, but there will be a driver or two out."

Maddie didn't know whether to be relieved or disappointed that he hadn't asked for her number or offered a ride. She wouldn't have accepted a ride, but she wouldn't have hesitated to give him her number. Then again, maybe it was a sign. She had big plans, and getting involved with someone on her first day in town was not one of them.

She said goodbye, leaving Jake behind as she made her way to the entrance and opened the rideshare app. The driver's arrival time was in ten minutes. Not bad. But the drinks had caught up with her, and she needed to find the restroom.

Making her way back through the crowded tasting room, she was glad there was no sign of Jake—that would be awkward. But just as she turned down the hallway, she spotted someone coming out of the bathroom and realized it was him.

He smiled down at her. "Are you following me?"

"Just looking for the restroom," she said, flustered.

"I was joking." Bending close, he confessed, "I've been kicking myself for not asking for your number."

"It's a small town," she said, ignoring how happy hearing that made her. "We would've run into each other sooner than later."

"Yeah, but I'd rather not leave it up to chance."

She didn't want to, either, even though it was silly to be this attracted to a man she'd only met a few hours ago. It had taken three dates with her last boyfriend before they'd kissed, and first she'd scoured his social media, learned the names of his parents and siblings and found out where he saw himself in the next five years.

All she knew about Jake was that he was on a nickname basis with her friends, an artist, had a sommelier brother named Andy and was miserable at guessing games. Oh, and that he didn't make a habit of picking up women. But was that just a line? Maybe he was an expert at hitting on ladies and knew exactly what to say to break down her defenses.

Maddie's confidence wavered, but his gaze dropped for the briefest moment, and this time she knew he wasn't eyeing her bracelet. He was looking at her lips, and suddenly it didn't matter if he was as sincere as he seemed or whether she knew what he did for a living or anything about his past. She wanted to kiss this man, and all that really mattered was whether he wanted that, too.

"I could give you my number," she said, heart pounding. "Or a kiss. Your choice."

Jake didn't hesitate. He bent and pressed his lips to hers. The feel of his mouth was bliss. Her hand instantly rose to his chest, fisting the fabric of his shirt, which was every bit as soft as it looked, and he groaned softly. The sound was electric, and she opened herself to him, parting her lips. He met her urgency, the sweep of his tongue stoking her desire.

Her skin was alight with sensation, awareness sparking through her at his skillful touch, his hand on her face angling her, ever so gently, to deepen the kiss. Until this moment, Maddie had never lost herself in a kiss, but she was completely under Jake's sway. His mouth captured hers, hungry, and she feasted on the sensation of lips. She pulled him closer, her boldness unleashed by his touch, and he broke the kiss to look down at her, his chest heaving, golden eyes shadowed in the dim hallway.

The distance brought reality crashing back. This hadn't been what she meant by turning over a new leaf. Her first time kissing a stranger and she'd done it in a town with a smaller population than the high school she'd attended.

Why hadn't she chosen to do something impulsive like this before, when her chances of running into her kissing partner again hadn't been astronomically high?

Because Jake is different, a voice piped up.

But she didn't believe in fairy tales. True love was something that developed over time, between two compatible people who wanted the same things out of life. This was just attraction, nothing more. Except she'd never been tempted to act on it before.

Overwhelmed, she took a step back and bumped into the wall, knocking off a framed photo. It fell to the floor and shattered. The scattered glass lay in broken pieces—just like her plan to start off on the right foot in Orchard Harbor. She bent to pick them up, but Jake took her arm, tugging gently.

"Let me," he said. "Listen—"

"Jake?" The voice came from behind them, and Maddie

jerked her head around to find his brother coming toward them, a concerned look on his face. "What happened?"

"Sorry, I knocked a photo off the wall." Her cheeks flamed with embarrassment at almost getting caught.

"My fault," Jake said. He crouched over the mess, carefully gathering the shards of glass. "I was coming out of the bathroom and startled her."

True, though not the whole story, and she was incredibly grateful for his composure. Maddie looked down at him, kneeling on the floor, pieces of broken glass cradled in his palms. Palms that had tenderly caressed her cheeks a moment ago. She wanted to flee, overwhelmed by emotions, but couldn't leave him with the mess. "Let me help," she said.

"All good." He avoided her eyes. "Andy will know where to find the broom and dustpan."

His brother nodded. "No worries, we've got it handled."

"You don't want to miss your ride," Jake added in what seemed like a pointed way.

Right. She shouldn't linger and make things more awkward. She wasn't about to let herself get tied up in knots over a kiss. Even if it was the best kiss of her life. And with a virtual stranger, no less.

But now he wouldn't even look her way, and this was exactly why she should've played it safe.

"Sorry again," she said. "Good to meet you both." Gosh, had it really only been a few hours ago? Mortified, she busied herself with buttoning her jacket to stop the urge to hide her face in her hands.

Jake finally looked up, but his expression was unreadable. "See you around, Maddie."

Not if she could help it. Even though everything about him drew her in, running into Jake again would be a very big mistake.

Chapter Three

Jake couldn't get the woman he met last night out of his head. Then again, he hadn't really tried, even though indulging in memories of their kiss might be setting himself up for disappointment since Maddie was bound to catch wind of his past, unlike his casual dates with women from out of town. But something about her had pushed him to take the risk and let someone in with the potential to get past his walls.

He never should've stayed to talk to her after he found out she was a local. No chance of their relationship going anywhere once she found out about his reckless reputation. But he'd gone and kissed her, in full view of anyone walking by. A mistake, even though it had felt so right. As a lifelong resident of Orchard Harbor, he knew how fast gossip flew. He didn't want that for her. Or himself, if he was being honest.

Maybe this morning's call from his boss was fate getting back at him for not thinking things through. He didn't believe in luck, but he did believe in consequences, and getting called out to this particular property sure felt like retribution for being impulsive.

Coffee in hand, he surveyed the run-down exterior of the building he'd once dreamed of turning into a gallery for the art guild. He'd steered clear of it for weeks. One of his colleagues at Wright Construction—an experienced foreman named Martin—was running this job, and Jake had work at three other properties. Why did his boss want to meet here, of all places?

A diesel pickup made a U-turn on the empty street and swung to a halt by the curb. Reese Wright climbed out, his dented travel mug in hand. The owner of the construction company had given Jake a job and hadn't rescinded the offer in the five years since, though Lord knows he'd have been well within his rights to let Jake go in those first few months.

He greeted Jake with a nod and tugged his ball cap lower over his blue eyes, squinting in the early-morning sun. "How're things going on the Hansom job?"

Their company had been hired to convert yet another family home into a vacation rental. Tourism drove their economy, but that didn't stop Jake from being resentful that the home of one his childhood friends, where he'd spent countless hours playing video games and watching football, would now be rented out by vacationers with no ties here. "On target to finish by the end of the month."

"Good, good," Reese said. "So you're free to take on another project."

Jake turned to his boss, surprised. "I hadn't heard of any new contracts coming in."

"Not a new one." Reese took a sip of his coffee. "Well, technically it is, since work hasn't started. But it's something we've had on the books for several months now."

Jake racked his brain for projects that hadn't been assigned and came up empty. It was too early for guessing games. Then again, maybe he shouldn't have stayed up so late last night playing them with a pretty stranger. "Where at?" His question came out grumpier than intended.

Reese didn't bat an eye. He was used to Jake's morning gruffness. "Right here." He lifted his salt-and-pepper bearded chin toward the brick facade in front of them. "We need someone to head up the caterer's renovation."

Jake had avoided looking at the building until now. He'd never learned the art of being a gracious loser; one of the few things he had in common with his dad. Chuck had always blamed bad luck on his losses in the casino and in life. But Jake was determined not to follow in his dad's footsteps.

The building had been an ice cream shop in his youth, but when the owner passed away, it had gone through a revolving door of tenants, making the transition from a T-shirt shop to a souvenir store to a café every handful of years. He'd envisioned it as something else entirely, but that wasn't his call to make.

Determined not to let his disappointment in losing the bid for this lease affect his work, he turned to his boss, but Reese was frowning down at his phone. "Trouble on the Bluff Street project. I need to head out, but the long and short of it is Martin's mother passed away."

"I heard," Jake said with sympathy. "Her funeral was last week, right?"

Reese nodded. "Martin needs to sort out her estate. He's going to be out of town for a few weeks. Maybe longer. And this project is time sensitive. The client has already sent three emails since she moved to town."

"She?" He didn't mean to be nosy, but he'd formed an unflattering picture of the person who beat him out. He'd imagined a cocky trust-fund bro who planned to strip any remaining character from the building and turn it into a franchise.

"Madelyn Briar," Reese said. *Madelyn.* Why did that name ring a bell? "She's anxious to get moving on this. Wants to be finished in six weeks."

Six weeks? Jake squinted at the building. Based on what he'd seen of the interior, twelve weeks sounded more doable.

Had Reese said she was a caterer? "The kitchen in there is bare-bones."

His boss looked up from his phone. "You've been over the plans?"

Shoot. He needed a reasonable excuse for why he was familiar with this property. He hadn't told anyone besides his brother and best friend about his failed bid. No sense in word getting around that he'd failed at something else. "Martin mentioned it."

"Glad you're not totally in the dark on this, because I want you to take over as lead contractor."

Jake should've seen it coming, but the directive caught him off guard. "I don't have much experience in commercial properties."

Reese gave him another piercing stare, and Jake resisted the urge to scratch at his collar. "For the past six months you've been breathing down my neck to take on more responsibility on the commercial renos we do."

He cursed his past self for being overeager to learn the ins and outs of renovating a commercial space, especially since he'd mostly wanted the extra experience for help on a potential gallery reno that was no longer in the works. "Yeah, but—"

"But what?" Reese crossed his arms, bulky in his tan work jacket, though a head shorter than Jake. "You don't want this? Say the word, and I'll pass it to Kevin."

Kevin had ordered quarter-inch tiles last week when they needed three-eighths. Much as Jake resented things shaking out the way they had, he couldn't let Kevin screw things up for a client. "I'll take it on."

"You sure?"

"I'm sure." He'd worked hard to rebuild his reputation, and he wouldn't let his personal feelings get in the way.

"Good." Reese ducked his chin in a nod. "Because the client's on her way, and I'm late for a permit meeting."

"But what about the plans? I know next to nothing about this project." He'd toured the building before placing an offer, but he didn't know anything about what the caterer wanted done with the property.

Reese was already walking toward his truck, phone to his ear. He half turned. "Already in your inbox. Just explain that you're new to the job and familiarize yourself later."

"Didn't you say she's been sending a bunch of emails?" Jake knew the type. Overinvested. Had watched a few episodes of home renovation shows and considered themselves an expert. But Reese had already climbed into his truck, the answer to Jake's question coming in a new email notification from his phone.

He checked the time. Ten minutes until the client was due to arrive. He'd need every spare minute to familiarize himself with the plans and remind himself that this was just business. The client hadn't outbid him on purpose.

The email was slow to download—service was spotty all over town, especially near the beach—so he turned to size up the building he'd been avoiding for a month and felt a wave of resentment. This would've made a perfect gallery for the art guild members. And now it would be turned into yet another place to eat. As if they needed any more of those in Orchard Harbor.

The streets were already lined with restaurants serving everything from pizza to homemade pie, though that was an oxymoron. He doubted this place would have anything unique to offer, but he wasn't a food critic, he was a contractor, and he'd make sure the job was done well, regardless of his feelings.

The windows were covered in brown paper so he couldn't get a good look inside. Giving up, he paced back toward the street and caught sight of someone who melted his irritation in a second.

Maddie rounded the corner, nearly running, a satchel bouncing off her hip. She was dressed in boots and a blazer, her curls swept into a low ponytail. Her face lit up when she saw him, but then she slowed, her steps hesitant. "Jake." Her greeting was a little breathless, and even though he hadn't been running, he was, too. "I know this is a small town, but I didn't expect to run into you again so soon."

He wasn't sure how she felt about this chance meeting. He'd assumed she'd hurried off last night because they'd nearly been caught kissing, but maybe she regretted the kiss itself.

"That's the problem with small towns," he said. "Hard to avoid anyone."

"Oh, I didn't want to…" She trailed off. "I love that about Orchard Harbor. It's why I moved here. To make connections."

Relieved, he smiled, forgetting his nerves for a minute because that was exactly how he felt. Even though some people held his past over his head, living in a place surrounded by friends and family more than made up for it. "I'm glad I ran into you. I'm still kicking myself for not getting your number. Though I'd make the same choice again, if I'm honest," he said, thinking of her offer, a kiss or her phone number.

She bit her lip. "I can't believe I actually said that. I'm not usually so impulsive."

"I believe you," he rushed to reassure her. She didn't have anything to be embarrassed about. "For what it's worth, I'm glad you were. I really enjoyed last night." At the time he'd thought she had, too, but her expression was hard to read.

"Same." She met his gaze, and the flicker of desire in her eyes there made him ask her something he might come to regret.

"Would you like to join me for lunch?" He couldn't pass up the opportunity to spend more time with her. "I have meetings this morning, but if you're free later, the restaurant at the Gull and Loon Resort serves great food."

He wasn't dressed for a fancy meal at the resort, but the owners were his best friend's parents, and they wouldn't care if he showed up in a denim shirt and paint-flecked jeans. Truth was, all the jeans he owned were either splattered with paint or wood stain or torn clear through.

But Maddie's face clouded over. "That's kind of you to ask, but I don't think it would be a good idea."

He could've sworn she'd been happy to see him a moment ago. "Can I ask why not?"

She sighed. "I just moved here, and I'm trying to get my footing. I do like you," she said with a sweet smile that somehow made it worse. "But I need to focus on work."

"Got it," he said, realizing he didn't even know what she did for a living. How did he feel such a strong connection for someone he knew so little about? No sense dwelling on it now.

He lifted a hand in goodbye and expected her to continue down the sidewalk, but instead she walked up to the building's entrance. He watched as she slid a key into the dead bolt, opened the door and stepped inside.

It took about two seconds for his brain to grasp the situation, and the moment he did, he muttered, "Figures." Today just went from bad to worse.

Maddie stepped inside the building she'd rented and closed the door, a mix of emotions churning in her stomach. She'd woken up filled with anticipation about seeing the future home of her catering business again.

Just seeing her name on the paperwork a few weeks ago had put her in tears, and actually being here, after knowing she'd almost lost out on this place due to an unexpected last-minute bid, should've had her doing a happy dance, but instead all she wanted to do was go back outside and tell Jake she did want to go out with him after all.

It had taken all her willpower to say no. He was even more handsome in the daylight, with rugged good looks and the casual confidence of a man who was capable of mastering any challenge.

But she'd spent a lot of time thinking last night—unable to sleep because the sensation of kissing him kept running through her mind—and decided now was not the time to get involved with anyone. Starting a business was a huge undertaking, and she needed to focus on that, not a beguiling stranger who might not be interested in the type of steady relationship she longed for someday.

She used to be open and trusting. After all, she'd met her two best friends during a chance meeting on vacation. But she'd learned the hard way that not everyone had her best interests at heart when a former friend had scammed her and stolen her identity, leaving her broke and betrayed. Even though Jake seemed like a wonderful guy, she couldn't prioritize her feelings for him over the work she needed to do to get her business up and running.

Forcing her mind away from the handsome man she'd left standing out on the street, she looked around the dim room. According to Celeste, who'd brokered the deal, the building had gone through many changes over the years. The last tenant converted it into a clothing boutique, and the fitting rooms along one wall were evidence of that.

The back held a run-down kitchen, which used to house a walk-in freezer, according to Tasha, who'd worked here as a teen when it was an ice cream shop. The building was a mishmash, but it was all hers. Maddie's heart raced at the thought. Or maybe that was the result of the mad dash up the sidewalk to make it to this meeting on time.

She prided herself on never being late. But this morning she'd slept through her alarm, and it wasn't until the sun streaked through the curtains that she finally popped out of bed. Thankfully, she'd laid out an outfit the night before: her sturdiest boots, a pair of jeans, and a blouse under her favorite blazer. An outfit that said "boss on a mission" and would look good with a hard hat, should that be required. She had no idea what touring the project would entail, but she wanted to be prepared for anything.

All her careful preparation had gone out the window the moment she ran into Jake. She'd known it would happen sometime, but less than twelve hours after their kiss was far sooner than she expected. Maybe the shock of seeing him again was the real reason for her breathlessness. Whatever the cause, she needed to collect herself before the contractor showed up.

As if summoned by her thoughts, a knock came from the door. Taking a deep inhale, she brushed dust off her sleeve from bumping against one of the shelves, opened the door and found herself face-to-face with the substantial frame of Jake Winn.

"Oh hi." She frowned, wondering why he was still here. Then she took in his work boots and paint-splattered jeans…

No. It couldn't be. Her eyes traced a path from his heavyweight canvas jacket to the hat that said WRIGHT CONSTRUCTION in bold letters. How hadn't she noticed that before?

He gave her a tight smile. "Allow me to reintroduce myself. Jake Winn, foreman on this project."

"But…" She tried to absorb this startling development. "You're an artist."

"I'm a man of many talents," he said, and there went that grin again. The one she'd found so appealing last night. Now it seemed a touch smug.

She narrowed her eyes. "I've been corresponding with a foreman named Martin."

"Unfortunately, he had to take a leave of absence. Personal reasons." He didn't elaborate, and Maddie's hackles rose.

She knew better than to take a stranger's words at face value. "If you'll excuse me," she said and shut the door in his face.

Scrolling to the Wright Construction contact in her phone, she hit the call button with shaky fingers. After waiting on hold for several minutes, she was told by the office manager that Martin was indeed out of town indefinitely, but that her contract would be handled by a very capable foreman. None other than Jake Winn. She thanked the woman, hung up and opened the door.

Jake was still standing there, hands in his pockets. He didn't glare at her like she expected, almost as if he understood her need to fact-check his story. That earned him some brownie points, but the whole situation still set her on edge. Had he known about this yesterday?

"Can I come in?" He didn't budge until she nodded.

Reality began to sink in that she'd kissed this man and knew next to nothing about him. She felt ridiculous. "How come you never brought up the fact that we'd be working together?"

"I had no idea," he said.

"Right. And you just expect me to believe you took over for Martin without knowing my name?"

"I didn't take over for him. I was assigned the project. This morning," he added pointedly. "All my boss told me was I'd be working with a caterer named Madelyn Briar. Maybe I should've put two-and-two together, but I didn't know your last name or even your full first name." He scowled, like all this was her fault. "Let alone what you did for a living. We didn't exactly get into details last night."

Put that way, she could see how he might be telling the truth. But it only made her decision to kiss him that much more unwise. "Guess that explains the paint." She gestured at the flecks of paint on his jeans. "Last night I assumed it was from your art."

"Art isn't something I do to pay the bills," he said, his voice gruff. "I never meant to give you that impression, but Andy was talking me up—which I never asked him to do, by the way." Rosy pink spots appeared on his cheeks. "He likes to brag about having an artist in the family, but construction is my job, and I've worked hard to get where I'm at. What about you?"

"What about me?"

He arched a sandy brow. "Are you an artist or a caterer?"

She let out an affronted huff. "Are you saying I lied to try to impress you or something?"

"Wouldn't blame you for trying to find common ground."

"Maybe that's something *you* do on dates," she said, gratified when he scowled. "But I'm an honest person."

"So am I. Which was why I'd never lie about being an artist."

"Neither did I. I'm a food stylist."

He took that in for a second. "You make clothes out of food? Wasn't aware that was a thing."

She blinked, then caught his meaning. "Not style as in fashion." Rubbing her forehead, which was starting to ache, she said, "Food is my artistic medium. I make dishes look appetizing in photos and videos."

"So you're the person responsible for the disappointment of expectation versus reality."

Of course he'd jump to that conclusion. "Not all food photographs well, but in most cases that has nothing to do with the quality."

He let out a noise that could only be described as a harrumph. "I'm still missing where the art part comes in."

So he was an art snob, after all. Good to know. "And gluing a bunch of recycled stuff together makes you qualified to judge?"

His nostrils flared. "I wasn't judging, I'm just trying to understand," he said, glowering at her.

Why was he so upset, anyway? "Are you really this mad

that I turned you down?" She hadn't taken him for that kind of guy, but she wasn't always a good judge of character.

He took off his hat and ran his fingers through his hair. "You think I'm upset about working with you because you don't want to go on a date with me?" He sounded hurt that she'd ever assume such a thing. "That's not it at all. I'm just having a hard time because this building was supposed to become a gallery for the art guild, but some out-of-towner placed a higher bid." He pointed at her. "You."

Things were beginning to make sense. "You wanted this building for yourself." That made things tricky. She'd never considered meeting the other person who wanted this space, let alone working with them. One downside of small-town life was you couldn't avoid anyone, as she was starting to learn firsthand.

He shook his head, his shaggy blond hair catching the streak of sunlight slanting in through the door. "Not for myself. I'm done selling artwork. But a lot of people in the art guild are looking to start a career."

Maddie remembered that his brother had mentioned Jake was vice president of the group. "Any artist from the guild would've been able to use the gallery?" That sounded like a whole lot of people who might hold a grudge against her.

"That was the plan," Jake said, confirming her fears. "Downtown Orchard Harbor gets a lot of foot traffic from wealthy visitors who would love to buy unique artwork for their vacation homes."

"Exactly the reason I was excited to lease this spot for my business," she said.

Hands on his hips, he countered, "You're not a local. What happens when you get tired of small-town life in a few years and decide to cut ties and move back home? The rent for a remodeled building will be sky-high, and likely the only one able to afford it will be a chain store or developer."

Trying to keep her cool in a situation that was spiraling beyond her control, she said, "My catering business will benefit the community. I'm not an outsider who will take my income elsewhere. And I worked hard for this dream." She'd spent years saving and rebuilding her credit after having her identity stolen and wasn't about to back down just because of one grumpy foreman. "While it's unfortunate your group of artists won't have this particular space, I'm here to stay. If you have a problem with that, maybe I should find a new contractor."

"No." Jake's eyes went wide. "I can do the work. I'd never let personal feelings interfere with business."

Maddie wasn't so sure. After all, he'd basically accused her of stealing this spot out from under him. "You're not going to sabotage me by installing the wrong kind of pipes or something because you're mad the guild lost the chance to turn this place into a gallery?"

"I'd never do shoddy work out of pettiness," he said, and she remembered his comment last night about being a man of integrity.

Something vulnerable in his expression tugged at her heart. "Okay." Fear of making another mistake had kept her stuck for too long. Wright Construction was accredited and came highly recommended by her friends. That, she could trust, even if she was on the fence about Jake personally. "But don't make me regret it."

He looked as if he had a few regrets of his own, and her stomach lurched at the realization that kissing her was probably high on that list. But he gave her a terse nod. "I'll do my best work. You have my word."

But was his word worth anything? That remained to be seen.

Chapter Four

Bang! Thud! Stomp, stomp, stomp.

Maddie sent a glare toward the ceiling and was rewarded with a shower of dust in her face. She sneezed and swiped it away. She'd left the catering business renovation an hour ago and headed back to her new home, the converted first floor of a house a few blocks inland, only to be confronted with more construction.

A short while after she'd come home from her unproductive meeting with Jake, she'd heard someone clomp up the stairs outside her door. After that, the whine of a power drill. And now this incessant hammering.

The lease mentioned ongoing renovations in the unit that occupied the upper half of the house. She suspected the price had been reduced due to other tenants not wanting to rent a place under construction, but she'd jumped at the chance to live in the beautifully restored lower level of a home near the main street that would've normally been far out of her budget.

Of course, that was before she faced the reality of constant noise. Settling into her new life had come with a lot of unexpected challenges. First, she'd had to reschedule the walk-through because her new foreman—the man she'd kissed last night—needed more time to familiarize himself with the plans. Now this. She flinched at the sound of hammering from upstairs.

But she shouldn't have expected everything to be smooth sailing. Experience had taught her to be patient, and a little noise and dust were small prices to pay for the joy of living within walking distance of her two best friends *and* a gorgeous beach.

Normally, she would've texted Celeste and Tasha first thing this morning to get their take on everything that had transpired since last night, but kissing a stranger was one thing. Kissing a stranger her friends had known since childhood was another. Last night, she'd let them know when she was home safely but hadn't mentioned Jake, and with the new development of working with him, she wanted to forget the whole thing.

She'd kissed a man who turned out to be exactly the kind of local her friends had warned her about. He'd insinuated that she was an outsider here to make a quick buck and leave town the moment things got tough. She imagined him going to the next meeting of the art guild she'd inadvertently outbid and asking the members to boycott her business.

What a mess.

To get her mind off things, she'd decided to work on a blog project she'd picked up. She often worked with professional photographers on food styling jobs, but for clients with a smaller budget, she took the photos as well.

Atop the kitchen table was a chopping block and a freshly cut orange. Jake had been right about one thing: in Maddie's line of work, nothing was ever as it seemed. Take the succulent orange. The juice dripping down the sliced fruit was actually spritzed water, thickened with glycerin. But on camera, the image was the perfect bite. Mouthwatering, appetizing, utterly delicious.

Outside of food styling, Maddie preferred things to be real and valued honesty over perfection. She'd take a bruised peach, ripe and heavy with juice, over an unblemished, flavorless fruit any day. That was why she was so excited to make the move to catering full-time, a career where visuals met taste. She would provide not only an elevated presentation but elevated flavors, too. And she wasn't worried about what a certain stuck-up foreman thought of her qualifications.

She picked up her camera again and aimed it at the orange, only then noticing a faint coating of dust on the previously immaculate surface. Letting out another growl of frustration, she dug through a few boxes in search of a dishcloth before giving up and using a paper towel to wipe off the dust.

Ignoring her grumbling stomach, she spritzed the orange and raised her camera again, only to be interrupted by a knock. What now?

She opened the door and once again found herself confronted with a now-familiar face. "Jake."

"Maddie."

"It's Madelyn, actually." She injected her tone with as much iciness as she could muster, considering the simmering heat that radiated through her at the sight of his handsome face. "Only my friends call me Maddie."

His face fell, and she almost took it back, but then she remembered how he'd insinuated her business was destined for failure. "What are you doing here?"

"Are you visiting a friend?" He peered over her shoulder, like he was checking for the real tenant.

"Nope, I just moved in." Why had he shown up on her doorstep if he hadn't expected to find her here?

"Of course you did." With a heavy sigh, he looked upward as if calling on the heavens for patience. But his expression slipped from frustration to wariness as he narrowed his eyes at the ceiling. "Did you feel a drip?"

She stepped out into the hallway and joined him in peering up at the entryway ceiling. Nothing unusual, except maybe…

She squinted at a discolored spot in the drywall, but Jake interrupted her inspection by clearing his throat.

"I didn't mean to interrupt. Just came down here to let you know it's going to be noisy for the next few weeks."

She cast a glance toward the varnished oak stairs, scuffed with boot prints and sawdust, finally putting two and two together. "That was you stomping around upstairs?"

His face flushed, a rosy hue overtaking his tanned complexion. "I wasn't stomping, I was working. I noticed something odd when I was working in the bathroom and—" Whatever Jake was about to say was cut short by a loud creak from above. As one, they looked up.

The spot she'd noticed a moment ago had spread, and the drywall was warped, almost as if the ceiling was bulging. A big drop of water fell down and splatted on the tip of her nose. She sneezed, the noise overtaken by another groan from above their heads, like a monster awakening.

"No-no-no-no-no," Jake said and darted for the stairs.

Maddie opened her mouth to ask what was wrong, but before she could, a huge chunk of plaster fell at her feet, and she let out a shriek.

He whirled around, eyes wide. "Maddie, watch out!"

No chance to be upset at him for using her nickname. The next moment he lunged toward her and swept her up into his arms, carrying her through the door of her apartment as a torrent of water burst from the entryway ceiling. She didn't know what to process first—the feel of his strong arms supporting her or the gush of water threatening to flood all her belongings.

Before she could wrap her head around what was happening, Jake kicked the door closed with his booted heel, as if that would stop the flood. He looked down at her, muscles flexing against her shoulder as he held her tight. "Are you all right?"

"Fine," she said. "What's going on?"

"Pipe burst." His mouth pressed into a line that pulled her attention to his lips.

Now was not the time to think about how his mouth had felt on hers, but she definitely was, and that needed to stop. "Could you please put me down?"

"Of course. Yeah." He shifted his hold, easing her legs down to the floor.

A trickle of cool water hit her bare toes, and she looked down to see water seeping under the door. She darted to the kitchen and was confronted by stacks of moving boxes. Where had she packed the towels? She tore open the nearest box and saw only dishes. The second held a blender and mixing bowls. Frustrated, she abandoned her search and raced toward her bedroom.

She pulled the comforter off her bed, scattering the throw pillows, and jogged back to the living room, where Jake was in the process of rolling up her rug. Momentarily distracted by the sight of his very nice butt, she blinked hard. Now was not the time to check him out. If the water reached the couch or boxes, all her stuff would be toast.

She tossed the blanket down on the growing puddle. Turning to help Jake, she was surprised to discover he'd already pushed the couch against the far wall and stacked the rug on top of it, safely away from the water.

Before she could thank him, he said, "Stay put. I'll fix this." Then he yanked open the door and darted into the hallway, pulling it shut behind him. She heard the squeak of boots on stairs. But it sounded like he was going down to the basement, not upstairs. Probably to shut off the water. Too late for that.

The duvet seemed to be sopping up most of the water for now, so she grabbed her phone to call Celeste. If there was anyone who could fix this, it wasn't Jake, it was her level-headed best friend.

Celeste answered right away. "I've been meaning to text you, but I'm packing for the conference." She'd mentioned an upcoming realty conference, but with all the mayhem, Maddie had forgotten. "You were out late last night. You didn't follow Tasha's advice, did you?"

"What, go wild? C'mon, you know me." Maddie forced a laugh. Sooner or later, she'd have to tell her friends about the complicated mess she was in with Jake, but right now she had bigger problems. "I'm actually calling because I need a plumber."

"You've only been in there a day, and something's already broken?" Celeste sounded concerned. "Good thing you got renters insurance."

"The thing is, it's not in my apartment per se." From the vent, she could hear muttered curses and the clang of pipes. "The entryway flooded and—" A loud screech came from below, and she risked poking her head out to check the damage. She was relieved to see the gush of water from above had slowed to a trickle.

Celeste was asking a million questions, and Maddie tuned back into the conversation, answering as best she could. "I'm fine, but I think a pipe burst. Water came through the hallway ceiling, and Jake's trying to fix it, but I get the sense he needs backup," she said as another string of creative curse words rose through the vent.

"Jake Winn?" Her friend sounded surprised. "How do you know him?"

Maddie sighed. That was not an explanation she wanted to go into right now. "He's remodeling the apartment upstairs."

"Is he okay?"

She wasn't expecting that question, but then again, if Jake had grown up with Tasha, Celeste must know him, too.

"He's fine, just a little wet." The image of him leaping off the stairs to get her to safety came to mind. That was the kind of move she would've expected from the sweet guy she met last night, not the grumpy man who'd shown up on her doorstep unexpectedly. Twice. Which one was the real Jake?

She pushed inconvenient thoughts of him aside. "My apartment is another story. I figured you'd know who to call with a plumbing emergency."

"Sure do. I already texted Lina, and she's on her way. Let me know if you need help with cleanup or a place to stay."

Maddie thanked her and was about to hang up when Celeste said, "I notice you didn't give me a straight answer about last night. I expect a full report next week after I get back from the conference." With that, she hung up and left Maddie to face a growing list of troubles that all began with a man named Jake.

Jake was staring at a giant hole in the ceiling, wondering how he wound up in this mess. Not only had the beautiful woman he'd kissed turned out to be the person who'd outbid him—and accused him of being the kind of guy who'd lie about his job to get a woman's attention—but to top it all off, she was his neighbor.

His best friend, Tom, was an attorney who'd recently inherited money after his grandmother's passing. He'd scored a deal on this house because the previous owner ran out of funds halfway through converting it into apartments. Jake's lease had been nearly up, and Tom had given him the option of living in the upstairs unit rent-free in exchange for finishing the remodel.

The arrangement had allowed Jake to bulk up his savings in a hurry, and in turn, he'd been able to apply for a loan to place a bid for the gallery space. But Madelyn had beat him to it. He knew it wasn't really a betrayal, but it felt like one. So did the way she'd questioned his motives for not explaining what he did for a living. As if she hadn't done the same thing.

But he was the one who had to prove himself. Well, he'd done it before, and he'd do it again. Right after he cleaned up this mess.

He went back upstairs to check for damage in his apartment. He'd stopped by on his lunch break to take out the old medicine cabinet and some shelving. Before he got started on demo, he'd put a load of towels in the washer.

The vanity would need to be changed out, too, but he was waiting for the plumber because he'd been worried about the condition of the pipes when he opened up the walls. Turned out his hunch had been correct. He hated being right.

He was shining a flashlight underneath the sink when a voice came from above him. "Tell me you didn't try to install a faucet without switching off the water."

He jerked upright, and his head whacked against the pipe. Wincing, he scooted out and saw his friend Lina, tool bag in hand. "How'd you know to come?"

"Celeste." Lina squatted down to peer under the sink. "Apparently, your neighbor is a friend of hers and said there was a plumbing emergency at this address. Looks like you were right about shoddy construction. What happened?"

"Pipes burst."

"I noticed," she said wryly. "What I'm wondering is why?"

"That's what I was trying to figure out." He narrowed his eyes at her. "And no, I didn't touch the plumbing. Probably should've held off on using the washing machine once I saw the condition of the pipes. That must be where the water came from."

"Didn't Tom have this place inspected?"

Jake nodded. "Everything came back solid."

"There's a hole in the ceiling downstairs that begs to differ."

"We might need to open up more walls." What would that mean for Maddie's apartment? Only time would tell.

Lina sighed. "Saving money is well and good, but you're living in a construction zone." She was all of five feet tall but had serious big sister energy. They'd worked together for years, and she'd become one of his best friends. "Is it worth it?"

"For free rent? I'd say so."

"What are you saving for, a boat? You'll need one if this keeps up," she teased.

The money he was saving on rent had been vital to his plan to renovate a gallery space for the guild. Now that his plan had fallen through, he was glad he'd kept it a secret. No one else would know his shot at redemption had failed. But even though he no longer needed the extra money, he'd never dream of not upholding his end of the bargain. "This is just a hiccup."

She rocked back on her heels. "You're lucky I was nearby."

"Not that lucky. You were supposed to be over last week. Might've caught this before the pipes burst."

"Take it up with your boss," she said. "He's the one who's got my company working on three houses at once right now."

That, he would not be doing. Especially since Reese had told him to think hard before tackling this reno on his own. He told Jake it wasn't about his abilities, but whether he should stretch himself so thin. But all these years later, Jake was still trying to prove himself.

The sound of footsteps on the creaky stairs had them both turning toward the door.

"Jake?" A voice came from the landing. *Maddie.*

He closed his eyes, stifling a groan. That woman was quickly becoming the bane of his existence. Without meeting Lina's inquiring gaze, he left the bathroom and yanked open the door.

Maddie stood there with the sleeves of her white blouse rolled up, curls coming loose from her bun, looking adorably disheveled. His grumpiness was overtaken by attraction, but he covered it up with a brief nod of acknowledgment. "Thanks for calling Lina."

"Oh." She looked taken aback. "No problem."

"Did the water reach your stuff?" He'd scooted the couch out of the way before running to shut off the water, but there had been a lot of moving boxes in harm's way.

She shook her head.

"Good. In that case, I need to wrap things up so I can get back to work." He began to shut the door, but she stopped him.

"What do you mean, get back to work? Aren't you working now?"

"Sort of. But this isn't a Wright Construction project." He leaned against the doorframe, searching for the simplest explanation to cut this short. "I'm fixing it up, but I also live here."

Her big brown eyes were full of skepticism. "You're messing with me."

His grip tightened on the doorframe. "Afraid not."

"I guess this is the universe making things even." She lifted both palms horizontally, like the scales of justice. "Move to a postcard-worthy town." One hand lifted higher. "Have a string of bad luck involving the first handsome stranger I meet." She raised one hand and lowered the other until they were equalized.

He didn't like what she was implying. "So I'm the downside?"

"You flooded my apartment," she said.

"Faulty pipes. I had nothing to do with it."

"That's supposed to make it better?"

He narrowed his eyes. "What about the kiss?"

"Too good to be true, obviously."

That brought an unbidden smile to his lips. "All I'm hearing is it was good." Her cute glare only made his grin widen. "No point in denying it now."

She shot him an adorably ineffective scowl. "Not good enough to make me forget you put a hole in the ceiling."

"Again, not my fault."

Maddie pursed her lips, clearly not believing him. "I can't handle a delay like this on my project, let alone the insurance nightmare."

"It's a renovation," he said. "Gotta be prepared for the unexpected."

"I took that to mean rotten floorboards or shipping delays, not contractor negligence."

Jake straightened up. "Now, hang on just a minute."

Lina stepped between them, tool bag slung over her shoulder. He hadn't even heard her come out of the bathroom. "No one's to blame for the flood except whichever company the previous owner contracted to do the plumbing," she told Maddie, who blinked in surprise. "We're dealing with poor workmanship, but not on Jake's part," Lina continued. "He only knows enough to catch plumbing mistakes, not fix them." She winked at him, and he ground his teeth.

"Whose side are you on?"

Grinning, she turned back to Maddie. "What I'm trying to say is that in his foreman role at Wright Construction, he'll be directing the project, and you'll be in great hands. He's supervised renovations on million-dollar properties."

Okay, Lina. Coming through with a buzzer beater in the fourth quarter. "*Multi*million-dollar properties," Jake added, and Lina elbowed him.

"Don't dig yourself in deeper," she muttered out of the side of her mouth. "Especially not before you give her the news."

Maddie had been watching them, a tiny furrow wedged between her brows, the same one that appeared during last night's guessing game. Even though a lot had changed since then, he still found her cute as heck. "News?" she asked.

Oh. Right. Jake had been so caught up in defending himself that he'd completely forgotten about what might be the worst part of today, at least for Maddie. "The water in the building will have to remain off for the rest of the day while Lina fixes the pipes and checks the extent of the damage."

Lina cut him a look, and he cleared his throat. "Maybe a few days. No more than a week," he said, glaring back at Lina. Worst-case scenario was usually the best policy when dealing with clients to keep their expectations in check, but after today's disasters, he didn't want to worry Maddie for no reason.

Her eyes went wide. "A week?" she said, her voice kicking up an octave.

Too late. "Um, possibly. The damage might extend into your unit as well."

"You're telling me I won't be able to shower for a week?"

"Or wash your hands or boil water," Lina added unhelpfully.

"But it might only be until tonight," he said, praying he was right.

Maddie let out a groan that was almost a growl. "Was this all part of a plan to make me feel unwelcome? Did you know all along that I was the one who outbid you?"

"What's she talking about?" Lina asked, and Jake's mind raced for an answer that would steer her from the truth. If anyone found out about his failed plan to help the guild, it would only add to the bad reputation that came from his former screw-ups and simply being Chuck Winn's son.

He decided to ignore Lina's question, hoping she'd forget it. "Renovations are messy. Get used to it."

"Yeah," Maddie said, glaring at him. "I'm starting to figure that out."

Lina scooched between them, offering a small wave. "Nice meeting you. Sorry it wasn't under better circumstances." With a twist of her lips, she headed down the stairs, leaving Jake and Madelyn in a stare-down.

She moved toward the door at the same time he did, and they bumped into each other. He took a step back. "After you."

"Oh, now you're a gentleman?"

"You seemed to think I was plenty gentlemanly last night," he said, unable to resist.

She lifted her chin defiantly. "Last night you hadn't accused me of undercutting locals or flooded my home." He held his tongue, barely. "And you expect me to think this is just a series of terrible coincidences?"

"You really think I would cause all this damage just to get back at you? I'm not that kind of person."

"I'm not sure," Maddie said. "All I know is you're not the man I thought you were." With that, she hurried down the stairs.

He'd been trying for years to prove he was reliable and trustworthy…only to make a whole new set of mistakes with the person he most wanted to impress.

Chapter Five

Maddie leaned against her door with an exhausted sigh, surveying the chaos of her living room. With the sofa shoved back and the end tables stacked on top of each other, the room looked like the world's most careless movers had ditched her stuff in a hurry. And instead of unpacking, she might need to find a temporary place to stay.

All thanks to Jake.

Last night, if she'd found out the cute guy she'd kissed was her upstairs neighbor, she would've thought it was a stroke of good luck. But that was before she discovered the real Jake was a grumpy, stubborn, apartment-flooding pain in the neck. Not at all like the kind, cheerful, laid-back guy she'd met last night.

Her stomach rumbled, and she checked her watch. Almost two o'clock. Just a few hours ago, she'd had to summon all her self-control not to say yes to lunch with Jake at the Gull and Loon Resort. She couldn't imagine sitting across a table from him now. They'd probably get in an argument before appetizers arrived.

But nothing was stopping her from going on her own.

So what if her first attempt at getting out of her comfort zone had been a mistake? New habits took time, and she was tired of being held back by doubt. She grabbed her purse, swung open the door and nearly collided with Jake's solid frame. Again.

With his tool belt over one shoulder and a ball cap pulled low over his brow, dark blond hair curling from beneath, he looked like the cover model for a construction hunks calendar. Except he wasn't shirtless, of course. Not that she was curious about what kind of muscles were hidden under the flannel. Checking out her hot neighbor was off the table.

Maddie's cheeks heated, and she lifted her gaze from his muscular chest, hoping to find something safer to focus on. But it was no help. His amber eyes were just as swoon-inducing as the rest of him. She'd have to find a way to deal with her attraction since it seemed like running into him was going to be a regular occurrence.

"Going somewhere?"

She straightened her spine, maintaining eye contact. She refused to let him know he still affected her. "Lunch."

"At the Gull and Loon?" His mouth slanted into a smug grin.

"Heard it was a great spot. Want me to bring you something?" she asked sweetly, wanting to get under his skin like he did with hers.

"You think I'd trust you with my food?"

Funny that he thought he had the high ground on trustworthiness. "Yet you expect me to trust you with my renovation."

His cheeks flushed red. "Yeah, well, I'd rather not swing the balance sheet more in your favor. What was it you called me earlier?" He rubbed his stubbled chin, making a show of trying to remember, then locked eyes with her. "Oh, right. 'The downside.'"

Maddie winced. That sounded meaner than she'd intended. It wasn't Jake she'd been upset at as much as her own decision to toss caution to the wind. If she'd behaved sensibly instead of kissing him, everything would be so much less complicated.

"Suit yourself." She pulled open the front door with the

stained-glass inset that she'd found so charming when she toured the place—back before she found out it came along with a cranky, infuriatingly attractive upstairs neighbor—and waltzed out onto the porch with as much airy dignity as she could muster, despite her urge to stomp like an annoyed teenager.

Served him right that the pipes burst and flooded the house. Except it wasn't just him getting the short end of the stick on that deal. Her fortunes were tied to his, at least until both renovations were done.

Maddie sat at a table overlooking the marina. She could see why Jake would pick the elegant hotel's restaurant for a date. The tranquil calm of sailboats bobbing on the water and seagulls soaring on the warm breeze was the perfect backdrop for quiet conversation.

Since it was in between the lunch and dinner rush, the restaurant was nearly empty. During summertime, Maddie knew from experience every restaurant in town would be bustling, but in early spring the lake water was still freezing and the weather fickle, so the town was relatively quiet on weekdays.

The server who'd shown her to her seat reappeared from the kitchen with a glass of water and asked if she had any questions about the menu.

"Actually, I'm ready to order." More like she was ready to eat the lemon slices if she didn't get food soon, but saying so wouldn't be polite. "May I please have the caprese grilled cheese sandwich and the soup of the day?"

"You don't want to check what it is first?"

"I'm trying to be more adventurous." Soup was safer than socializing with strangers. Baby steps.

The waitress smiled. "I like that attitude. Are you enjoying your stay?"

“Oh, I’m not a resort guest. I recently moved to town.” Recently, as in hadn’t updated her license or unpacked but long enough to have made an enemy out of an influential local.

“Oh really?” The server gave Maddie a discreet once-over, as if reappraising her in this new light. “What brings you to town?”

A love of Lake Michigan, wanting to be closer to her best friends in the world and the desire not to let one mistake keep her stuck forever. Yes, she’d trusted the wrong person and lost a lot of money in the process. But she’d rebuilt her savings, and she was here, ready to start the life of her dreams. Food styling was a great creative outlet and had been a lucrative career, but her real passion was making delicious food.

That answer would be way more than the waitress bargained for, so she went with the easiest explanation, vowing to work on sharing more about herself on a day she felt less emotionally drained.

“I’m opening a catering business focused on charcuterie boards and picnics.” Her business cards were in her purse, but she wasn’t sure if now would be a good time to offer one. She didn’t want to sell herself short, but she also didn’t want to seem pushy. She wasn’t just in town to network, after all. She wanted genuine friends. A community.

“Cool. I bet folks will eat that up.” The waitress chuckled. “No pun intended.”

Maddie smiled. “Here’s hoping. But first I have to get my kitchen up and running.”

“Are you operating out of your home?”

Maddie shook her head again, not sure whether to feel proud or foolish that she’d gone all-in on this venture. “I leased a spot down the street, actually.”

The server let out an impressed whistle. “That’s prime real estate.”

"So I've heard. Apparently, I outbid a local who wanted the place." She paused, regretting that she'd shared that tidbit.

"What do you mean by that? You're a local, too."

Maddie opened her mouth to protest, but the waitress added, "Orchard Harbor is your home now. Don't let anyone tell you otherwise."

Maddie felt the tension of the day's events dissipate. "Thank you. I needed that reminder."

The server started toward the kitchen, then turned and said, "If you have business cards, you might want to leave some with the concierge. I think a lot of our guests would be interested in catered picnics."

The prospect of a partnership with a cornerstone business went a long way to ease the sting of Jake's words. If only Maddie could banish the memory of how his lips felt on hers just as easily.

The week had started out amazing thanks to meeting a beautiful stranger, but everything had gone downhill from there. The one bright spot was they hadn't needed to do extensive repairs on the pipes. Lina had pinpointed the problem and confirmed the rest of the plumbing was up to code. He'd been excited to tell Madelyn the good news, but she merely thanked him and shut the door in his face. Fine.

Several days had passed since the house had flooded, and Jake had spent all his spare time on cleanup and patching the hole in the ceiling. Lina worked overtime, too, installing new pipes, and between them, the plumbing was fully fixed by Monday. But the extra work meant he hadn't had any time to go over the plans for Maddie's reno. The added distraction of living in the same house as her hadn't helped, either.

One evening he'd been playing music while he worked. Maddie had switched on the TV at increasing volume until he finally stomped downstairs to ask her to turn it down. He wasn't really bothered, but getting a glimpse of her adorable scowl had been worth it.

In retaliation, she'd started blasting music at 6:00 a.m. Since he couldn't sleep with the noise, he figured he may as well start demolishing the kitchen cabinets the next morning. To the tune of heavy metal. When Maddie arrived at the door in her pajamas and bonnet to tell him to knock it off, he hadn't been as annoyed as he'd made it seem. In fact, he'd had to hold back a grin at how cute she looked when she was grouchy.

Last night was quiet, and while he kind of missed their bickering, he'd finally been able to go over the plans for her reno, staying up late, making notes and confirming Martin's timeline and materials. When he finished, he'd been tempted to go downstairs and tell Maddie that he was ready for the walk-through, but given their usual doorway arguments, he decided an email would be the safer choice. Especially since seeing her was a reminder of how their kiss had lit him up in ways he'd never felt before.

She responded to his email right away, confirming she could meet the next morning. He tried not to think of her in the apartment below, cuddled up in the corner of her couch wearing the ruffled pajama shorts that had given him a glimpse of her stunning legs while she typed out a reply on her phone.

He'd shown up for their meeting the next morning a full fifteen minutes early, ready to prove he could be a professional about the situation, only to find the front door open and Maddie already inside, looking gorgeous as always.

She'd obviously learned how messy construction sites could be because instead of the blazer she'd worn last week, she had on a fleece jacket, the cuffs sliding past her wrists and making her already small frame seem even tinier. She looked delicate, but he already knew that behind her exterior was a woman who wouldn't back down from a fight.

"Nice you could finally find time to do this," Maddie said, proving he was right to be on edge.

"I'm early," he said, trying to keep his voice even.

"Yeah, but it's been days. I can't afford delays in the project."

He gritted his teeth. "Understood, but this project was handed to me last-minute, and my other renos had time-sensitive things that needed to be finished up." Not to mention that he'd worked around the clock to fix a mess that wasn't his fault, no matter what Maddie thought.

Instead of accepting his comment for the reasonable explanation it was, she crossed her arms. "Will it be like that moving forward? Maybe it would be better if someone who's not so busy took this on."

A valid question, but it got right under his skin and stuck, like a splinter. "Won't be a problem," he said. "I give all my projects equal priority, and I've rearranged the timing to make everything work." He couldn't have her reporting to his boss that he'd been unprofessional. Reese had taken a chance on him when no one else would, and he'd never give him a reason to regret that.

"I'm here now." Jake would prove himself through hard work, his usual currency. "Let's get started."

Raking her eyes over him in a quick sweep, like she was sizing him up, she finally nodded. He blew out a relieved breath and followed her through the room, still cluttered with the previous tenant's clothing fixtures and display cases.

She started off by mentioning that she wanted to reuse some fixtures, and if it had been anyone else, he would've shared the name of a shop that did excellent furniture restoration.

But his plan today was to say as little as possible. Couldn't get into trouble with his mouth shut.

He bit his tongue about the areas he'd pinpointed for improvement while going over the specs. Though the contractor he'd taken over for was more experienced, Jake had an eye for detail. But he figured Maddie wasn't interested in his opinion, so he kept quiet, nodding along while she explained her vision for the remodel.

Most of the space would only need cosmetic upgrades, but the kitchen would require the bulk of her budget. All new commercial-grade appliances, new floors, plus shelving and storage space for the unique items she'd require, from specialty cutting boards to picnic baskets.

She pointed at the ceiling, talking about lighting, and his gaze caught on her slender fingers, remembering how they'd felt pressed against his chest when the energy between them shifted from flirtatious to sheer, intense passion in an instant.

"Good so far?" she asked, and he came back to reality with a snap to find her watching him with narrowed eyes. So unlike the needy look right before their lips met on that first night in the winery. He managed a nod, and she moved off again.

When they came to the kitchen, the door to the storage closet was stuck tight. Maddie yanked a couple times, but it wouldn't budge.

"Here, let me," he said.

She sent him a glare. "I've got it." On the next tug, the door flung open, and she tumbled back with the force of it, toppling into him.

He caught her on instinct, wrapping his arms around her. Her head fit against his chest, his upper body curled around her protectively. He caught the aroma of roasted coffee beans and vanilla in her hair, inhaling on instinct before his brain caught up, and he gently let go.

She whirled around. “Thank you,” she said. “But maybe don’t make a habit of scooping me up.” Lifting her chin, she brushed her hands down her jacket in an effort to collect herself, and he grinned.

“I would if you’d stop tumbling into my arms.”

“I didn’t tumble,” she said with a little huff.

“You’d rather I let you fall next time?” he asked. “Or get drenched by questionable water?”

She put her hands on her hips. “You’re infuriating, you know that?”

“Well, you’re—” He stopped himself. He was about to tell her she was adorable. Not something he could say about his client, let alone the woman he was on thin ice with.

“What?”

“Nothing.” He waved a hand toward the open pantry. “Carry on.”

With another suspicious glance, she did so, rounding out the walk-through with her plans for the kitchen space. Most of the ideas were excellent, but the flooring she’d picked wasn’t as durable as other options, and he would’ve liked to raise the idea of extending the counter space and switching the positions of the appliances to maximize efficiency.

With any other client, he would’ve brought this up during the design stage, but he’d been handed this job late in the game, and he’d already made a mess of things. Better to just go with the plans as written than risk getting into another argument, tempting as it was to verbally spar with her.

So he kept his mouth shut and told himself it was for the best. Back out in the main room, she tugged on her coat in quick, jerky motions, almost dropping her bag in the process.

“Want me to hold that for you?”

“No need,” she said.

"Is everything all right?" He couldn't seem to help being too interested in this woman for his own good.

She let out a frustrated-sounding breath. "I know things are bound to be awkward, but I had hoped we could put it behind us."

"We have," he said. "Or I have, at least." She, on the other hand, seemed to be itching for a fight.

"Really?" She'd managed to get her coat on, but the collar was flipped, and he shoved his hands in his pockets against the urge to fix it.

She tracked the movement. "This is what I'm talking about. You're so flippant about all this."

He cocked his head. "Flippant?"

"Yes," she said. "Standing there casually, like none of this is important. You've barely said a word all day. When I spoke with Martin, he offered feedback. Let me know if I was on the right track."

Somehow keeping quiet had backfired. "But the design is finished."

"Sure, but I figured once you got a look at the space…" She broke off. "You know what? Never mind."

"No," he said, straightening up. "If it's opinions you want, I've got them."

She arched a brow. "Oh really." Her sarcastic tone made it sound like she was calling him out for not doing his homework. That may have been true in high school, but working in construction was his passion. He was committed to this and damned good at it, and she didn't have the right to act like a straight-A student who'd gotten stuck with him for a group project.

"Yes, really." He pointed at the front windows. "These are single pane. Probably fifty years old. Plenty of room in the budget to install new ones and cut back on your energy costs."

Without checking to see if she followed, he walked to the kitchen. "You want vinyl flooring in here, which is technically fine. But ceramic tile would be much more durable."

Maddie frowned. "I discussed that with Martin, but he said vinyl would be cheaper and quicker to install."

"So you'd rather cut corners in order to open sooner?"

"I didn't say that."

"As for the kitchen layout—"

"I designed that," she said, interrupting.

"As for the kitchen layout," he repeated, crossing his arms. "The flow is all off. You'll be doing most of your prep at the counter, yet you've got the range in the middle. It's inefficient."

"And you know this from your extensive work in food service?" she asked.

Her sarcastic tone grated on his nerves. "I know it from years of doing kitchen renovations. You might think you want two separate prep areas, but this will make things harder."

"Good to know you're the expert on my profession," she said.

He threw up his hands. There was no winning with her. "You wanted my opinion. I'm giving it to you."

"Yeah, well, I take it back." She pulled her keys out of her pocket. "I think we're done here."

"You're not going to consider any of my ideas?"

"The windows, maybe," she said. "But just because you've renovated a few home kitchens doesn't make you qualified to comment on my workspace."

A few kitchens. More like dozens. And he'd done plenty of commercial renovations, too. But he'd been underestimated often enough to know the only way to prove himself was through his actions. "Got it. I'll stick to the plans, then."

"Sounds good." She fired the words like a fastball.

"Great," he shot back.

Things with Maddie were heating up, but not at all in the way he'd imagined the night they met. At least he was cured of his inconvenient desire for her. Kissing Maddie was the last thing on his mind. All he wanted now was to prove her wrong.

Maddie left the meeting with Jake and immediately texted her friends. When she was upset, the best way to turn the day around was to cook for people she cared about.

Maddie: Who's up for lunch?

Celeste: My flight was delayed, so I won't be home until evening.

Tasha: That's the worst! Stay hydrated and we'll see you soon. Maddie, want to get takeout and eat at the beach?

Maddie: Yes to the beach, but no need to order food. I'll bring lunch.

Celeste: I'll just be here eating my overpriced airport food. :) Lol. Don't share any juicy gossip without me!

Maddie: Wouldn't dream of it.

She'd planned to tell her friends the whole story of what was happening with Jake, but without Celeste there, she was relieved to have a few more days before the embarrassing truth came out. Glancing around her kitchen, she decided the baguette she'd baked the night before would make a great sandwich base. She topped it with ham, roasted red peppers, baby spinach and smoked gouda before cutting it in half.

She wrapped the two sandwiches in parchment paper, then packed them into a picnic basket along with fresh fruit and a cucumber salad. Tasha loved salt-and-vinegar chips, so Maddie stopped at the specialty grocer on the way.

Once she arrived at the beach, she spotted Tasha laying a blanket on the sand and made her way over.

The town's lighthouse stood guard at the end of a concrete walkway stretching into the lake, the deep red a contrast to the bright blue sky and sparkling water. It was hard to stay upset surrounded by so much beauty, but when Tasha asked how the morning's meeting had gone, Maddie felt her earlier frustration surge.

"Can you believe he had the nerve to tell me I don't know what I really want when it comes to my kitchen?"

"Didn't you ask his opinion?"

Her friend clearly wasn't grasping the tone in which Jake had delivered his *opinions*. He'd seemed thrilled at the opportunity to tell her where she'd gone wrong in the reno plans.

"I did." Maddie passed her friend a cold can of sparkling peach juice. "But he didn't have to insinuate that I don't have a clue what I'm doing."

Tasha crunched into a potato chip, then said, "Well, he's worked in construction for years."

"Yeah, but I've worked in catering for years."

"Last time we talked, you were really happy with Martin's input. What's changed?"

Oh. Right. Maddie hadn't mentioned that the foreman in question was Jake. Or that he wasn't just her foreman. Celeste's conference and the arrival of Tasha's nephew had given her an excuse to avoid filling them in on all the details.

Shifting her eyes away from Tasha's penetrating gaze, she looked out over the placid water. No waves today, just a serene expanse of blue. This would be the ideal moment to explain, but then again, she didn't want to turn the entire meal into a conversation about her love life.

Plus, Celeste wasn't here, and she'd promised not to share any juicy gossip. Better to stay quiet. No hurt feelings, and she wouldn't have to recount the embarrassing details twice.

"You're right, I was really happy with the original consultation," she said, not mentioning that she was no longer working with Martin. "I think I'm just nervous that it's all getting real." Not a *total* lie. She was nervous, but she was also aggravated that she'd gotten herself into this situation with Jake.

She'd meant to get back on solid footing today with him, but then he'd shown up in that same faded flannel he'd worn the night they met, the one whose softness she could still remember grasping, pulling him closer as his lips parted hers, and it was all downhill from there.

"I get it," Tasha said. "When I opened the salon, I was a nervous wreck. Remember how you guys had to talk me out of ordering that sequined ball gown for the grand opening?"

Maddie laughed, glad for the change of subject. "It was definitely giving more beauty pageant energy than salon-grand-opening vibes. You could totally have made it work, but your nerves do tend to manifest in outfit choices you regret."

"Like how I was so stressed about delivering my speech as class president that I decided sewing tasseled tiers onto my graduation gown would be high fashion?"

"I wasn't going to bring it up, but..." She remembered how Tasha had called her while hiding in a bathroom stall before the ceremony. Maddie had been in the middle of glazing pottery during art class in her hometown two hours away—her own high school graduation was a week later—and made an excuse to go out to the hallway so she could soothe her friend who was moaning about how she couldn't show her face in the tragically altered gown. Luckily, Celeste, who'd graduated the year before, had saved hers. She rushed home to get it out of the closet, and the day had been saved.

That was their friendship in a nutshell—Tasha making bold moves that sometimes backfired, but worked out more often than not, Celeste coming through with a clear head in a crisis, and Maddie offering support. She was used to being the steady one and didn't want to admit she'd done something impulsive that had backfired.

When Tasha had left Orchard Harbor to chase her dreams in Chicago after high school, their friendship had evolved. Maddie had no longer been the only one who was geographically distant, and they'd grown even closer as they made a point to be present in each others' lives, from meeting up in Orchard Harbor to helping Celeste plan her wedding to summer weekends together in the city.

Both friends had driven hours on short notice to help Maddie pick up the pieces when she'd discovered her identity had been stolen. The friendship that began on a crowded beach in high school had weathered a decade of big changes, and Maddie couldn't wait to see what the next ten years brought.

"How are Izzy and the baby?" Maddie asked. Tasha's sister and the newborn had to stay at the hospital for several days due to his early arrival, but both mom and baby were back home resting according to the latest texts.

"They're doing well. Let me know when would be a good time to come over and help unpack. I have two appointments this evening, but later this week would work."

They made plans to reach out to Celeste and set it up, with Maddie promising to make it worth their while by serving new recipes she was testing. Once they'd finished their picnic, Tasha had to head back to get ready for her next client, but Maddie wanted a few more minutes of peace and sunshine. It was too chilly to walk along the shoreline, so she reclined on the blanket and let the sound of the waves ease the stress of the day.

On the way back to her car, she snapped a photo of the red lighthouse at the end of the pier for social media. Inspired by the idyllic surroundings, she filmed a quick update about the renovation process with the lake as background. She'd planned to do it on-site after the walk-through, but her topsy-turvy feelings toward Jake had derailed her.

She wrote a quick caption and posted it on her business account. She was surprised to see a like come in right away from the inn's profile. A moment later, she received a notification that they'd begun following her. She'd talked to the concierge like the waitress suggested, and he'd taken a stack of her business cards.

Feeling giddy, she did a little dance right there on the beach. Jake might not want her here, but she had other Orchard Harbor locals on her side.

With a fresh sense of purpose, she cast one last look at the sparkling blue water stretching to the horizon and headed home. Time to get back to work. One grumpy foreman wasn't going to slow her down.

Chapter Six

Jake swung the sledgehammer and landed a blow on the wall in front of him. It felt good to make progress after the roller coaster of the past two weeks. A mix-up with the permits had resulted in another delay. Add that to the time it had taken for him to go over the plans, and they were already way behind schedule.

The boards in front of him caved in, revealing the mirror on the opposite wall. The last tenant had put in fitting rooms for customers to try on beachy clothing. Taking the partitions down would give Maddie a wide-open space for a counter and display case, plus live-edge shelves for the selection of picnic baskets and blankets, as well banquet-style tables for customers to taste samples.

Pretty fancy for a catering business, but that was what the tourists loved. And what the tourists loved brought money to the local economy. Work for his crew meant savings for his own dreams. He'd tried to convince himself that his secret hope that Maddie would manage to beat the odds and stay in business had nothing to do with an irrational desire for her to stick around and everything to do with the fact that stable commerce was good for the town.

But the truth was he wanted her here, despite everything. He swung hard, hoping to dislodge pesky thoughts of the woman he had no business being interested in.

The wall collapsed with a thud, and Jake stepped back, waving his hand to clear the dust. The rest of the crew was taking out old appliances from the kitchen. He'd triple-checked that the electrical had been shut off, standard procedure, but he was being extra careful with every step of this reno. He needed to restore his reputation in Maddie's eyes.

Resting the sledgehammer against his leg, he paused to listen. Up until now he'd heard the squeak of metal on tile, grunts and the occasional shout as the men worked. But all he heard at the moment was the low hum of conversation. Had they run into a problem?

He stepped through the debris of splintered boards, his steel-toe boots providing protection from nails and broken glass. His safety glasses were covered in a fine coating of dust, and he took them off, tucking them into his collar. He patted his back pocket for his phone to check the time, but it wasn't there. *Huh.* Scanning the room, he walked toward the others. "Hey, guys, seen my phone?"

A familiar feminine voice answered. "This what you're looking for?"

His head snapped up, and he found himself face-to-face with Madelyn, once again popping up when he least expected it. She was wearing that blazer again, the one that made her look sexy and in control, a dainty silver necklace visible at her open collar.

His eyes slipped from down her legs, curvy beneath her jeans, to her ballet-slipper-style shoes. The leather looked soft and delicate, no match for a rusty nail or sharp edge of exposed metal that could be lying around. What was she thinking, walking around a reno in those?

"How'd you get in here?" The question came out as a challenge, the words scraping past a throat dry with worry. If she got hurt, he'd never be able to live with himself. Bad enough she blamed him for flooding her apartment, but if she got injured on his watch? His blood turned to ice at the thought.

She hooked a thumb over her shoulder, the copper bracelet she'd worn on the night they met flashing beneath her sleeve. "The back door was open. These two, uh…" she said, squinting at the crew like she was trying to remember their names. "Neil?" she asked the youngest guy on the crew, who nodded encouragingly. "And Terrence, right?" His buddy gave her a thumbs-up. *Traitor*. Maddie turned back to Jake. "They told me I could come on in."

"They should've run it by me," he said. "We're in the middle of demo and—"

"Yeah, I know," she interrupted. "That's why I'm here. For a progress update."

To check up on him, she meant. He crossed his arms, his worry edged out by the desire to prove to this woman, once and for all, that her renovation was in good hands. "Why, exactly?"

She copied his pose, chin high. "I have a lot of money invested in this. It's my responsibility to make sure things are going well."

"That's where you're wrong," he said through gritted teeth. "It's my responsibility to do things right. All you've got to do is sign off when I'm done."

Her dark brows shot up. "Oh, is that right? I'm just supposed to stay away and trust you to do a good job?"

There she was, throwing that word *trust* around like he'd done something to break it. "You're the one who hired us. Either you trust your own judgment, or you don't." Was that the problem? Had she been burned in the past?

Before he could explore that hunch, she said, "I trust Wright Construction. I read testimonials, and my friends vouched for the company." She took a step forward, bringing them almost chest to chest.

This close, she had to tilt her head back to look him in the eyes, but she didn't seem intimidated in the slightest. That shouldn't have stirred his blood, but damn if he didn't flash back to the moment before he'd kissed her in the winery. She'd had that same reckless look right before their mouths met.

"It's you I don't trust." The words yanked him out of the memory like a jab to the most tender part of his heart. "You've done nothing but make a mess of things since we met."

"If I recall, we both made a mess of things together," he said, the response spilling out before he could think it through.

Her eyes flashed, and she let out a sound half between a groan and a growl, and dammit, he was one second away from kissing her again. "I'm talking about the flood, and you know it."

"For the last time, that wasn't my fault. The pipes were worn clear through." He stepped back, putting space between them before his thoughts went haywire again. "Nothing like that has ever happened on a project of mine. Ask the guys." He gestured toward where Terrence and Neil had been standing, but they were gone.

Where was his backup when he needed them? First they'd let Maddie in without the proper safety attire. Then they'd abandoned him when he needed a vote of confidence.

"Oh, I'll take their word for it," she said. "Just not yours." With that, she spun on her thin-soled heels and Jake fought back a wince, watching her storm out without so much as a glance at the hazard-strewn floor, her head vulnerable without a hard hat.

"Well, shit."

"You can say that again," Terrence said, stepping back inside with a glance over his shoulder at Maddie stomping off. He leaned against the door, his denim shirt streaked with grease from carrying out the stove. "There something going on between the two of you we should know about?"

"Nothing I can't handle," Jake said.

"You sure about that, boss?" Neil appeared beside Terrence, casting a worried glance over his shoulder. "Because my sister gets that same look right before she rats me out to my parents."

A low chuckle came from Terrence. "He's not wrong," he said. "You're about to be in trouble with the boss." He lifted his chin toward where Maddie had her phone out and was jabbing at the screen.

Jake's stomach dropped out. Yanking off his hard hat, he rushed outside and jogged past the rented dumpster to where she stood by her car parked on the street. She was digging through her purse, phone tucked between her shoulder and chin.

He waved to get her attention and whispered, "Maddie." Remembering she'd told him not to use her nickname anymore, he tried again. "Madelyn, I mean. Hang on. Please, let me explain." How, he wasn't sure. Every time he talked to her, he made things worse. But he had to try.

She didn't hang up but met his eyes and shrugged in a get-on-with-it gesture.

"You could've been hurt." Worry sharpened his tone. "Walking in unannounced without the proper gear is asking for trouble."

She lowered the phone, hand cupped over it to muffle her voice. "I told you, the guys let me in."

He tried not to roll his eyes. "Neil's just a kid." About the same age as Jake when he'd started construction work in earnest—barely twenty, though worlds more responsible than he had been. "And Terrence is too nice to say no. He probably thought he could keep you from getting hurt."

"And you don't think he would?" she asked.

"I don't think anyone could stop you if you put your mind to it."

Her lips twitched at that, curving into a smile, and he sensed an opening. "If you want to visit the site, you should call first."

"I shouldn't need permission to visit my own shop." Her brown eyes met his in challenge.

"You're going to have to give up some control," he said, "for your own good. Until the remodel is done, it's my domain. The crews need space to work without worrying about interruption. One wrong swing of the hammer, and you could've been seriously hurt."

"Then maybe you should keep me updated on what's going on so I wouldn't have to stop in."

"I send updates every week," he said. "Demolition is barely underway."

Her posture deflated, and even though he was glad she seemed to be coming around, he didn't like seeing her look dejected. "I was just excited, I guess. I wanted to document the process for my social media account."

That snapped him back to attention. "You put yourself in harm's way just to get selfies for social media?"

"It's for my business," she said. "Keeping followers up to date with progress will build interest."

He knew that was common practice nowadays, but the whole thing seemed silly to him. Next thing you know she'd be asking him to install a time-lapse camera in the ceiling to catch the whole process on camera.

"Did you get Terrence and Neil to sign off on that?" Who was he kidding? They'd probably jump at the chance.

"I was in the middle of asking them when you barged in."

Barged in? Granted, yes, it was her name on the lease. But she'd hired them to renovate, which meant that for now, he was in charge. He had every right to do whatever was necessary to make sure things ran smoothly, and that included not allowing Maddie to get hurt while taking selfies at the job site.

"Well, make sure you get their permission before posting anything," he said. "And don't share any photos that include me." He didn't care either way, but he wasn't feeling particularly generous.

"Gladly," she said, her tone jagged as lake ice in January. "Anything else?"

"I'm not denying it's your right to come and go as you please." His skin itched under her prickly gaze, and he was all too aware she was on hold with the office manager, his future at Wright Construction on the line. "But there's going to be a lot going on. It would be much better if you could let us know ahead of time before you plan to stop by." There. That sounded reasonable.

"You don't think I can take care of myself?" The words came out as a challenge, but her expression looked more hurt than anything. As if she desperately wanted him to see her as strong and capable.

Why couldn't he manage to say the right thing? All he wanted was to keep her safe. "It's not that. Accidents happen, even with precautions." He thought about the time a guy who'd been on the job twenty years had lost focus and driven a nail straight through his hand. "I wouldn't be able to live with myself if you got hurt on my watch."

"If you're worried about me suing, don't be," she said.

He let out a growl of frustration. This woman was twisting him up in knots. "I'm not worried about liability." He stepped closer, nearly undone by the gentle scent of vanilla that clung to her skin. "I'm worried about *you*."

Maddie's mouth fell open, like she was stunned by his admission, but then he heard a voice on the other end of the call, and she half turned, lifting the phone to her mouth again. "Hello? Yes, I'm still here."

Jake's stomach clenched. Too late. She was going to tell Reese how unprofessional he'd been. The worst part was, he deserved it. He'd risked everything he worked for just because he couldn't get his feelings under control.

She was murmuring into the phone with her back to him, but loud enough for him to catch pieces of the conversation. "I was calling about a project under contract with your firm, but I was able to talk with the foreman assigned to it. Yep. Jake Winn." She nodded. "All good. Yep. Great."

A moment later, she ended the call. He wanted to hug her, but instead he said, "Thank you."

She nodded, expression softer than before. "Just make sure you send those updates. I don't like being kept in the dark." With that, she got into her car and drove away.

He'd dug himself out of a hole, but if life had taught him anything, it was that trouble was never far away. And Maddie felt like all kinds of trouble.

He grinned. *Bring it on, Madelyn Briar.* He'd always loved a challenge.

Maddie drove away from Jake, purposefully avoiding the rearview mirror. If she looked back, she might get that suspicious tug in her chest, the one that had prompted her to assure the office manager her questions had been answered, and she didn't need to speak with the owner of Wright Construction after all.

How did things with Jake always manage to take a turn for the worse? All she'd wanted to do was post an update about the renovation—*her* renovation. But he had to go and accuse her of inserting herself where she didn't belong. Of putting herself in harm's way, as if she weren't a grown woman.

But there'd been something desperate in the way he'd chased after her that showed he didn't understand how things kept getting jumbled up between them, either. That maybe he had her best interests at heart, despite his words coming out gruff and ornery. And then he told her he cared about her.

Well, not exactly. He'd said he was worried about her. But the look in his eyes when he'd said it had melted away her frustration.

Didn't hurt that he looked better in a hard hat than anyone had a right to, and when he'd taken it off to glare down at her with those sparkling amber eyes… Well, she could admit she might've fired back to keep from dwelling on how his rugged handsomeness affected her.

But now she'd lost out on the chance to film content. She was trying to build interest in her business before the grand opening. Social media wasn't the only way to get the word out, though. She'd spent the last week visiting local businesses and giving out her card. She'd found a beautiful necklace to give her mom on Mother's Day while chatting with the manager at one shop and ate her fill of ice cream at another, despite the weather being too cold to enjoy the patio seating. While she ate, she'd discussed stocking pints of their locally made ice cream as an add-on for picnics.

But today's excursion was a personal one. She needed to find a place to work where she wouldn't be interrupted by random hammering throughout the day. There seemed to be no rhyme or reason to when Jake worked on the apartment upstairs, other than he never used power tools at night or early morning except the first week when they'd been going back and forth, trying to one-up each other with the amount of noise in their apartment. She knew he was trying to respect her sleep schedule, but the pounding in the middle of the day when she was working on spreadsheets or photoshoots wasn't helpful, either.

More often than not, she found herself going to the Harbor Bridge Café, but she couldn't keep paying for coffee every time she needed a quiet spot with Wi-Fi, at least not until she was making a profit from the catering business. Especially since there only seemed to be one barista and she was always too swamped to chat, so Maddie couldn't even use the excuse of networking.

What she needed was a quiet place to do her work that wouldn't put a dent in her savings. Turning onto a street lined with stately historic homes, she parallel parked in front of the library. The building featured a peaked roof and walls of windows.

A bulletin board in the entryway caught her attention. Flyers for everything from language learning clubs to sailing classes were tacked to the board, and she caught sight of a neon flyer advertising the Orchard Harbor Art Guild.

"That's a great organization, whether you're new to art or a professional," said a voice behind her, and Maddie turned to find a tall woman, probably early thirties, standing behind her. She wore wide-leg trousers and a crocheted sweater in shades of bright pink, with an Orchard Harbor Public Library lanyard around her neck.

Maddie's gaze shot between the board and the librarian. "Thanks. But uh… I'm not sure that's the one for me." Or that she'd be welcome. "I was actually looking to see if there are any cooking classes or supper clubs."

"A foodie?" The librarian grinned. "Me, too. I actually host a monthly cookbook club here at the library."

"Now that's the kind of book club I can get behind." Maddie instantly realized where she was and tried to walk her statement back. "Not that all books aren't great—"

The librarian gave a soft laugh. "No worries. That's one reason why I host the club, besides getting to taste great food. It brings people into the library who might not otherwise stop in, and we have a lot of resources to offer the community besides books." Her dark eyes sparkled. "Just so you know, reading recipes counts, especially on a food blog. I mean, I feel like I have to skim through an entire autobiography every time I'm looking for an answer to a simple question, like how long to hard boil eggs."

Maddie smiled, grateful that the librarian was so laid-back. She had hazy memories of being shushed by librarians on school field trips and scolded for not turning in her books on time, but then again, she had barely stepped foot in a library as an adult. She should probably hold off on forming opinions about the profession.

"I'm Maddie," she said. "I'm opening a catering business, so my interest in the food-related clubs isn't entirely altruistic."

"Oh yay!" The other woman's smile didn't waver. If anything, it grew bigger. "It's awesome to hear there will be another woman-owned business in town. I love to see it."

Her welcoming attitude went a long way toward smoothing Maddie's ruffled feelings after the morning's interaction with Jake. "Thank you, I'm excited to be here."

The librarian tilted her head, looking thoughtful. "You know, we host monthly cooking classes. They're a hit with the senior residents. If you'd like to sign up to be a demonstrator sometime, you could pass along info about your catering business during the class."

"That sounds fantastic."

"Great! I could email you what dates we have available, and we'll go from there." She headed toward the front desk, and Maddie followed. "My name's Shreya, by the way."

Maddie jotted her info down on the piece of paper Shreya

provided and took the flyer with the upcoming cookbook club dates, then gratefully accepted a tour of the library. They ended in front of the nonfiction section, and Shreya was showing her where to find the cookbook selections for the March and April meetings when she was called to the front to help with checkout.

“I hope to see you back soon,” Shreya said.

“Definitely. It was great to meet you.” Maddie took not only this month’s cookbook pick but the next one as well. The conversation had left her brimming with ideas and optimism. Maybe she could even offer charcuterie-board-making classes at the shop. She couldn’t wait for the first book club meeting.

Despite the argument with Jake and the failed mission to get content for social media, today had been a success. Tasha and Celeste were right—networking really wasn’t so bad after all. Most people in town had been more than welcoming. As long as she steered clear of the art guild members, who were no doubt disappointed she’d stolen their gallery space, her future here looked bright.

Jake sat at a round table next to the president of the art guild, Gloria. They were watching his friend Garrett’s presentation on how to use social media effectively as an artist. He owned a local glassblowing studio that offered tours and had a big following on social media. The topic was an unwelcome reminder of how he’d messed up Maddie’s plan to raise interest in her business by sharing videos of the renovation process.

Guilt ate at him, but he tried to focus on the slide on the projector. Tonight’s topic wasn’t useful for him since he wasn’t interested in promoting his art, but he wanted to support Garrett, and he did his best to attend every meeting, regardless of the topic. He wasn’t just here to learn; he was here to stay connected. He’d acted out after his father walked out on their family in high school—leaving behind a wife and sons who'd lost their home thanks to his mountains of debt—and it had cost Jake a lot of friendships and goodwill.

For several years, he stayed on a course of bad decisions and regret until he finally realized he was punishing himself for his father's mistakes. Finding the courage to join the group had made him feel like he'd done a full one-eighty, from angry kid to a man on a mission. His goal? Prove to everyone that he wasn't a dishonest fraud like his dad.

The members of the art guild had welcomed him from his very first meeting, but not everyone in town was so quick to forgive.

Making amends to those he'd personally wronged had been top priority. But creating a gallery space for local artists would've been a contribution to the town that the naysayers wouldn't have been able to overlook.

Sure, Maddie had unknowingly derailed his plan. But maybe it was for the best. Renovations always uncovered unexpected issues, and his budget hadn't been very big. He was just glad he'd only told Andy and Tom. The fewer people who knew he'd failed, the better.

Garrett wrapped up the presentation to the sound of applause. Gloria stood and thanked him for the information. She'd been an art teacher at Orchard Harbor High School until her retirement a few years ago, and it showed in her command of the room. Now, her oil paintings were sought-after throughout the region. She directed everyone to help themselves to refreshments before the business meeting convened.

Jake expected to find the usual array of baked goods from the Harbor Bridge Café, but there were only prepackaged donuts and cookies.

"No scones or muffins today?" he asked Garrett. His

friend's straight brown hair was pulled into a bun, his beard on the shaggy side.

"Heard the café is shorthanded. Elise is focusing on coffee and small batches only for the time being." Garrett bit into a donut and made a face. "We need to look elsewhere for snacks in the meantime because these donuts are not it."

Jake had to agree. "Elise has spoiled us, that's for sure." The packaged donuts left a waxy film on his teeth that had him reaching for a cup of coffee. Maddie popped into his mind. He'd never tasted her food, but he assumed someone who poured their life savings into opening a catering business knew their stuff. Plus the smells that wafted up the stairway each night were heavenly and made his frozen dinners a whole lot less appealing.

"I might know of someone who could provide treats." The moment the words left his mouth, Jake willed them back. Why had he brought Maddie into the mix? The guild was his safe space, the one place he didn't feel judged. Besides, her commercial kitchen wasn't up and running yet. No way she'd be able to make enough food to feed a crowd in her apartment.

But Garrett was looking at him with interest. "Oh really? Who?"

Too late to back out now. "I'm working on a catering business renovation and from what I can tell, the owner's cooking is top-notch."

"You mean your neighbor?" Garrett said, and Jake nearly dropped his coffee. His friend chuckled. "Don't look so surprised, man. Word travels fast. Maybe you could score us a discount on snacks."

Small chance. She'd probably up her prices if the request came through him. "She's working on opening a business. You know how hard that is." Garrett had worked for years to get his glass-blowing studio off the ground. "She deserves to be paid what the food is worth."

"Couldn't agree more," his friend said. "I was messing around." Garrett bit into another donut and winced. "Hopefully your neighbor can help because I don't think I can handle another month of these store-bought treats."

Neighbor. People had started to head back to their seats, and Jake took the excuse to follow suit before Garrett asked him any more questions about Maddie and discovered his feelings ran a lot deeper than neighborly.

He made small talk with the others at the table, and a few minutes later, Gloria called the meeting to order with a clap of her hands. "We have some important business to attend to, so let's get to the next portion of the meeting before any of you sneak out the back." She lifted her chin toward a table across the room. "Looking at you, Laurel."

Laurel had been in the act of folding up her napkin and laughed. "You know I've got to let Daisy out," she said, referring to her pug.

"This won't take long," Gloria promised. "But we need to discuss the Orchard Blossom Fest. As you all know, submitting a piece to display in our booth isn't mandatory, but even if you're not looking to sell a piece, it's a great motivation to finish off a project. You'll get eyes on your work, plus we give out awards and prizes to everyone who enters."

She went on to explain more details about the event.

Jake settled back in his chair. At his first festival six years ago, his nerves had been sky-high. He'd expected his entry to be ignored or maybe even poked fun at, but to his surprise, he'd received three offers to buy the piece and interest from local gallery owners. His brief stint of producing work at high volume taught him that wasn't what he wanted out of art, but he still made something for the art guild's booth every year to support the group.

The room was suddenly quiet, and he felt everyone's eyes on him. For a split second, he thought they might've found out about his secret bid for a gallery space. Honestly, he felt relieved to have it out in the open, but then Garrett said, "Think you can put in a good word for us?"

Jake frowned. He must've missed something.

"With the caterer," his friend prompted. "We could use another food vendor for the festival."

While Jake was processing this, Gloria spoke up. "I was looking at Madelyn Briar's website, and she plans to open a few weeks beforehand. Since you're already working with her, we thought you could be our point of contact."

"Sure," he said, though hearing the invitation from him might make Maddie more likely to decline. "I'll talk to her."

"Great." Gloria beamed at him. "With that taken care of, let's move on to discussing booth rentals. Patti, can you share an update?"

The meeting continued, but Jake was no longer listening. All he could think was how Maddie had somehow managed to infiltrate every part of his life in less than a month. It was clear he hadn't thought things through before kissing her that night.

If only he could find it in himself to regret it.

Chapter Seven

If cookbooks had been on the required reading list in school, Maddie would've been a lot more interested in writing book reports. She'd spent the past few days immersed in the cookbook club selection, scribbling notes and dreaming up ways to adapt the recipes.

She had a treasured collection of favorite recipe books, but this chef was new to her. The glossy photos made the food appear melt-in-your-mouth delicious. Great job by the food stylist. She tried out several recipes before settling on one to bring to the meeting that fit the small-bites aesthetic of her catering company. Nothing wrong with staying on brand, especially since her brand was perfect for get-togethers.

The meeting was held in a multipurpose room at the library. This month's theme was Garden Party, in a nod to the start of spring. Vases bursting with tulips sat at the center of each round table, and the place settings were porcelain with an ivy border. The whole thing looked like a grown-up tea party. Maddie was in love.

She placed her homemade fig crackers topped with goat cheese and bacon jam next to what must be a carrot cake since it was decorated with piped buttercream carrots. Clearly, she wasn't the only skilled cook in attendance. She snapped a few photos of the food and decor for a social media post, giving herself a minute to settle in before going to say hello to everyone.

Though she hadn't managed to get over being wary of strangers, opening up to new people was getting easier. She reminded herself that these people were her neighbors and potential friends. At least she hoped so. Having one enemy in town was more than enough.

Looking around, she locked eyes with an auburn-haired woman in a floral dress and fluffy cream cardigan, who smiled, beckoning Maddie to the open seat next to her.

"I'm Britta," she said when Maddie sat down. "I saw you taking photos and figured this must be your first time. The group goes all out for these, but us old hats have gotten used to it."

Maddie smiled, not sure if being singled out as new was a good thing or not, but she was used to it by now. "I'm Madelyn Briar," she said. "This is actually my first book club, period. I'm not much of a reader, but recipes are an exception."

The woman seated across the table smiled at her. She was wearing a yellow gingham vintage-style dress with puffed sleeves, her hair pulled into a high ponytail with curly bangs. "I'm so glad you gave it a try. I'll read anything, but food makes everything better."

"Crystal is a local author," Britta said. "She writes comfy mysteries."

"*Cozy* mysteries," Crystal said with a resigned note to her voice that told Maddie this wasn't the first time she'd had to correct Britta. She turned to Maddie, and her brown eyes sparkled like she was imparting a secret. "They have recipes in the back."

Maddie grinned. "Now you're speaking my language. I'd love to check them out. My friend Celeste is a big fan of cozy mysteries, and she's been telling me to give the foodie ones a try."

"You're a friend of Celeste's?" Crystal asked. "She's been so supportive. I can always count on her to show up at my local events."

Maddie wasn't surprised to hear it. Busy though Celeste was, she always came through for her friends. "Celeste is part of the reason I moved here," she said. "I've been friends with her and Tasha Grant since high school. I grew up inland but met them on summer break one year. Tasha convinced me to finally go after my dreams and open a catering business," she added, noticing that it felt easier to say each time she got the words out.

"Ooh." Crystal half rose out of her seat, looking at the table with all the food. "Which dish did you bring? I'll have to try it first."

Maddie felt tempted to brush off the compliment, but she needed to get used to talking confidently about her food. "I put my own spin on the fig puff pastries from the hors d'oeuvres section. I'm going to specialize in upscale picnics and charcuterie boards, so I figured it would be great to try out some new recipes that I could use once my tasting room opens."

"Love that idea," Crystal said.

"Well, some of us are mere amateurs," Britta said, breaking in like she'd been waiting for an opening. "But I hardly think that makes our food less appealing."

"Definitely not," Maddie told her. "What did you make?"

"The carrot cake."

"That looks fabulous." Maddie was grateful not to have to fib. "I'm excited to try it."

"I'm excited to try everything," Crystal said. "If you'll excuse me, ladies, I'm going to go fix a plate."

Eager to sample the food, Maddie scooched her chair back

to join Crystal, but Britta jumped in with a question. "Did you say you were opening a tasting room? That's a unique idea for a catering business." The way she said *unique* made it sound more like *weird*, but luckily, Maddie was prepared for this question.

She'd had to justify her business plans to her parents, who were supportive but anxious for her not to take more risks after finally rebuilding her credit. They'd seen her struggle after the scammer stole her identity, and it took a lot of convincing to show them that she didn't just want a safe career; she wanted fulfilling work.

Well-meaning friends like Celeste had also questioned her choices. Her friends and family had wanted to make sure Maddie didn't make a business move she'd regret. Even though their worry sometimes made Maddie feel like they doubted her, it had also pushed her to think long and hard about each step. As a result, she was confident in how she'd chosen to go about opening her business.

"Think of it like a tasting room at a winery," she explained. "The primary goal is to benefit from foot traffic. Impulse buys from couples looking for a romantic date to end the evening or families who forgot to pack a cooler for a day at the beach or a hike, that sort of thing."

Britta's expression softened from judgmental to intrigued, which gave Maddie the confidence to keep going.

"I'm also looking to tap into the vacationer market, people who wouldn't necessarily hear about my business through word of mouth."

Britta was nodding along. "That does sound like a solid idea. But you'd have the most visibility downtown, and retail spots there aren't cheap."

Maddie smiled. "You're telling me. Luckily, Celeste helped me find a great deal on place that just needs a little fixing up."

"That's a bold choice, but I commend you for taking the risk," Britta said.

Maddie wasn't sure whether that was a backhanded compliment or a forward-handed insult, but she was going to give Britta the benefit of the doubt. She didn't seem mean-spirited, just opinionated.

"Thanks. I have a great company handling the renovation." She wasn't about to reveal her issues with Jake to a stranger, let alone someone who seemed ready to pounce on any weakness. "Wright Construction came highly recommended."

"Let me guess—Martin Nash? He handled my friend's renovation when she opened a doggy boutique."

"Originally, I was working with Martin," Maddie said. "But he had to take a leave of absence, and Jake Winn took over."

Britta's blue eyes went wide. "Jake?"

"Yes, why?"

"I'd be careful is all. Jake's the town bad boy. Or at least he was. Got up to all sorts of trouble in school, vandalized stuff. He got fired from every job he ever had until Reese hired him."

"The owner of Wright Construction?"

Britta nodded, taking a demure sip of tea. "He hired Jake when no one else would and must've talked some sense into him. Jake turned things around after that, though a lot of us question whether the change is genuine."

Normally, Maddie wouldn't put any trust in gossip, but was it so farfetched? The apartment had flooded on his watch. Even though she believed it wasn't his fault, wouldn't an experienced contractor have caught the problem before it got to that point? Plus, he'd basically chased her off the property when she'd dropped by unannounced.

At the time, she'd believed his explanation about being concerned for her safety. But could it be he didn't want her to take a closer look at what was going on in case she spotted poor workmanship?

She'd never live it down if she made another bad judgment call, but she couldn't bring herself to believe the worst of Jake. They'd bickered, but beneath the arguments she felt an undercurrent of lingering attraction. "He made it sound like his work was highly sought after."

Britta let out an undignified snort. "Hardly. Don't get me wrong, Wright Construction is outstanding, but Jake specifically?" She shook her head. "He has his share of friends. But folks around here have long memories, and he devoted a lot of time to being up to no good. Plenty of people I know wouldn't trust him to set foot in their house, let alone renovate it."

A sense of justice pushed Maddie to stand up for him, even as Britta cast doubt on her opinion of him. "People can change." She was hoping to, after all. To become the person she'd been before her life got turned upside down.

"Sure they can," Britta said, not sounding like she believed it. She took a sip of tea. "And Jake's not a bad guy. But I wouldn't say he's trustworthy, either."

Could Maddie's first impression of him have been so wrong? Maybe the Jake she'd met the second day was the real him. Cocky and quick to judge, rather than mild-mannered and self-confident.

Maddie excused herself to go get a plate of food before the book discussion began, but she'd suddenly lost her appetite.

All night, Maddie thought about what Britta had said. Jake came home later than usual, and she was upset at herself for paying such close attention to his schedule. She'd heard the front door close, then a pause before the creak of the stairs signaled he was going up to his own apartment.

Had he been thinking of knocking on her door? But why?

They'd stopped feuding over noise levels, and he'd been sending updates through email just like he promised. He'd even attached photos and a few short clips he said she could use for social media. She'd grinned when she saw the selfie of Terrence and Neil. None of himself, and she told herself not to be disappointed.

She needed advice on how to handle what Britta had revealed, but when she texted Tasha, her friend couldn't chat because she was at her sister's house again. The baby had colic, and it was all hands on deck. Celeste was free to meet up for coffee in a couple days. Maddie was tempted to call her parents, but they were already worried about her. Their overbearing concern was well-meaning, but she needed to prove she could take care of herself. She wasn't a naive young woman anymore.

The next morning, she'd come to a decision that she wasn't going to do anything about what Britta had told her. Gossip wasn't any more trustworthy than a first impression. Celeste and Tasha would've told her if there'd been a reason to avoid Jake. She'd move ahead with her task for the day, which meant making a decision about an accent wall she'd been considering.

She headed to the cabinetry shop and lumberyard a few blocks off the main street. The store had a hand-carved wooden sign hanging out front, and a brick walkway in a herringbone pattern led to a two-story converted home with dormers and crocuses in window boxes. Very quaint and welcoming.

Inside, a man in a canvas half apron stood behind a gleaming wooden counter. He had a combed-out afro and freckles dotted his cheekbones. He smiled at her from behind black-framed glasses. "Welcome in. How may I help you today?"

His warm greeting helped ease the ache of worry that had knotted her chest. "I'm looking for reclaimed wood for a project. Would you happen to have any samples?"

"I can do better than samples. I'll show you our current stock, if you don't mind stepping back out into the cold?"

Maddie never left home without the proper attire, and in the spring that meant layers. She'd slipped a crewneck sweater over her tee and topped that off with a jacket and silk scarf before heading out. "Not at all," she said, and the man smiled.

"Follow me, then." On the way through a bright showroom lined with cabinet options and handles in all types of finishes, from brass to painted ceramic, they passed an office where a woman sat squinting at a computer, glasses tucked into her blond hair. The man leading Maddie paused and asked, "Could you please keep an eye on the front?"

She pushed back from the desk with a distracted smile. "Sure thing, Spencer."

The back of the shop opened into a small clearing overhung by trees, and beyond that stood a three-sided barn. Underneath the open-beamed ceiling, stacks of wood were arranged on rows of deep shelves. Even from here, she caught the enticing scent of fresh-cut wood.

He stopped and said, "If you're doing a large-scale project, we might not have the inventory to suit your needs, but we do have a variety of reclaimed wood in smaller quantities."

"I'm still making up my mind." Maddie didn't want to get his hopes up for a sale. "But the wall I'd need covered is sixteen feet long and nine feet high." She'd studied the plans often enough that she had the dimensions memorized.

"Shouldn't be a problem," Spencer said. "Would you like me to walk you through the space, or would you rather explore on your own?"

She nibbled her lip. It was always tough to make decisions with people watching.

He must've sensed this, because he stepped back. "Take

your time. If you need help, give me a buzz." He pointed to a doorbell by the back door.

"I probably won't be purchasing any large quantities today, but I'm also looking for something smaller." She held out her hands to indicate a size that would make a good backdrop for photos. Sometimes she liked to create a cozy cabin setting for pictures of hot chocolate and lattes.

"Hmm," he said. "Are you looking for something you can repurpose for a piece of furniture?"

"Actually, I plan to use it as a photo prop. I'm a food stylist."

"Food stylist, huh?" He looked at her thoughtfully. "What does that involve?"

He sounded curious, not skeptical, which was a welcome change. "I make sure food looks appealing in photos. I do a lot of freelance work with restaurants for websites and menus, that sort of thing."

Spencer broke out in a grin. "I know of a few local restaurants you could help in that department. You didn't hear it from me, but the pizza place's menu looks like crime scene photos, not food."

She chuckled. "I've seen my share of sketchy-looking menus, trust me. If you ever hear of them asking around for help with an update, feel free to mention my name."

"I'll bring it up the next time I stop in. I worked there three summers as a kid, so Alan won't mind the suggestion coming from me." There was a thud from inside the shop, and Spencer glanced over his shoulder. "Better get back in there. But check the bins in the back corner. That's where we keep the smaller pieces of barnwood."

He hurried away, and Maddie stepped inside the large shed, inhaling deeply and letting the earthy scents calm her. Sawdust swirled around her boots, kicked up by the breeze, and she stuck her hands in her jacket pockets. Strolling slowly, she glanced around at the rows of stacked lumber. Pausing by a shelf of what looked like old barnwood, she reached for one and pulled back when a splinter jabbed her thumb. "Ouch," she said aloud into the empty space, shaking her hand to ease the sting.

"Might want to refrain from handling the wood unless you have the proper protection." The voice was low and rich with a hint of teasing, and it sent a thrill through her, even though she should've learned by now.

Maddie turned to see Jake in one of the aisles, standing by a wheelbarrow full of two-by-fours.

"I'm beginning to think you're following me," he said with the same smirk she'd found endearing that first night. How had things changed so much in a few short weeks?

"I could say the same." She raised her brows in challenge.

He crossed his arms, biceps bulging against his denim shirt. "I come here all the time. Last I checked, caterers don't usually visit lumberyards."

"Shows what you know about my job," she said, aware she sounded childish and wondering what it was about him that brought out her competitive side. Normally, she'd never bicker with someone she was working with. Something about him made her reckless when she'd worked so hard to be careful.

"Since my contractor told me to stay out of his hair—" she gave him a pointed look "—I decided to focus on the design elements of the project. I'm thinking of putting a reclaimed lumber wall in the tasting room."

"Wood paneling would make the space look smaller," he said.

"Martin didn't seem to think so." Though Maddie was inclined to agree. She'd been leaning toward a more elegant vibe with custom wallpaper, but she didn't want to give Jake the satisfaction of agreeing with him.

"Martin's old school. He never goes against what the customer thinks they want."

"Sounds like a good policy," she said.

"Except when the customer is wrong."

"I don't think that's the saying."

He frowned at her, mouth a tight line in his stubbled jaw. "The saying doesn't take into account customers having unrealistic expectations or being just plain misinformed."

"An accent wall is a matter of taste."

He took hold of another piece of wood, pulled it out and hoisted it smoothly onto the wheelbarrow. "Just trying to save you from regrets down the line."

"The only thing I regret is going with Wright Construction." She tried not to watch as he unbuttoned his cuffs, rolling up his sleeves with efficient turns. His nonchalance irked her, almost as much as the sexy flicks of his deft fingers. The same fingers that had caressed her cheek so tenderly the night they met.

Shoving aside the thought, she hitched a thumb over her shoulder toward the main building. "Spencer seems to have a lot of connections in town. I bet he knows another reputable company."

Jake froze, amber eyes locking on hers. "We have a contract."

"You don't even want to work with me."

"Doesn't mean I don't want the work," he said.

This man was infuriating. "What about me? You think I want to spend the next few months working closely with you? There's got to be someone else at Wright Construction to take it on."

"Only my boss, and he has a full slate of contracts. You want out?" he asked. "Good luck finding another company to work with you."

"What's that supposed to mean?" Realization hit her like an icy wave. "You're going to turn people against me?"

"Wouldn't have to." He feigned nonchalance, but his shoulders looked tense. "It's a small town. Not a lot of options, and we've built up a good reputation, whereas you're the newcomer."

Pretty rich, coming from a guy with a bad past. Then again, he was probably counting on an outsider not knowing the gossip. "Guess that's how you get people to work with you," Maddie said. "Lack of choices."

Jake's frown turned into a glower. "People choose us because we do good work."

"Wright Construction, sure. But you personally? I'm betting most people wouldn't work with you if they had a choice." She echoed Britta's words, and saying them aloud felt like a low blow he didn't deserve.

Sure enough, his expression slipped into something that looked less angry and more hurt. A flash of the kindhearted man she'd met at the winery. Then his gaze turned steely. "You think you can do better? Go ahead and find another contractor."

She'd been bluffing. She didn't want to go through the hassle of finding someone else. "You'd probably love that. But I won't give you the satisfaction of backing out."

"If it's your deposit you're worried about, I'll cover it." His jaw was set, like he meant it.

"You're that confident I won't find someone better?"

He didn't flinch, stance wide, looking down at her. "There isn't anyone better. So, yeah. I'm that confident."

"Maybe I'll just have to broaden my search. Look outside Orchard Harbor."

"Sounds about right." He grabbed the handles of the wheelbarrow and started walking away.

"What's that supposed to mean?" She hurried around to face him, not ready to let him have the last word.

"You say you're loyal to this place, but you haven't even been here a month and are already ready to pull jobs from locals and hand them to someone else."

"That's not fair. I want to be a part of things, but I can't do that if you're standing in my way."

He made a sweeping gesture, bowing at the waist. "Then by all means, find my replacement." His eyes swept up to meet hers, and her stomach fluttered with something akin to butterflies. Probably the after-effects of too much adrenaline.

"You're not worried about losing the money?"

His expression clouded over. "Like you said, what's losing the work compared to not having to deal with you?"

His words stung, but what hurt even more was knowing years had passed and she still couldn't trust herself to be a good judge of character.

This made one thing certain: falling for Jake Winn would've been a terrible mistake.

Chapter Eight

Jake was in his studio, tinkering. Andy and his wife, Carmen, let him use the barn on their property a few miles outside town, nestled in the rolling hills that were home to the apple, cherry, peach and plum orchards the town was named for. The crickets were out, which should've been his signal to head home. Grab dinner and a shower and make sure they were on track to move forward with the next step on Madelyn's project.

Demolition was finished, but the wiring needed an upgrade, and they were waiting on the electricians. They needed to keep the walls open, but could work on flooring in the meantime. If he put a rush on the more durable tile, maybe he could convince her to go that route. Except he might not get a chance to do any of that since he'd goaded her into looking for another contractor.

But dang it, she'd said he wasn't trustworthy. He'd been so hurt by the insinuation that he'd pushed her away, and now he was in real danger of Reese finding out he'd screwed up.

Instead of going home to mope, he'd come here to get some perspective. He'd started making art as a positive outlet for his resentment over his father's absence. Somewhere along the way it had become part of who he was.

Lately, though, he'd been too busy to spend much time in his makeshift studio, but he'd salvaged an end table from a recent demo and was thinking of putting an inlay on the top.

He was sifting through the bin of bottle caps he'd found on the beach when his brother walked in through the big sliding door.

"You didn't stop by the house to say hi," Andy said.

"Didn't want to disturb dinnertime."

"You mean you didn't want to get pulled into a tea party with Katie."

Jake chuckled. "I never mind teatime. Especially not when she raids the pantry."

"Does what?" his brother asked. "Never mind. I shouldn't be surprised, knowing that girl. Gets it from you." Jake had always been the mischievous one, while Andy toed the line.

His brother had been about to graduate when their father's gambling problem came to light. Andy had taken it in stride, changing his college plans like it was no big deal. Jake had resented him for not being more upset, before he learned better. Andy had been hurting, too, but as the oldest, he'd felt responsible. Their mom, Donna, had been so blindsided that she hadn't known how to support either of them.

But things were different now. She'd healed and was a steady presence in their lives. And Jake had long since taken responsibility for the choices he'd made back then.

"You've been scarce since that night at the winery. Been seeing that woman I caught you kissing?" Andy's matter-of-fact question snapped Jake to alertness so quickly he dropped the bin of bottle caps, and they scattered across the floor.

"You saw?"

His brother cracked a grin. "Nah, but I had a hunch, and you just confirmed it." He stooped to scoop up a few of the bottle caps by his feet. "Since she's the first woman you've shown interest in for a good long while, I decided I'd best stay out of it."

Glowering, Jake picked up the half empty bin. "Knew I should've gone out to the bar that night instead of drinking overpriced wine."

"I figured you'd be thanking me, since you wouldn't have been there to meet her if not for me. Did you get her number?"

"No, because someone—" he raised his brows meaningfully "—interrupted us."

Andy rubbed his jaw. "Sorry, man. But I'm sure you'll see her around. Or wait, isn't she Tasha's friend? You could ask her if Maddie's open to hanging out again."

"She's not." Jake busied himself with picking up bottle caps. Maybe his brother would get the hint and leave.

"Don't tell me you already messed things up."

Of course Andy would assume it was Jake's fault. It was, mostly. But still. "I ran into her again and asked her out. She wasn't interested, and that was before things got complicated."

"How can it possibly be too complicated with someone you just met?"

"She lives in the apartment below me. It got flooded the day after we met, and since I'm doing the reno upstairs, she blamed me at first."

Andy's green eyes went wide. "Not a great second impression."

"That's not the half of it." No getting around it; Jake would have to tell his brother everything. He explained the situation, from discovering he'd be working for Maddie to arguing when she'd shown up unannounced at the jobsite, then running his mouth and potentially losing out on the contract. He felt queasy just thinking about telling his boss he'd cost them the lucrative contract, but he'd tackle that problem when he got official word from Maddie that she was taking her business elsewhere.

Andy whistled. "You weren't kidding about complicated."

"I'm not the only one at fault," Jake said. "She called me inept, even though I had nothing to do with the pipes bursting."

"Was this before or after you accused her of being a greedy entrepreneur who only cared about profits?"

Okay, yeah, that hadn't been cool of him. "I overreacted because I was shocked to have to work on the space I'd lost out for the gallery," Jake said. "It's still a sore spot."

"You should tell the other guild members what you had planned. You don't have to do it on your own."

"They already voted to table the idea, and I tried anyway. Telling them would just make me look foolish."

Andy didn't look convinced. The only other person who knew he'd put in a bid was his friend Tom, and neither of them thought it was a good idea to keep his plan a secret. But they'd both made good choices their whole lives. Neither of them understood what it was like to have to fight to earn back their reputation.

"I hate that you felt like you needed to try to prove yourself in the first place," Andy said. "You've turned things around in a major way, but sometimes I feel like you're still punishing yourself for your past mistakes."

Jake retrieved another stray bottle cap from under a shelf. "They took me in and supported me even before I got my act together."

"And in turn, you've done so much for the group. Mentored young artists, worked to do more community outreach. You're already a valuable member without creating a gallery space."

Jake knew that, but he'd also wanted to fully step out from his dad's shadow. "I know, but sometimes I feel like half the town still thinks I'm a big screw-up. I wanted to prove I could make a plan and follow through." A gallery space would've brought in more tourism dollars, but it was probably for the best that he wasn't taking on such a big project alone.

"First of all, half the town doesn't hate you. Just a few vocal people putting misplaced anger on you. You're not the one who borrowed money and didn't repay."

"No, I'm just the kid who acted out and didn't live up to people's trust in me."

"You *were* that kid." Andy emphasized the past tense. "A kid who'd lost his dad and his home and was hurting. Now you're a grown man who owns up to his actions."

"Or digs himself in deeper," Jake said, thinking of today's encounter with Madelyn. "I want to keep things professional, but every time I see Madelyn, I make a mess of things." He took the full bin and slid it back into its spot.

His brother eyed him thoughtfully. "Maybe it's because you want more than a professional relationship with her."

"I did, but that ship has sailed." Every time he was around Maddie, his thoughts got jumbled up. He wished they could go back to their first meeting when everything had been easy and straightforward.

"You of all people should know there's always a chance for a do-over."

Normally, Jake would agree. All it took was one good choice, then another. But he felt like he'd blown his chances with her every step of the way. "All I can hope for now is to salvage our working relationship," he said.

"All right, then apologize," Andy said. "Whether or not she decides to keep working with you, you'll be seeing a lot of each other in the weeks to come because you're living under one roof," his brother said. "May as well do all you can to mend things."

Jake had already come to that conclusion, but hearing it from his brother cemented it. He was good at patching drywall and repairing cracked tiles. Fixing relationships was a skill he was still working on, but Madelyn was someone worth trying for. And maybe she'd change her mind about finding another contractor.

If not? Well, he'd have to admit where he'd gone wrong to

his boss. Wouldn't be the first time, but Reese had stuck with him through worse.

With a jolt, he realized he cared less about losing face in front of his boss than losing out on a chance with Madelyn.

Jake was right. Maddie had to expand her search beyond Orchard Harbor. Her head hurt from spending hours checking business ratings and customer reviews. She'd already been through this months ago and was fully satisfied with Wright Construction, right up until grumpy Jake stepped in.

She half wanted to give up just to save herself the trouble, but every time she considered that option, his smug face popped into her mind. She knew he'd gloat in that cocky and unfortunately sexy way of his, and she refused to give him the satisfaction. Celeste had connections through her real estate work, and they'd finally found a time to meet for coffee.

Ensconced in a sunlit corner of Harbor Bridge Café, Maddie kept watch for her friend. She'd invited Tasha to meet up, too, but one of her clients had made a last-minute appointment for a silk press. Maddie half expected Celeste to cancel as well. Her friends still hadn't found time to come over to her apartment, and though Maddie was mostly done unpacking, she craved their input on how she could go about decorating the space.

Celeste was the hardest to pin down. She'd always worked long hours since she'd been the breadwinner in her marriage, but lately Maddie wondered whether she was filling her time with work to avoid admitting she was lonely. Opening herself up to love after her ex's infidelity would be daunting, and Maddie understood the urge to put up walls; she'd done that for years. But she was trying to learn how to trust again, and Celeste wasn't quite there yet.

The line for coffee was slowing down. The pastry case was usually empty by the time Maddie arrived, but today she'd managed to snag a lemon poppy seed scone and was gearing up to introduce herself, but the barista disappeared into the back room the moment she'd finished Maddie's drink. She was beginning to think making a connection with this particular Orchard Harbor business was a lost cause.

She'd finished the delicious scone—tart, with the subtle, nutty crunch of the poppy seeds—and Celeste still hadn't arrived. She was just about to check her phone to see if she'd missed a text when her friend stepped inside, elegant as always in a belted linen dress with a wool coat draped over her shoulders as if she'd walked in off a Parisian street, an effect only heightened when she ordered a double shot of espresso and the last remaining chocolate croissant.

While Celeste waited for her food, she shot Maddie an apologetic grimace before making a call. Arriving at the table with her plate, she said into the phone, "I'll get back to you when I hear from the seller. End of day at the latest, all right? Talk soon." She hung up with a relieved-sounding sigh and sank into the chair, eyeing Maddie's green iced tea topped with purple foam and a sprinkling of lavender buds. "Ooh, is that the matcha-lavender latte?"

Maddie nodded. "The lavender lends a fruity, floral taste. Pairs well with the earthy matcha." The vibrant hues of the green tea and lavender foam looked especially fitting for a warm spring day. "But it's almost too pretty to drink."

"Like everything you make," Celeste said.

"Yeah, but I haven't mastered latte art. It's something I've been wanting to add to my repertoire."

"You should talk to the owner, Elise," Celeste said. "I bet she wouldn't mind showing you sometime."

"Wouldn't mind showing her what?" a voice said, sounding peeved, and Maddie looked up to find the barista approaching the table, a mug and saucer in hand. Great, she owned the place? Maddie was more certain than ever that there would be no chance for a partnership, judging by the woman's surliness. She and Jake would make a good pair, though the thought gave her an annoying pang of jealousy.

Celeste smiled. "Maddie was just saying she'd love a lesson in latte art."

Elise crossed her arms. "Sure, if she's looking for a job. In case you hadn't noticed, we're short-staffed. Don't exactly have time for free lessons."

"I noticed your pastry case is usually sold out. It must be hard to keep up," Maddie said with sympathy.

The café owner softened. "I've had trouble finding help in the off-season."

Maddie wished she could help out. The extra money might come in handy, though she had income from freelance work.

"We'll spread the word that there's a job opening," Celeste said, giving Maddie a meaningful look, as if she knew she'd been considering offering to help.

"Sorry I snapped at you," Elise said, addressing Maddie. "I'm just so frazzled lately, and I hate disappointing customers who come in looking for their favorite treats."

"Your drinks more than make up for it," Maddie said. "This latte is delicious. What brand of syrup do you use?"

Elise smiled for the first time all morning. "I make it myself using organic lavender."

"The quality really comes through." This might be the opening she'd been looking for. "I'm opening a catering business down the street, and I'd love to partner with you to include café beverages in picnic orders."

"That sounds tricky." But the café owner looked intrigued. "How would we coordinate orders? Would you be providing the containers for the drinks? Taking paper cups on a picnic sounds like a recipe for disaster."

"I plan to offer reusable cups and thermoses. Customers would pay a deposit for the picnic basket and tableware, refundable upon return." She wanted to be both eco-conscious and provide an experience beyond the everyday. "We would only offer café beverages as an option for orders placed more than a day in advance. And there's no rush to settle things now," Maddie added. "We can revisit the idea once you're fully staffed."

Elise looked relieved. "I'd like that." A group of elderly men walked in, and she said, "Stop by on your way out, and I'll give you my information." She went back to her post behind the counter with a bounce in her step.

Celeste regarded Maddie with the kind of mothering stare she knew all too well. "You were going to apply for the job on the spot, weren't you?"

"The extra money wouldn't hurt, and she's clearly in dire straits."

"You've got such a soft heart," Celeste said. "But you don't need to add anything else to your plate."

Maddie knew her friend was right. "I'm just glad she doesn't resent me. Every time I came in, she'd hurry to the back room after she made my order. I thought maybe I'd made another enemy in town."

Celeste finished her espresso and set the mug on the saucer, no trace of red lipstick on the white ceramic. Maddie would have asked what brand it was, but no doubt it would be well out of her price range. "What do you mean?" Celeste asked.

Maddie knew the moment had come to spill, but Celeste had spent years warning her not to be so trusting after she'd fallen for a scam filling out what she'd thought was an apartment lease. Later, she discovered she'd been tricked into divulging all her personal information to someone she'd only known a few months.

Telling Celeste she'd trusted Jake enough to kiss him without asking even the most basic of personal questions, like what he did for a living, meant she was in for a big helping of *I told you so.* Maybe she could avoid a lecture if she stuck to the business side of the story.

"You know how Jake Winn is my upstairs neighbor? Well, he's not just my neighbor. Martin got called away, and he took over as foreman on my project."

"Why didn't you mention that before?"

Because she'd kissed him and made a fool of herself. But that wasn't a conversation for a crowded café.

"I've been planning to, but we've all been so busy," she said, hoping Celeste wouldn't get suspicious. "Did you know I went to a cookbook club meeting at the library last night? I met Crystal and checked out the first book in her latest series."

"About time you give foodie mysteries a try," Celeste said. "And I'm glad you two met—she's great. But you're not going to distract me from the lowdown about Jake. Has he done something unprofessional?"

Oh, he'd done some very unprofessional things all right. But that was before they'd met in a business capacity. "Let's just say he wasn't happy to be assigned my project, and he's made that very clear."

She ran down what had happened, starting with the day after their kiss. It wasn't exactly relevant to them working together, and what advice would Celeste give besides to avoid him, which Maddie was already planning to do? As much as two people living under the same roof could avoid each other. She'd confess the whole truth once the three friends finally found time to all hang out together.

When she finished, Celeste said, "I had no idea the art guild was looking to open a gallery. I could've helped them find a good location."

"You would've helped them rent the place over me?"

Celeste gave her a get-out-of-here look. “Of course not. Besides the fact that you’re my best friend, your building has relatively low ceilings, which works just fine for your needs, but I could’ve helped them find something much more suited to a gallery.”

“Are you going to reach out?” Connecting people with the right properties was Celeste’s passion, but Maddie couldn’t help wanting to avoid the members of the art guild. At least a few of them must resent her, if Jake’s reaction was anything to go on.

“After how Jake treated you?” Celeste’s smooth forehead crinkled in consternation. “If anyone else in the group wants my help, they know where to find me. But I’m not going out of my way to work with them when their vice president made my friend feel unwelcome.”

Maddie felt an unexpected pinch of guilt. Jake’s reaction to finding out she was the person he’d be working for had stung, but she’d thrown her share of barbs. Called him unqualified and negligent. Thrown his supposed bad reputation in his face at the lumberyard, even though it was hearsay.

“So you don’t think it’s out of line to look for a new contractor?”

Celeste wiggled her hand in a so-so motion. “I see why you want to make a switch, but Wright Construction is the best. Not just in town, but the whole region. There’s a reason Tasha chose them to remodel her salon.”

Maddie had been overwhelmed by the idea of renting a fixer-upper building, but going with a company Tasha had a great experience with had made her feel more comfortable. Then Jake had gone and ruined everything. “What about the second best?” she asked.

Celeste hesitated, like she didn’t want to offer what she knew. “Atlas Construction. They operate out of a town north of here. They do solid work, but…”

“But what?”

"Do you really want to back out of your contract with a great local business just because you and Jake got off on the wrong foot?"

They'd gotten off on the right foot, actually. So right that Maddie had been floating on air. Then she'd fallen back to earth the next day.

"I can handle not being Jake Winn's favorite person," she said, though her stomach did an odd flip at the thought of not being special to him.

"Not just Jake." Celeste glanced at the customers waiting to order, her long, black hair gleaming in the sunlight coming through the café windows. She lowered her voice. "Lots of people work for Wright Construction. The owner, Reese, is well respected in the community. You wouldn't just be firing Jake. You'd be firing the whole company."

Maddie swallowed a gulp of tea, the bitter notes of matcha suddenly outweighing the sweetness of the lavender. Making enemies was the opposite of her goal. What she wanted most was to put down roots in the community, but Jake's orneriness was making that task harder. "The last thing I want to do is hurt anyone's finances, but Jake should've considered his responsibility to the crew when he dared me to look elsewhere. If the only thing wrong with Atlas is that they're not Orchard Harbor locals, then that's unfortunate, but I'm not the one who's being unreasonable."

Celeste leveled a look at her that said otherwise. "Things haven't gone smoothly, I get it. But I can see how he might be a little put out. Remember how much it sucked to lose out on the first few properties you tried to lease?"

Maddie bit her lip. She'd been so disappointed when her first choice slipped through her fingers that her mom had insisted on treating her to a spa day. While she was grateful for her mother's concern, at the time it had felt like more proof her family thought she couldn't handle the stress of being a small business owner. "I didn't blame the people who got the properties."

"No, but you also didn't have to work for them." Celeste raised her hands, sensing Maddie was about to argue. "Look, things are bound to be weird. But is it so wrong that the man wanted to make sure you didn't get injured on his jobsite?"

"*His* jobsite?" Maddie asked. "It's my shop. And I didn't go running wild."

"I still don't understand how keeping you safe is a strike against him."

"I may have misjudged that situation." She remembered how worried he'd seemed underneath his tough exterior. "But I can't trust him to have my best interests at heart."

Celeste tapped her manicured nails on the side of her mug thoughtfully. "Okay. But my advice? Don't tell the owner of Atlas that you originally hired Wright Construction. If you end up changing your mind, at least you won't be burning bridges."

That made sense, and Maddie felt relieved that she wouldn't be locked into a decision yet. But that had nothing to do with the appeal of a certain handsome foreman and everything to do with keeping her options open to make the best choice for her business.

Yesterday, a series of minor emergencies kept Jake from connecting with Maddie to say sorry. Full of restless energy last night, he'd opened the plans for Maddie's catering business and analyzed the kitchen layout from a new perspective. Now that he knew she'd designed it herself and it wasn't just a recommendation from Martin, he could see why the setup would work for her since she'd be packaging items to go.

With that off his mind, he made plans to reach out to several tile specialists and call in favors to see if he could get a discount on sturdier flooring. Even after everything, he wanted the best for her. Part of it was professional integrity, but there was no denying how much he longed to make her smile.

The quest to fix things needed to start with an apology, so today he was determined to catch her first thing in the morning. He'd be juggling work at two houses, but things were on hold at Maddie's project until she made her decision about whether to continue working with Wright Construction. He'd told his boss they were waiting on her flooring choices, which was partially true. He still hoped to convince her to go with the more durable flooring, if she accepted his apology, that was.

He'd combed his hair and messed with it in the mirror for five minutes before giving up and putting on a baseball hat. Not much he could do about his outfit since he was headed into work after talking to her, but he did knock the mud off his boots before heading downstairs, breathing a sigh of relief to see Maddie's car still in the driveway.

He hurried over to Harbor Bridge Café to get one of their white chocolate pistachio croissants for her before they sold out. Judging from the delicious smell of roasted coffee beans wafting up the stairs each morning, he knew she was a coffee drinker, so he ordered two cups of the house blend to go, then rushed back to the house.

Maddie's car was gone.

He let out a frustrated sigh. There went his chance to sweeten the apology. He would've cursed his bad luck, if he believed in that sort of thing. Since he didn't, he chalked it up to bad timing and took a big bite of the croissant. Couldn't very well let it go to waste.

Once he finished chewing, he found her number in the emails they'd exchanged and dialed before he lost his nerve.

"Hello?" Her voice had the wary, tentative tone of someone answering an unknown caller, and he noticed she didn't give her name.

"Hi, Maddie," he said, then cleared his throat. "Er, Madelyn. This is Jake."

"Jake Winn?"

Did she know a lot of other Jakes? Or was that her way of reminding him they weren't on friendly terms anymore? Like he could forget. "Yes. I was hoping to catch you before you left."

"You were already gone this morning," she said.

"I was out getting coffee. For you."

"For me?" Her voice sounded distant. "Why?"

He was making a mess of this. "I wanted to bring you breakfast and apologize. I should never have made you feel like you're not welcome here, and I really do want the job. I take full responsibility for baiting you into switching contractors, but could you reconsider?"

Nothing. Not a sniff or a snarl or the quick comeback he was used to. Damn, he'd really screwed up this time. "I can give you a list of clients whose renovations I've handled in the past. Give them a call and see for yourself if my work is up to your standards."

Silence. Frowning, he lowered the phone. She'd hung up on him.

Message received. He'd hit rock bottom on the well of second chances. Nothing left to do but get on with things.

He headed to the vacation home they were renovating. Today a pool company was coming to break ground, and cabinets were being delivered. A string of small emergencies pulled his attention from Maddie, and a few hours later, when he was inspecting the backsplash, his phone buzzed with what felt like the hundredth call of the day. He answered without looking.

"Tell me you're on your way back." He'd sent Neil to the hardware store to pick up the darker grout the homeowner had requested.

"You're still mad I wasn't home this morning?" Maddie's voice.

Jake stood up so fast he banged his head on the cabinet. "Ouch!" Rubbing the back of his head, he said quickly, "I thought you were someone else." Then he remembered she'd hung up on him. "Did you decide to hear me out?"

"The call dropped. I was on the beach, and service is terrible."

"Oh." He leaned back against the counter, feeling sheepish.

"Did you think I did it on purpose?" Her voice was teasing, and he could picture her pretty lips curving into a grin that made her dimples pop.

"Figured you didn't want to hear my apology."

"Oh, is that what you called about?" She was for sure smiling now; he could hear it in her voice. "I definitely want to hear that."

"Too late, you missed it." Was he smiling, too? Dang it, he was.

"No chance of a repeat performance? Or that coffee you mentioned?"

"That depends," he said.

"On what?"

"Are you in a basement or a tunnel?" He smirked. "Just want to be prepared in case you 'accidentally' hang up on me again."

"You're a pain, you know that?"

"So I've been told."

"Are you going to apologize or not?"

"I'm sorry," he said, sobering up. "Really sorry. I got defensive and lashed out at you, and that was wrong."

"Hold on, could you repeat that?" She raised her voice, like the service was sketchy. "You're breaking up."

He kept a straight face, barely. "Funny."

"You really think I'd hang up after hearing that?"

"I had a lot more planned."

"Now I'm really bummed my phone cut out," she said, and he wished he hadn't missed her this morning. It had been too long since they'd had a conversation where they weren't trying to one-up each other.

"I was going to say how finding out I'd be working with the woman who rocked my world that night at the winery threw me off guard and I've been trying to find my footing ever since, but that's no excuse."

"It threw me off, too." Her voice was soft, and he wondered if she remembered that passionate moment as vividly as he did. "But I didn't accuse you of shady business practices." She paused. "At least not at first." Her chuckle reached his ears, and he caught himself smiling again.

This was the connection they'd had at the beginning. He hadn't imagined it. There was something between them. Something they could find their way back to. At least he hoped so.

"Does that mean you're willing to give Wright Construction—" he heard the front door open and lowered his voice, not wanting any of this to get back to his boss "—another chance?"

Maddie sighed, and he tensed. "I wish we'd talked sooner. I'm walking into a meeting right now with another construction company that came highly recommended."

"Who?" The word scraped past gritted teeth. Somehow, he knew before she even said it.

"Atlas."

Of course. They were the only other large-scale construction firm in the area. Still, he had to ask. "Can you cancel it? I'm willing and ready to work with you."

"And I appreciate that, trust me." Here came the *but*. "But I'm trying to build relationships in the community, and backing out of a business meeting at the last minute wouldn't reflect well on my integrity."

"What about backing out of a contract?" He hadn't meant to bring it up, but did it really have to be Atlas? He stood no chance if she found out about his history with them.

"You pushed me into a corner, Jake. You practically dared me to go elsewhere."

He wanted to bite out that she'd backed him into a corner first, but he heard voices in the hall. Neil, talking to one of the guys installing the maple hardwood flooring.

"Fine. But keep an open mind, okay? I think we could make a good team." Judging by their fiery chemistry the first night, it was either that or be bitter rivals, and he would have a lot more fun being on Maddie's good side.

A moment of silence, and he imagined her biting that plump lower lip of hers, the one he'd relished tasting. Finally, she said, "I will. Your apology means a lot. But if Atlas seems like a better fit, I'm going with them. I have to do what's best for my business."

That, Jake understood. It was why he'd swallowed his pride and called her in the first place. She wasn't out to get him. She was just someone working hard to meet her goals. A very beautiful—very infuriating—businesswoman.

"Oh, and Jake?"

"Yeah?"

"If I do decide to stick with Wright Construction, you'd better be on your best behavior." Why did her stern tone make him suddenly weak at the knees?

"Don't worry," he said. "I know how to play nice."

Chapter Nine

After Jake's apology, Maddie regretted following through on her decision to book a consultation with the other construction company. What she'd told Jake was true, though. She wanted to build a strong reputation as a business owner, and that meant not canceling a meeting at the last minute.

She would give Atlas Construction a fair shot, but working with Jake suddenly didn't seem so horrible. In fact, spending more time with him using the excuse of working together sounded way too appealing.

She remembered their delicious kiss all too clearly, and desire had unfurled at his promise to "play nice." How had such innocent words conjured up thoughts of all the naughty ways he could make good on that promise? But now was not the time to let her emotions run the show.

With a renewed commitment to being cautious, thanks to her chat with Celeste, she'd dug deep into Atlas Construction, making sure the business was on the up-and-up. She'd cross-checked phone numbers, addresses, their social media presence and business ratings. Before Jake's apology, she'd felt comfortable moving forward with a meeting, but now she just wanted to get it over with.

But twenty minutes past their meeting time, Damien still hadn't shown up. To pass the time, she was texting her mom, who was anxious about the slow progress and what it meant for Maddie's budget.

Finishing the text, she looked up to see a middle-aged man approaching her shop with a frown. He had a clipboard and shiny leather shoes. "Interrupting something?" he asked as if she'd been the one over half an hour late to the meeting.

"Just keeping myself busy while I waited," she replied with a flat smile.

"Sorry. I got caught up with my last client. They're making an addition to their home to accommodate an indoor pool." It came out as less of an excuse than a flex, especially paired with the appraising glance the man cast at the run-down exterior of her building. "So we'll be turning this into a catering business?"

There was no "we" yet, but Maddie refrained from saying that. "This will be my catering business, yes." Without Jake there, she decided to err on the safe side and not lead him on a tour in case they needed a hard hat, but she opened the front door and let him look inside while she ran down an overview of the work she'd need done, along with the timeframe.

"You have a lot of specific ideas." Damien frowned at the gutted room. "And something tells me we're not the first construction company you've met with."

Uh-oh. She'd planned to keep her contract with Wright Construction under wraps like Celeste advised, but hadn't expected such a direct statement. "It's a big decision," she hedged.

His smile was more of a sneer. "Look, I don't mind you getting quotes from multiple companies, but let's not waste our time if you're committed elsewhere."

Did he know she'd been working with Jake's company?

At her silence, he added, "You should know word travels fast around here. I'm not surprised you're considering jumping ship. Wright Construction does decent work, but from what I hear, you got saddled with Jake Winn."

That caught her attention. First Britta, and now she was hearing about Jake's poor reputation from another contractor. It wouldn't be the first time she'd misjudged someone, but it was more than just a gut feeling. Tasha and Celeste both trusted him, and that mattered more than two strangers' opinions. "I'm not here to discuss my dealings with another company."

He held up a hand. "Fine. I get it. But since you're new around here, I figured you deserve to know what you're getting yourself into. Jake's not reliable. He's cocky and doesn't take the job seriously. It's why he doesn't work for us anymore."

He didn't…what? Her jaw dropped, and Damien's smirk reappeared. "Oh, you didn't know? He got his start with us, but we couldn't keep him on. In fact, no one wanted to hire him after that. But the owner of Wright Construction has a soft heart. Took a chance on Jake, but you know what they say. No good deed goes unpunished." He gave a short chuckle, but Maddie didn't join in. Her mind was racing with what she'd just learned. Why hadn't Jake mentioned he'd worked for Atlas?

The reason seemed obvious: he'd been fired. Of course he'd kept it to himself in hopes Maddie wouldn't find out.

"I can see I've given you food for thought." Damien's smarmy smile made another appearance. "We'll be happy to provide you with a quote based on what I saw today. Keep in mind it's not just about the money, but quality of service, which you'll find at Atlas. Wish I could say the same for Wright Construction, but anyone who employs someone as negligent as Jake doesn't have my vote of confidence."

Maddie was too stunned to do much more than thank him for his time and shake his cold hand. She watched him walk back to his sleek sports car and tried to process what she'd learned.

She wasn't sure what to believe, but couldn't shake the feeling that the owner of Atlas Construction wasn't altogether trustworthy, either. While she was mulling it over, Tasha texted.

Tasha: Hey ladies! Sorry but I won't be able to make it tonight. The baby isn't sleeping well and Izzy is still worn down.

Celeste: No worries, we'll reschedule!

Maddie: Give them our love!

Tasha: I will, but I'll probably barely see my sister. With Ben back at work, I'll either be holding the baby so she can rest or doing some batch-cooking.

That gave Maddie an idea. She had a decision to make, and she did her best thinking in the kitchen.

A car backed out of Tasha's driveway just as Maddie pulled up, probably a client. People came to Tasha for everything from natural styles to weaves and special-occasion makeup. She'd moved back to Orchard Harbor a couple years ago after nearly a decade of working in a high-end salon in Chicago, homesick and ready to be near family again. She'd bought an old Craftsman house and was slowly remodeling it, starting with the front porch she'd converted into a salon.

Setting down the large cooler full of food for Izzy's family, Maddie let herself in through the modern glass door. To the right, upholstered chairs flanked a low table piled with magazines. A coffee machine and clear-front mini fridge were in the corner next to a potted plant. A pair of styling chairs sat in front of a large mirror and vanity stocked with supplies. Soft music flowed from a speaker, and a bubbling fountain added to the ambience.

The room had windows on three sides, showing evidence of its previous incarnation as a front porch, but it was wholly transformed. Tasha's positive experience with Wright Construction had made Maddie feel like she'd be in good hands. That was before she'd met Jake.

As she retrieved the cooler, her friend emerged from the house with a broom and dustpan. Her face broke into a warm smile. "You're surprising me with food again? A girl could get used to this."

"One of the perks of living in the same town. But most of this is for your sister. I wanted you to be able to spend time with her and the baby tonight instead of cooking."

Tasha wrapped her in a hug, broomstick and all. "You're the sweetest." She pulled back. "What did you make for me?" she asked with a twinkle in her eye.

"Nothing fancy, just a berry salad with honey-lime dressing to go along with crème fraîche mashed potatoes, lemony asparagus and seared chicken breast." Maddie opened the soft-sided cooler slung over her shoulder to show Tasha. "I packed it in individual containers so you could have it for lunch all week." She planned to stop at Celeste's office next.

"This looks divine." Tasha pointed at the glossy berries topped with sprigs of mint visible through the bowl's clear lid. "My version of a fruit salad comes from cans, maybe topped with sliced bananas if I'm feeling extra."

"Nothing wrong with that," Maddie said. She wasn't a food snob, and she knew how tough it could be to find affordable fresh fruit. "I'll put this in your fridge," she said.

When she came back out onto the porch, Tasha was sweeping loose hair out from under the styling chair. "I can't believe the three of us haven't found time to get together yet. I don't mind helping my sister out, but I hope things settle down soon."

"How are Izzy and the little one?"

"Exhausted." Tasha looked tired, too, but her hair was immaculate as always. She'd plaited her twists into a braid that draped over one shoulder. "Now that they're back at home, we've all been pitching in. I'm headed over after my next client, but she won't be here for another half hour, so you came at a good time." She swept the loose hair into a dustpan.

Maddie wanted to offer to help tidy up, but experience told her Tasha would turn it down, so instead she grabbed a can of sparkling water out of the mini fridge and plopped onto the nearest chair. "In that case, I could use some advice on a tricky situation."

"Oh?" Tasha's voice hit the exact note of curious anticipation that made it so easy for her customers to bare their souls. She had a reputation for knowing all the gossip in town, though she didn't divulge secrets and only shared innocent news with close friends and family. Maddie was sure her friend would know the truth about Jake and his involvement with Atlas Construction.

She filled Tasha in on everything that had gone down with her and Jake professionally, including what Britta had told her about Jake's bad reputation and how the owner of Atlas validated that opinion.

Tasha had finished sweeping and was sipping a drink of her own by the time Maddie was finished. She sucked her teeth. "No offense, but Britta doesn't know what she's talking about. Her sister was in the same grade as me and Jake, but she's a few years older, and a lot of the rumors were exaggerated."

Maddie's heart lightened at that, but she told herself to play it cool. "Yeah?"

"Definitely. I mean, Jake got up to trouble, I'm not denying that. He often skipped school, and after graduation, he jumped from job to job." She must've noticed Maddie's face at hearing that, because she waved a hand. "He was going through a lot. From what I hear, things didn't end well with Atlas, but I don't know the whole story. All I know is he started working for Wright Construction not long after and turned things around. He's even on the board of the local art guild, and they've got a great reputation for community service."

That much Maddie knew. But did holding down a job and being a leader in a respected community organization mean that Jake was someone she could trust with her future? Her business future, specifically. She couldn't let herself think of a personal future with him, not after how complicated things had become.

Her friend was eyeing her like she sensed there was more to the story, and Maddie couldn't hold back any longer. "There's one more slightly relevant detail."

Tasha coolly sipped her soda, giving Maddie the space to talk.

"I kissed him."

Spluttering, Tasha managed to say, "Jake?" She coughed. "Girl, why didn't you lead with that?"

"Because I was embarrassed. It was at the winery—"

"Your first night in town?" Tasha shrieked, but her eyes were sparkling. "Maddie Briar, I didn't think you had it in you."

Maddie fought the urge to bury her face in her hands. "I didn't know it was him at the time. After you and Celeste left, a group of people crowded in and basically took over the table.

Jake swooped in and, well, saved me." He'd been so grumpily gallant, it had charmed her.

"I love this for you," Tasha said.

"It wasn't that serious."

"Says the woman who kissed him for his troubles." Tasha bounced her eyebrows, but Maddie glowered.

"You want the rest of the story or not?"

Tasha mimed zipping her lips closed.

"We got to talking, and when I discovered he was an artist, I told him how art plays a part in my work, too, though I didn't mention the business." That part was still new, and she felt shy bringing it up. "One thing led to another, and we ended up hanging out for a few hours. Then, when I was on my way out, we bumped into each other again and—"

"Your faces just collided?" Tasha smirked.

"No, it was very much intentional." And she couldn't quite bring herself to wish it never happened, even though she'd spent the past few weeks reaping the chaotic consequences. Given another chance, she'd do it again. Which was why she couldn't allow herself to think of Jake that way. "It was a pretty amazing kiss. Life-altering, honestly. Though for all the reasons it shouldn't have been, because, well… You know the rest of the story."

"No wonder you reacted the way you did when he called you out." Tasha made a face. "The nerve of that man to give you the best kiss of your life and then do a total one-eighty."

"Hey, I never said it was the best kiss of my life."

"Your face did," Tasha said. "I wonder if you're more upset at him or at yourself because you finally let your guard down and it backfired."

"Of course I'm upset with myself," Maddie said. "It's humiliating to think I had a connection with someone only to realize I was totally misguided."

"But he did apologize, and since you didn't agree to work with Atlas Construction, I'm guessing that means you have doubts?"

"I want to trust him," Maddie admitted. "Besides the fact that I want to be on good terms with local businesses, I also hate to think my judgment was wrong again."

Tasha frowned. "That jerkface coworker took advantage of your trust, yes. But it was years ago, and you learned from the experience. You've been careful ever since. Too careful, if you ask me."

Easy for Tasha to say. She hadn't lost her savings and had to live with her parents for years while she rebuilt her credit. Maddie wished she could go back to the carefree person she'd been before her identity was stolen, but she knew firsthand the destruction that could unfold when she let down her guard. "I just don't know how to strike a balance between caution and trust."

"By keeping your eyes open. Don't give away your heart on a whim, but don't smother your feelings, either. You didn't declare love to Jake or move in with him. It was just a kiss."

"Actually…"

Tasha's light-brown eyes went wide. "We really do need to talk more."

"Not that." Her cheeks burned furiously. "But the wild thing is we're kind of living together. He's my upstairs neighbor."

"And you're just now telling me?"

"There was a lot to share! It got lost in the shuffle," Maddie said.

Tasha looked at the can in her hand. "Remind me to grab something stronger next time you come over."

"See why I need advice? Jake's reputation aside, do you think it's just too complicated to stick with Wright Construction, or should I give him another chance?"

Tasha blew out a long breath. "That's a loaded question, and my next appointment is in…" she pulled her phone out of her apron and checked the time "…oof, fifteen minutes. Come chat with me about it while I pack up a few things to take to Izzy's house."

Maddie followed Tasha through the sturdy teal door that separated the rest of the house from the salon. Bright colors and patterns were complemented by chrome accents and unique furniture. The whole house felt like an extension of Tasha's vivacious personality. She pulled a bottle of red wine from a rack that looked like it was made of driftwood, inlaid with a mosaic of beach glass.

"Is that new?" Maddie didn't remember seeing the unique wine rack on her last visit.

"It's the berry-infused red wine we tried the other night," Tasha explained, sliding the bottle into a canvas tote. "My mom has been with my sister and the baby all day, so I figured she deserves some pampering as well."

"I meant the wine rack," Maddie said. "It's such a beautiful statement piece."

"Not surprised you'd think so, after hearing you kissed the craftsman who made it." She gave Maddie a teasing grin. "It's one of Jake's designs."

Maddie took a closer look. The artistry was evident. The elements had been seamlessly blended to form a piece that was both exciting and functional, highlighting the way waves and sand had smoothed the edges of the glass and softened the wood grain into an almost satin finish.

She couldn't resist reaching out to touch it, imagining the same skillful hands that had traced her curves bringing this piece to life.

Tasha cleared her throat. "You're thinking about him, aren't you?"

Maddie looked up guiltily. "Hard not to. He made a big impression on me that night. But even if he was still interested after everything, throwing romance into the mix is definitely a mistake." Part of her wanted to take the risk, but that wasn't an option with how Jake felt about her now.

"I agree," her friend said, surprising her. She expected that advice from Celeste, but Tasha was a big fan of taking chances. "Jake isn't a menace like a lot of people in town think, don't get me wrong. But he is impulsive, especially when it comes to things he's passionate about. I've always felt like he was a kindred spirit."

Tasha was incredibly passionate and bold, which some people mistook for arrogance, when in reality she was one of the kindest people Maddie had ever met.

"You need someone steady," her friend continued. "Especially now. Your life is going to be full of upheaval, and adding a guy to the mix would be messy even without the drama you two have shared. Maybe it's for the best that things went down the way they did."

First her friends had acted like she couldn't handle an hour on her own at the winery, and now Tasha was implying she wouldn't be able to juggle work and a new relationship. Even though her friend's advice echoed her own fears, Maddie didn't like the implication that she wasn't strong and capable.

She held the tote bag open as Tasha added some herbal tea and fuzzy socks. "So I should move forward with him as contractor and pretend the kiss never happened?"

"I can vouch for his character, but at the end of the day, you'll have to decide for yourself whether you want to work with him." At least Tasha wasn't strong-arming Maddie into a decision. "As for the romance, you have trouble sending your meal back at restaurants when it's not what you ordered, yet you keep getting in arguments with Jake? It sounds like he brings out the worst in you."

It might seem that way, but to Maddie it felt like he'd lit a long-dormant fire in her. Every man she'd dated before had been a solid, safe choice. All those guys were good on paper, but she'd never felt a spark like she did with Jake. Sure, they'd argued, but he'd apologized and given her space to make a decision that might cost him the esteem of his boss.

Maybe a guy who checked all the boxes wasn't as important as someone who lit her up, made her feel the kind of passion she'd only ever seen in movies.

Tasha slung the bag over her shoulder, and Maddie blinked herself out of her thoughts. "It's a lot to think about, but I see your point."

Tasha looked like she wanted to say more, but the bell above the salon door chimed. "Shoot, my client's here. I wish we had more time to talk, but we'll make it happen soon. Especially since you live just down the street now and not two hours away."

Maddie's heart lifted. No matter what happened, her friends had her back.

She felt relief knowing her professional judgment hadn't been wrong. But the jury was still out on whether her heart could be trusted.

Jake had spent the afternoon driving between jobsites. He was too stressed thinking about Maddie meeting with Damien to stay in one place and needed to check progress on each renovation anyway.

He couldn't stomach the thought of her choosing Atlas Construction. Anyone else, he'd understand, but Damien was not just anyone.

Working at Atlas had been his personal rock bottom. Life

after his dad left had been rough, but Jake had been a grown man by the time he started working for Damien. Young, yes, but old enough to be held accountable for his actions. Remembering how he'd treated work like a joke back then had his heart rate up, and he jogged out to his truck to grab a toolbox to keep his guys at the lake house reno from noticing something was wrong.

The moment he shut his truck door, he saw someone familiar crossing the yard. "Okay, now I know you're following me." He'd meant to sound stern, but he knew his face gave him away. How was Madelyn able to make him melt even when she'd probably come to tell him he'd lost the contract to the closest thing he had to an enemy?

She grinned back, and his heart gave a happy leap. "This time, yes," she admitted. It was an unseasonably warm day, and she was wearing a flowy dress, the short sleeves fluttering around her arms. "I was going to call, but I ran into Lina at the house, and she told me you'd be here. This is the kind of conversation I'd rather have in person."

He glanced around at all the activity. Bricklayers were taking advantage of the sunshine to put in new columns for the front porch, and workers moved in and out of the house carrying tools, lumber and supplies. Not a very private place to get fired.

She stepped closer, like she could tell he was on edge. "Maybe we could go for a walk, if you've got a minute?"

"Sure," he said, relieved.

She started toward the road, but he reached for her elbow to lead her in the other direction instead. It was a casual gesture, but the moment his fingers touched the soft skin at the inside of her arm, he was transported to their kiss. The caress of her lips, her tongue… He stumbled on the torn-up sod near the house, and Madelyn caught his waist, steadying him.

His cheeks flushed with embarrassment but also longing. Her soft body was pressed to his side, and her hair smelled like lilacs.

All too quickly, she let go. "Where are you taking me?"

"To see the million-dollar view." He smiled down at her. "Figured I owe you one." He led her along the side of the sprawling cottage to the edge of the bluff, where the dune slanted down to a sandy beach. Beyond, sparkling teal water gave way to deep blue.

She let out a gasp, and he pinched his eyes shut, trying not to think of how that breathy sound had felt against his mouth. "I didn't realize the lake was so close," she said, and he dared to open his eyes again, taking in the view.

Lake Michigan stretched before them, framed by trees set against a clear sky. A wooden staircase led down to the beach. It was in need of sanding and a fresh coat of stain, but sturdy. He let her go first, not wanting to block the view with his tall frame.

She paused at the landing to take a pair of sunglasses out of her tote and slip them on her face. "I could get used to this view."

"Best part of this job," he said and lifted his chin toward the mansion on the bluff above them. "Great scenery while we work."

"Maybe I'm in the wrong industry," she said.

"But won't you be delivering picnics to people on the beach?" Jake realized he'd shown his hand the moment he spoke.

Madelyn clearly did as well, because she turned to him with a smile. "How did you know?"

He lifted his hat and ran a hand through his hair. May as well own up to it. "Checked out your website." Standard practice when they did commercial renos. But he hadn't done it just for business reasons. He was curious about her, even though she'd probably come to tell him to get lost.

"I'm surprised you were interested." Her curls lifted in the breeze, brushing her delicate throat. "Since you think food styling is all about deception."

Guilt punched through him. No wonder she wanted out of the deal. "I was talking nonsense. What you said about my art..." He cut himself short. This wasn't her fault. "I get touchy about my creations. I used to call it tinkering. Something to kill time. But even though I take pride in it now, a lot of the guys I work with still give me crap about being an artist. I know they're just messing around, but it's hard not to take it personally. All the tired stuff about what's manly and not. Wish I could say I cared less, but I'm still getting there."

He dug his thumbnail into the weathered gray wood of the railing, feeling ashamed. Not about his art, but how he'd acted toward Maddie. "I turned that insecurity onto you. For that, I'm sorry."

Her brows rose. "Not to let you off easy, but I hate that you had to deal with that." Behind her sunglasses, her eyes flashed up toward the house, like she wanted to go give his crew a piece of her mind, and he couldn't help but grin at her feistiness. "Anyone and everyone can be an artist. People who think otherwise are ignorant," she said. "But as for your apology, consider it accepted. I was out of line, too. My emotions got the best of me, partly because of..." She cleared her throat. "You'd just asked me out, and the one-eighty left me scrambling."

He opened his mouth to apologize again, but she held up her hand.

"We both said things we regret. Let our tempers get the best of us. Not that it was cool of you, but I'm guilty of the same.

I made fun of your art, but I really do think it's amazing, like I told you at the winery."

At the mention of that night, his eyes dropped to her lips and found them parted, plump under a faint sheen of gloss that he knew tasted like ripe strawberries. He gulped and raised his gaze. "You haven't even seen it."

"Actually, I have. At Tasha's house. She owns a wine rack you made, and the work is incredible. I don't think it's silly or a waste of time. I was just lashing out."

"You never struck me as the lashing-out type." Even during their fights, he saw a wariness in her eyes, a desire to hold back.

She gave a short laugh. "The funny thing is, I'm not." Behind the dark lenses of her sunglasses, her gaze connected with his. "You have a way of getting under my skin."

He knew exactly what she meant. He'd been determined to act professional when Reese passed the job onto him. Then he'd found out the building was hers, and it was like a string attached to his heart had been yanked.

"Guess it's a good thing we won't be working together, then," he said. Might as well get the bad news over with before he got any more misguided ideas.

"I thought you wanted me to keep an open mind," she said.

"You met with Atlas. I'm sure Damien had plenty to say about me, and none of it good." He was ashamed thinking back on his time at Atlas Construction. Calling off sick whenever he felt like it. The delayed timelines that had cost clients money. He'd never done shoddy work, when he bothered to show up. But he'd been unreliable and selfish. "Truth is, I would've fired one of my guys long before he let me go. Whatever he told you is true."

"And what about now?" Maddie watched him expectantly.

"Haven't missed a shift in five years. Been lead foreman for two. I take this job seriously."

"Then I see no reason why I shouldn't stick with Wright Construction." She leaned an elbow on the banister. "I let Atlas know that I won't be needing their services. Damien was less than professional, and—"

"In what way?" Jake's senses leaped to high alert. If that jerk had done anything to make her feel uncomfortable, then he'd have a lot to answer for.

"Nothing like that. But his comments about you weren't fitting for a business meeting. I have no interest in working with someone who tries to win a contract by throwing their competition under the bus."

"For what it's worth, I gave him good reason to hold a grudge."

"Still not okay," she said. "I'm learning to trust my judgment again, and it's telling me to steer clear of Damien." He wondered what she meant by not trusting her judgment, but was in no position to probe. "If it won't bother you to work on a building that you wanted for yourself, then I'm ready to move forward."

"Not for myself. I wasn't planning to sell pieces in the gallery." He wanted her to understand he wasn't mad about missing out on something that would benefit himself; it was for the art guild. Then again, he had been trying to get back into the town's good graces, so maybe it was one and the same. "But to answer your question, yes, I can let it go." He realized he already had. He thought of it as Madelyn's place now.

She stuck out her hand. "Then it's settled. I can't wait to see how things turn out."

Clasping her hand in his, he gave it a firm shake, trying not to remember the way those same fingers had twisted in his shirt, pulling him close. "We'll do right by you, Maddie." He cleared his throat. "Sorry, Madelyn."

"Maddie's fine." She grinned, flashing her dimples. "After all we've been through, I'd say we're back on a nickname basis."

He smiled down at her, feeling the same sense of relief as when he kicked off his heavy work boots after a long day. From an unexpected kiss to business partners, his dealings with Maddie were a roller coaster, and even though he'd always been a fan of thrills, he was pretty sure she wasn't. For her sake, he hoped there were no more twists and turns ahead.

He'd had more than his share of second chances in life, but getting to work with Maddie topped them all. He wouldn't make a mess of things this time around.

Chapter Ten

Exhausted from a week full of decisions about her business, Maddie was lying on her couch Saturday night, staring at the ceiling, where faint music and occasional thuds came from Jake's apartment. She was confident sticking with Wright Construction was the best choice, but seeing Jake on the beach today also made her long for a personal connection with him.

Just when she'd finally convinced herself it was time to stop envisioning him with his shirtsleeves rolled up, gripping whatever tool that was causing that racket in his strong hands, someone knocked at the door.

She hauled herself up off the sofa and went to see who was paying her an unexpected visit, grateful she hadn't bothered to change into pajamas yet. But when she opened it, she realized it wouldn't have mattered if she had. Her two best friends in the world stood on the other side of the door.

"Did I mess up the days? I thought we were having dinner tomorrow," Maddie said.

"That was the plan, but Celeste and I ran into each other at the grocery store and decided it was past time to hang out." Tasha breezed inside, a casserole in her oven-mitt-covered hands.

Celeste held back. "Are you okay with us showing up here unannounced?"

"More than okay," Maddie assured her. "But all I have is leftovers."

"Don't worry, we've got it covered." Tasha set the foil-covered dish on the counter. "Lemon chicken and zucchini with orzo," she said. "My mom is in full grandmother mode and made, like, six of these."

"Aren't they supposed to be for your sister?"

"She won't miss this one," Tasha said with a glint in her eyes.

Maddie gaped at her. "Tash!"

"Kidding. Izzy said that with what you made and Mom's food, they've run out of freezer space." Tasha pulled the foil from the dish, and citrus-scented steam rose from a delicious-looking dish topped with lightly charred lemon slices. "Between you and me, though, I think Izzy just prefers your cooking."

Celeste set the tote bag she was carrying down on the round kitchen table. "I like both Maddie's and your mom's cooking," she said diplomatically, and Maddie agreed. She'd had dinner with the Grants often enough to know Tasha's mom worked wonders in the kitchen.

Celeste started opening the cupboards one by one. "You're so organized already." She turned around, scanning the room. "Where are all the boxes? I thought we could help you get settled in."

"I needed to keep busy."

"Oh, and your freelance work plus getting ready to launch a catering business isn't enough?"

Maddie shrugged. "There's plenty for you guys to help me with, like hanging pictures."

Celeste looked triumphantly at Tasha. "Told you my tool kit would come in handy."

"Better point her to the nearest picture frame, quick," Tasha told Maddie. "She's been dying to break out her stud finder and tape measure."

Celeste's husband had been a DIY extraordinaire who took care of all the odd jobs around the house with his ample spare time. He was often unemployed since he always found reasons why all the available positions weren't worth his time or excuses to quit when he did get hired, which put the burden for providing for them solely on Celeste's shoulders. Then he used her long hours at work as an excuse for cheating.

In the aftermath of his affair and their subsequent divorce, Celeste had taken it upon herself to learn how to tackle household projects. But Maddie couldn't help but wonder what steps she'd taken to mend her heart.

"Will do," Maddie said. "But first let's eat." She found a vase for the flowers Celeste had brought while her friends grabbed plates and a serving spoon. They sat down around Maddie's small kitchen table with the food and glasses of wine, the bouquet of daffodils lending a cheerful touch.

Celeste scooped a serving of casserole onto her plate. "I know we surprised you by showing up like this, but we decided a girls' night was long overdue. Especially since I've been wondering if there's more to the Jake situation than you let on."

Maddie looked at Tasha, who shook her head. "I didn't say anything."

"So there is something going on," Celeste said. "I know you still have trouble trusting people after what happened. But I could tell there was more to it than that."

"You're right. It's been complicated enough living in the same house as Jake while working together on my renovation, but on top of that..." *Just say it.* "I kissed him."

"What?" Eyes wide, Celeste turned to Tasha. "Are you hearing this?"

"I found out earlier today."

"So I'm the last to know." Celeste sat back, mouth pursed.

Maddie didn't blame her for feeling hurt at being left out. "I figured if I mentioned it when we were talking business at the coffee shop, you'd just think I wanted to find a new contractor for personal reasons."

"Probably a good call. The owner is nosy as all get-out, too," Tasha said supportively.

"Seems to be a common trait in Orchard Harbor." Maddie couldn't help but think of Britta. "Anyway, when I asked Tasha for advice about Atlas, I realized I had to give her the whole story, like I should have with you. Plus, she would've got it out of me anyway. You know how she is."

"Like a badger," Tasha said with a proud smile. "Or maybe a fox. Take your pick of any tenacious, perceptive, adorable woodland creature."

Celeste snorted, and Maddie let out a laugh. "But seriously," she said. "The real reason is I was embarrassed. I mean, you know me. I don't kiss strangers. I don't even talk to them if I can avoid it."

Her friends chuckled, but then Celeste said, "You might not know him well, but he's not exactly a stranger. He's your neighbor, and you're working with him."

"I didn't know any of that when I kissed him…" here came the hard part "…that first night at the winery."

"You kissed Jake the same night you met him?" Celeste's arched brows rose.

Maddie nodded, mortified.

"Our girl finally stepped outside the box," Tasha said proudly.

"And look where it landed me." A thump sounded from above their heads, and they all looked up. On instinct, Maddie dropped her voice. "Just my luck that the only time I ever do something like this, it turns out he's my contractor-slash-neighbor."

"A pretty nice arrangement, under other circumstances," Tasha said.

"Well, under these circumstances, it's a nonstarter." Maddie speared a lemon slice with her fork. "You should've seen the look on his face when he found out the woman he'd chatted up was actually the woman who stole the property he wanted for a gallery."

"Which I still don't understand." Celeste swirled her glass of wine thoughtfully. "He only ever sells his art to friends and family. Why was he so keen on a gallery?"

"Apparently, he was the one renovating it on behalf of the guild," Maddie said. "Maybe he felt more invested because of that. All I know is I was public enemy number one to him." Good thing they'd finally turned a corner that afternoon. She just hoped they could maintain this truce.

"Not at the winery you weren't," Tasha said, but relented when Maddie shot her a glare. "Just saying, if he kissed you, he must've been into you." Her expression turned sly. "Come to think of it, who made the first move? We need details."

Maddie's cheeks blazed. She'd known this was coming, but still. "It was mutual. He asked for my number, but I offered him a choice. My number or a kiss."

"Bold move." Tasha took a bite of orzo and added, "It's always the quiet ones."

"Oh stop." But Maddie took a sip of wine to hide her grin. Just thinking about kissing Jake made her want to do it again, which was absolutely off the table now that she'd decided to keep him on as foreman.

The thud of footfalls on the stairs had Maddie cocking her head to listen. Her friends froze when a knock came at the door.

"Is that him?" Celeste mouthed.

"Of course it's him," Tasha said at full volume.

"Shh." Maddie wished she could melt into the floor.

"Are you going to answer it?" Celeste asked.

"If she doesn't, I will," Tasha said, shrugging when Celeste glared at her. "I'm just saying, no reason to leave him standing there all night."

No way around it. She didn't want to leave him hanging, but the idea of talking to him with her friends looking on was mortifying. She went to the door, very aware of both sets of eyes on her as she pulled it open.

Sure enough, Jake stood in the entryway. Unlike usual, he wasn't dressed in jeans and a work shirt but had on a soft-looking T-shirt, and his bare feet peeked out from under the gray sweatpants he wore low on his hips. He looked every bit as appealing in lounge clothes as he did in a hard hat with sawdust on his shoulders.

"Hey." His gaze flicked upward, over her shoulder, and he must've caught sight of the others because he dipped his chin in a quick nod of hello. "Didn't realize you had company. I won't keep you. But I was cleaning out the kitchen cupboards the other day and I found this." He handed her a cookbook. "Not that you need any help in the cooking department, but I thought you might enjoy having it."

The pages were stained, and the binding was loose, but she recognized it instantly as a favorite from her childhood. "My dad used these recipes all the time, but his copy got lost." She smoothed a hand down the familiar cover. "Thank you."

He gave a half smile, and she wanted to rise on her tiptoes and kiss the corner of his mouth where it dented his cheek. Wanted it so fiercely that she had to grip the doorframe to stay in place.

She cast a glance at her friends. "Want to come in for dinner?" It was the polite thing to say, but she also craved more time with him, she realized.

"I don't want to intrude."

From behind her, Tasha said, "If you want to come back another time when you have Maddie all to yourself, just say so."

"I don't—" He thrust a hand through his hair, cheeks crimson. "I mean, dinner sounds great. But you're busy. I'll leave you to it." With that, he turned and went upstairs.

Maddie returned to the table and slumped in her chair. "Well, that couldn't have been more embarrassing."

"Which part?" Tasha took a sip of wine. "Bringing you a token of his affection or the way you two were staring into each other's eyes like there was no one else in the room?"

"He was just being neighborly."

"My neighbors let me borrow their shovel in the winter, but they don't look at me like I'm dinner and dessert all in one when they do it."

"Much as I hate to agree with Tasha when she's being messy," Celeste said with a grin, "can't say I disagree."

"You really think he's into me?"

"He kissed you, did he not?" Celeste asked as if that was proof enough.

"That was before all this." But looking down at the well-loved cookbook in her hands, she couldn't help but wonder.

Celeste was watching her, her dark eyes sharp in the low light. "You like him."

Maddie wanted to deny it, but on the heels of his apology and seeing him at work, all strong and capable, and on the beach, hair ruffled in the breeze… "He barely tolerates me."

Tasha blew a noisy raspberry. "Puh-lease. It sounds like he'd gotten himself all worked up to not like whoever outbid him. It wasn't personal."

Celeste took a pensive sip of wine. “Do you think his apology was genuine?”

“I do.” Maddie didn’t hesitate. “He even told me about his bad track record at Atlas before I brought it up.” Though she sensed there was more to the story, but didn’t want to push him. His personal life wasn’t her business, and he’d told her enough on a professional level to make her trust him.

“But is that enough?” Celeste asked.

“Weren’t you the one who told me not to make hasty decisions or believe Britta’s gossip? Why are you playing devil’s advocate?”

“Because I don’t want you to get hurt,” Celeste said. “When you came to me for advice, I didn’t know the full story. And now that you’ve decided to stick with him…” Her mouth pulled into a worried frown. “I’m just worried you might have more personal than professional reasons for choosing to stay with Wright Construction.”

Maddie bristled. “That’s exactly why I didn’t tell you. I know I’ve made poor judgment calls in the past, but I made a practical choice. I want to build a good rapport with other local businesses, and like you said, Wright Construction is well respected. Part of moving here was learning not to be afraid of putting my trust in people again.”

“Trusting your coworker wasn’t a mistake,” Tasha said. “She pulled you in with kindness, and anyone would’ve fallen for it.”

“Not everyone would’ve put their banking and social security information into a sketchy lease document forwarded by someone they’d only known a few months.”

Tasha set down her wineglass. “It was going to be your first apartment. You didn’t know how the process was supposed to work. Give yourself some grace.”

“But also keep your eyes open,” Celeste added, and Tasha

nodded in agreement. "I'm glad you're on good terms with Jake again, but it's probably not the best time to get involved with someone, especially not with all the complications. There are plenty of single guys in Orchard Harbor. When the time is right, you'll have another chance."

Maddie wanted to protest, but between the renovation and building a life here, she had enough on her plate. Romance would make things trickier, and now that she and Jake had sorted things out on the business side, the smart choice would be to let go of her feelings for him.

Jake hoped he was wrong. Carefully, he pried up a piece of warped linoleum in the kitchen of Maddie's project to reveal the flooring underneath. "Shit." Asbestos tile.

The presence of asbestos in the flooring they planned to pull up meant they'd need to halt construction until it was taken care of. Rising, he braced himself to make the kind of call he always dreaded. He'd rather go for a swim in Lake Michigan in January than tell Maddie about another setback. But as foreman, he was always the one to break bad news.

He stuck his tongue in his cheek, waiting for her to answer his phone call. He hadn't seen her since he'd brought over the cookbook last week, probably because he'd been spending most evenings at his studio. Resolving things with Maddie had filled him with inspiration, and he'd begun a new mosaic.

The call went to voicemail, and he left a message. She texted a moment later, telling him she was working at the library and would be over soon.

Ten minutes later, she met him in front of the building, looking tense, and he hated to be the one to ruin her day.

"Asbestos." The dreaded word made Maddie's frown deepen. "We need to bring in a remediation team to properly dispose of the old tiles and make sure there are no particles in the air. It won't be cheap."

"How much?" she asked.

"Enough to put a big dent in your contingency."

Her mouth pulled into a firm line, but she nodded, tucking a curl behind her ear. She wore her hair loose today, springy curls framing her face. "Okay, but we planned for this."

"Losing the contingency this early in the process isn't a great sign. There's a lot of work to do, and we still haven't sourced some of the high-end kitchen appliances you wanted. Maybe it's time to think about finding places in the budget to cut back while we still can."

"I chose those appliances because of longevity. I plan to be in business for a long time."

Jake sniffed. He didn't want to dash her hopes, but the tourism industry could be tough. "If business is still good in a few years, you'll be able to upgrade."

"If?" Maddie cocked her head. "You don't think I have a chance of making it, do you?"

"I never said that." Jake shoved his hands in his pockets. "I want you to succeed. It's just that tourism slows down in the winter, and—"

"Restaurants are likely to fail, I know. But I have a strong concept and can always pivot as needed."

He believed her, and what did he know about the food industry, after all? "Charcuterie is having a moment," Jake said, repeating what his sister-in-law had mentioned when he told them about Maddie's business. "I'm sure being on trend will bring in a lot of customers."

"On trend?" Maddie's voice rose another notch. He could feel the conversation spiraling, and he wasn't sure where he'd gone wrong. "Pretty sure people have been having picnics for decades. And yes, charcuterie is having a moment, but catering is an evergreen service."

Wasn't trendy a good thing? Apparently not. "I was trying to give you a compliment."

"Oh really? Because you seem pretty set on reminding me that my time here in Orchard Harbor isn't permanent." Her eyes flashed with indignation, but then she stopped, brows tugged inward. "Wait, did you say a compliment?"

He grinned. "Yeah. I don't know much about fancy food or small plates or whatnot. But I have a feeling a lot of the wealthy people who vacation here will. Isn't that what you're counting on?"

"Guess I'm not used to you being nice to me."

Hearing those words, his heart lurched. "Let's fix that."

Her lips curved into a teasing grin. "What do you have in mind?"

He found himself stepping closer until they were toe-to-toe on the sidewalk. Except this time, he had no intention of arguing with her. "I was thinking maybe a do-over of that first night."

He reached out and gently took hold of her chin. Dipped his head and dropped a kiss on those parted lips.

Her hands found his chest, but instead of pushing him away, her fingers twined in the fabric of his jacket, pulling him closer. He explored the sweetness of her mouth, every bit as tempting as he remembered. When he deepened the kiss, she let out a little gasp that shot a bolt of desire straight through him.

Another gasp, louder this time, came from somewhere over his shoulder, and he belatedly realized they were making out in the middle of town at ten o'clock in the morning. They broke apart, and he darted a guilty glance over his shoulder to see they'd been caught by Geraldine Pullman.

"Jacob Winn, I thought that was you." The petite lady blinked at them from behind purple glasses. She was wearing a knit hat and woolen scarf, despite the sunny warmth. "Kissing on the sidewalk, and before noon on a Monday." She tsked, then her thin lips lifted in a mischievous smile. "Gonna introduce me to your sweetheart?"

He half turned toward Maddie, certain she wouldn't be okay with the title of sweetheart.

She looked startled but stepped forward and held out her hand. The same hand that seconds ago had been pulling him closer, molding their bodies together, but he shoved that alluring thought aside.

"Madelyn Briar," she said. "I'm new in town."

Miss Geraldine gave her a slow once-over before taking her hand. "Well, Miss New-in-town, I'm Geraldine Pullman. What brings you to Orchard Harbor? Is it this handsome young man?"

Maddie met his eyes, then quickly darted her glance away. "I'm here to open a catering business. This is my shop," she said, nodding toward the butcher-paper-covered windows.

"Hmm." Miss Geraldine gave the building a critical glance. "I've heard you're handling the remodel, Jake." Her tone implied she'd jumped to all sorts of conclusions, and he opened his mouth to set the record straight, but no better explanation came out.

Maddie seemed to be having the same problem, and Miss Geraldine chuckled. "If you're worried I'll spread your secret, don't be. It's yours to tell when the time is right."

"But there's no secret," Jake said, finally finding his voice.

"Mmm-hmm." Geraldine divided a glance between them. "Next time, maybe just conduct your personal business inside, eh?" She waggled her white brows.

"Have a good day, Miss Geraldine," he found himself saying, his years of training in good manners winning out.

She put up a thin hand in a wave, continuing on toward the post office with decisive steps.

Maddie grabbed his arm, pulling him into the alley.

He had a flash of what sorts of good trouble they could get up to before his brain caught up, and he realized she hadn't tugged him in here for *that*. Her eyes were wide, and she most definitely was not thinking of a repeat performance.

Bummer, because he didn't think Miss Geraldine's advice was half bad.

"What just happened?" Maddie hissed. The adrenaline of being caught making out by a matriarch of her adopted hometown was receding, and her limbs felt weak. Or maybe that was a result of another earth-shattering kiss with Jake.

"Are you okay? You're trembling." Jake sounded concerned, and she hated that he always seemed to worry over her, but in this case, it was justified.

"I need to get out of here." She was pretty sure her shop was off-limits because of the asbestos, but she needed a minute to process things in private.

"Come with me." He looped his arm around her shoulders and steered her toward the other side of the alley. The space between the buildings was neatly paved, with bright murals on both sides, but right now it felt like the walls were closing in.

"Where are we going?" she asked Jake when they came out onto the tree-lined avenue behind her building.

"My company is working on a residential project on Apple Blossom Street. But we're waiting on some countertops. No one's working today, so we can talk in private."

That sounded like a solid plan, so she allowed him to continue to lead her across the street, down one block to a gorgeous Cape Cod-style home.

He led her through the open garage—which on second glance was missing a door entirely—and into the house. Everything was framed out, but the floor was still plywood, and the whole place smelled like sawdust. She inhaled happily before she realized it smelled so good because it reminded her of Jake.

Embarrassed, she pulled away. "Will she really keep it to herself, do you think?" The look in his eyes was answer enough, and she groaned. "We seriously got caught by the town busybody?"

"Miss Geraldine isn't the only busybody in town," Jake said, and Maddie immediately thought of Britta. Could've been worse, she supposed. "But she won't be able to resist telling at least a few of the others," he admitted.

She let out a defeated sigh, and he surprised her by wrapping her in a hug. She hadn't expected it, but couldn't deny it was comforting, like they were in this together.

"Why'd she have to jump to conclusions?" Her question was muffled against the soft flannel of his shirt, and she felt his chest move in a quiet chuckle.

"Might've had something to do with your lips on mine."

"Your lips on mine," she countered.

"That's what I said, isn't it?"

"Humph."

He let out another soft laugh. "Stubborn."

"Takes one to know one."

"Well, yeah," he admitted, not sounding too bothered about it. "The question is…" his voice was a comforting rumble "…what're we going to do about it?"

She pulled back enough to look at him, secretly pleased that he didn't let go entirely, just slipped his hands to her lower back to accommodate the space between them. "Do about what?"

"The fact that by lunchtime at least three of the town's biggest gossips will know there's something going on between us," he said. "I'm sorry I put you in this position."

"Wasn't just you." She forced herself to meet his gaze, even though talking about this might've been the most embarrassing thing she'd ever done. "I wanted the kiss, too," she said, blushing. "But maybe next time, we should take Miss Geraldine's advice."

"Next time?" His mouth quirked up in an adorable grin.

She wanted to roll her eyes at how he'd chosen to focus on that part, but found herself smiling instead. "What I meant is, the night we met, we kissed in full view of anyone who might've walked by. Today we got carried away on Main Street. What's next, a town hall meeting?"

"Never been to one of those," he said thoughtfully. "But my guess is it would liven things up." She glowered, but he just grinned. "We should be more careful if it, um...happens again." His eyes dropped to her lips. "But in the meantime, how do you feel about people knowing about it?"

"I don't see how it's any of their business," she said. But she could see how the news would spread. Jake was well-known in Orchard Harbor. And now he'd been spotted in the arms of a newcomer. Of course people would talk. "But I have to admit, I'm not thrilled about word getting out that I kissed a stranger on the street."

"Are we strangers?" Jake's voice dropped into a husky register, and her heartbeat quickened. "That might've been true a few weeks ago, but I'd say we're long past that."

"Be that as it may," she said, trying to block out the thud of her racing pulse, "I don't have the benefit of the doubt. No one knows me."

"Tasha and Celeste know you," he said. "The guys on my crew know you. They've been pestering me ever since you stopped by about how we should make more videos for your social media."

"They're right," she said.

He shrugged as if he wasn't sold, but then he added, "And I know you. Or at least I'd like to."

She wanted that, too. Wanted to have another date with Jake and discuss all the things they didn't have a chance to on that first night. To hold hands on the beach and get another kiss goodnight.

But then she remembered her friends warning her to stay focused. Kissing Jake had derailed her, not once but twice.

She pulled away, her heart lurching at the flash of hurt in his eyes. But her friends' advice echoed in her mind, along with the very real demands on her time. "I can't be in a relationship right now. Not that you're even asking." She might be reading into things. But she did need to be clear. For him and herself. "But right now I should focus on getting my business up and running. I can't be distracted."

His eyes searched her face, then his chin jerked down in a quick nod. "Got it." He stepped back, shoving his hands into his pockets.

She wanted to pull him close again, feel the comforting weight of his arms around her and the coaxing pressure of his lips. To banish that yearning, she said, "Hopefully it'll blow over if we don't give people anything else to talk about."

"You're overestimating the amount of interesting gossip around here. But yeah, people will let it go eventually."

"In the meantime, it's probably best if we're not seen together."

Something clouded Jake's expression, but he nodded again.

"Shouldn't be too hard to avoid each other, other than the whole living under one roof complication."

"That and the whole working together thing." Things had gotten hopelessly complicated, especially now that she couldn't deny she still had feelings for him. But if people wanted to be that nosy, it wasn't her and Jake's problem. "Not much we can do about that. As long as no one catches us kissing again, I think we're good."

"Right." His eyes swept over her face for a split second, and suddenly she wished they'd kissed again before they made the deal to avoid each other. Too late now.

She shook her head to clear it. "I'll leave first, and then you can follow in five minutes," she said.

"Why do you get to leave first?"

"Fine," she said, grateful to go back to the familiarity of bickering. It would make it much easier to avoid him if he was getting on her nerves. "You go, I'll stay."

"You can't be here alone, it's my jobsite." He sighed. "Right. Yeah. I guess I need to stop being so ornery."

Her eyebrows twitched upward. "Ya think?"

He shook his head. "Don't go getting all sassy now."

"Or what?" The flirtatious words slipped out, and she jammed her mouth shut, turning to go before he could answer. Avoiding him was going to be much harder than she thought.

Chapter Eleven

Jake plopped onto a stool at Driftwood Tavern. The rooftop bar overlooking the inlet was a favorite spot for tourists but this time of year he could grab a drink and enjoy the view without wading through a crowd. A cool breeze came in off the lake, and he set his beer on the coaster before it blew away.

Only a few other people were sitting outside tonight, which was just how he liked it. After a day spent dealing with shipping delays and cracked countertops, he needed to decompress. For a while, living in a town where everyone knew everyone else's business had felt suffocating. But having people he'd known all his life be there for him no matter what was a gift he'd never take for granted again.

Maddie didn't have that, and if she wanted to keep her distance so she could focus on building her own support system here, she deserved that chance. He wouldn't stand in her way, even though their latest kiss left him wishing more than ever that he hadn't screwed things up.

A few people had stopped by his table to say hey, but for the past hour or so he'd been alone. That peace wasn't due to last, because familiar laughter floated up from the restaurant below. A moment later, his best friend, Tom, came upstairs, suit jacket over one arm and tie loose, his russet-red hair still perfectly styled despite what had probably been a thirteen-hour day at the law firm.

"Thought you might need something to soak up the beer," Tom said, placing a platter of appetizers on the table.

Jake picked up a fried pickle. Dubious but willing to give it a go, he popped one in his mouth, then winced at the combination of briny pickle and greasy batter. He finished chewing, then called over his shoulder, toward the bar, "Norm, why can't you fry something that's meant to be fried for once? Potatoes maybe?"

Norman shouted back, "You've got no culinary aptitude, Winn. I'll come to you for advice when I need to put a fresh layer of lacquer on the bar top," he joked.

Grinning, Jake turned back to the table and caught Tom in the act of sneaking a swig of his beer. He clicked his tongue in frustration. "Dude, c'mon."

Tom waved a hand at the food he'd brought up, like it was a fair trade. Complaints were pointless with his best friend, so Jake just grabbed a piece of bruschetta.

"Long day?" Tom asked when he'd finished gulping most of Jake's drink.

"You could say that."

"I could tell." Not surprising, since they'd been friends since kindergarten. "Is it the Connery project? I told you not to go with the Carrara marble."

Jake sat back with a huff. "Everything you know about remodeling comes from watching house flipping reality shows."

"Sure, sure, rub your years of experience in my face."

Getting close to a decade. And that only counted his years working in construction. Growing up, he'd helped with his dad's ever-present projects around their house on weekends. After everything went down, Jake had wanted nothing to do with it for a long time.

"Figure you'd be more grateful, considering those years

of experience are helping me renovate your investment property." Jake was kidding, but Tom's expression turned serious.

"Actually, I've been meaning to talk to you about something," Tom said. "I snagged a deal on another house last week. I'd like to hire you in an official capacity this time around."

"I haven't seen any houses for sale recently around town."

Tom dipped a fried pickle in ranch. "It's not exactly in town." Excitement shone in his hazel eyes. "It's on the lakeshore."

Jake let out a low whistle. Those were multimillion-dollar properties. He hadn't realized Tom had that kind of money.

"Don't get too excited," Tom said. "It's in pretty rough shape."

"But the property alone…" Even undeveloped beachfront lots commanded upward of a million dollars.

"The owner wanted out. Something to do with cutting personal ties. Celeste told me it had been on the market for three years with no movement. Still wasn't cheap, but man, so worth it."

Jake was just happy he had a roof over his head. At one point in time, that hadn't been a given. He couldn't imagine buying a house on the lake, but he was happy for his friend. "Can't wait to see it. Just don't expect Reese to cut you a deal on reno costs now that he knows you're loaded," he said with a grin.

Tom laughed. "I know your crew will do right by me. Speaking of, how're things going at the house? I haven't received any complaints from the other tenant since the pipes burst, so I'm assuming you haven't been bothering her with construction noise."

Jake knew Maddie would come up sooner or later. "I keep it to daytime hours. But she's been plenty bothered." He'd gone through enough boyhood mayhem with Tom to know he was an iron trap when it came to ratting people out, so he caught him up on everything that had happened since he'd met Maddie, ending with their encounter with Miss Geraldine but leaving out the mention of making out on the sidewalk.

"But why would Miss Geraldine assume you two were dating?"

"You know how the older generation is. Can't be with a woman without a chaperone and all that."

"You're friends with plenty of women," Tom said. "What aren't you telling me?"

Jake stuffed a fried pickle into his mouth, sacrificing his taste buds to get out of answering the question.

Tom loosened his tie and sat back, like he had all the time in the world.

Knowing a lost cause when he saw one, Jake swallowed around the lump in his throat and said in a rush, "She caught us kissing."

Tom's eyes went wide. "Unless your methods have vastly changed, I don't remember that being part of the renovation services you offer clients."

"Shut up, man. This is serious." Jake leaned closer. "We didn't mean to get caught, but—"

"But this is Orchard Harbor, and secrets travel fast, let alone acts done in daylight on Main Street." Shaking his head, Tom said, "What were you thinking, Jake?"

He hadn't been thinking, obviously. "There's something about Maddie. She makes me feel…energized." But not in the way he had been, aimless and needing an outlet. She made him feel creative. Passionate. "I've been spending more time on my art."

"Maddie, that's her name?"

Jake nodded. "Madelyn, but her friends call her Maddie."

"That's what you are? A friend?"

"I don't know, man, that's the thing." Jake sat back in his chair, feeling the familiar fizz of confusion and yearning take hold. "We seem to be either arguing or kissing, there's no in-between."

"This isn't the first time it happened?" Tom asked with his usual quickness.

Shoot. Jake would have to be more careful. Telling Tom about the kiss on Main Street was one thing; that was public knowledge. But what happened at the winery was between him and Maddie only. He didn't want to violate her trust. "All I'm saying is I'm not sure if we're even friends. With me working on her reno, we need to keep things professional, and this is the opposite of that."

"I'd say so. You're basically Orchard Harbor official," Tom said, chuckling. "No way you're getting out of this one."

"Our plan is to avoid being seen together until the gossip dies down. Maddie just moved here and isn't looking for a relationship." He hadn't been, either, until he met her.

"Too bad," Tom said. "Would probably be easier if you were an actual couple."

"How so?"

"Kiss your client? That's news. Kiss your girlfriend, and that's no one's business but yours."

Jake could see his point. Even so, a relationship was off-limits. They'd stick to the plan and avoid each other. As much as two people sharing a house and a jobsite could.

He had a feeling they'd fixed their professional problems just to tumble into a whole bunch of personal trouble.

Maddie hadn't seen Jake since their kiss last week. She hadn't heard him much in the evenings, either. He might be out with friends, but part of her wondered if he was in his studio, wherever that was.

She missed him, but it wasn't fair to seek him out, not when she was the one who'd suggested they keep their distance. It helped that work was halted on her project until the asbestos was taken care of, even though she hated falling behind schedule. Her savings would only last so long, and large-scale food-styling gigs were hard to come by in this area. At least she'd recently heard back from Spencer that the owner of the pizza place was ready to update his menu with Maddie's help.

To stay productive, she'd also been testing recipes for her own menu and had just pulled a tray of apricot scones out of the oven when her phone vibrated on the table. Pulling off her oven mitts, she picked it up and saw a new message in the group text with her friends.

Celeste: I did some sleuthing, and things are not looking good.

This time, she'd told them right away about getting caught kissing Jake. Hiding things had only left her feeling lost. Unsurprisingly, they were on board with her plan to steer clear of Jake, although she wasn't 100 percent sold on the idea herself.

Keeping her distance had been even more difficult than expected. She wanted to explore their connection, wanted the feel of his lips on hers again, but her judgment had led her astray in the past.

Tasha: Same. Folks are talking, and I think you need new plan. I don't have any clients this morning. Want to meet up for bagels and coffee?

Celeste: Wish I could, but I have showings.

Maddie: Next time, Celeste! Tasha, wanna come here instead? I unpacked my espresso machine, and I baked apricot scones.

Tasha: You had me at espresso.

Celeste: Now I'm even more bummed to miss. Keep me posted, ladies!

Maddie: We'll save you some scones.

Tasha: One. We'll save you *one* scone. Maybe. ;)

Smiling, Maddie set the phone down so she could snap a few photos of the scones. She foamed milk for a latte, then set a scone on a plate and added the mug, a tea towel and a bud vase with a daffodil she'd picked from the patch in the backyard to the table.

But the photos turned out too dim, so she carried the tray to her room, which had more natural light. She'd opened the windows that morning to let the fresh air in, and a breeze stirred the gauzy curtains. Fetching the piece of reclaimed wood she'd bought, she laid it on the bed and put everything on top. She decided to shoot from above in hopes it would pass for a rustic table and raised her camera to her eye.

A loud knock startled her, and she nearly dropped the camera onto the food. Grumbling, she hopped off the bed and yanked open the front door, expecting to see her best friend. Instead, the sight of Jake in all his rugged, flannel-clad glory greeted her.

"Oh, hi." Seeing him again after so long made the ache in her chest grow bigger. Keeping her distance was looking less and less like an option.

Hands in his pockets, he asked, "Got a minute?"

Not really. Tasha was due any second, but she hated how hesitant he looked, like she was going to turn him away, when all week her mind had been full of him. "I don't have long, but come in. I need to take some photos before the foam on the latte deflates."

She went back to her bedroom, trying to play it cool. Was it weird to invite him into her room like this? Maybe. But she'd spent a lot of time getting the latte art just right, and she didn't want it to go to waste. She took a few photos, then checked them in the viewfinder.

"Is this for your catering business or freelance work?" Jake asked.

Out of the corner of her eye, she noticed he was leaning against the doorway, thumb hooked into his belt loop, and it took all her concentration not to focus on how effortlessly attractive he was.

"I'm updating my website," she said. "When I do food-styling gigs, I usually work with a professional photographer. But I take the photos as well from time to time." She frowned at the thumbnail.

"What's wrong?" He came closer, and she showed him the images.

"I was trying to make it look like the food was laid out on a table. The kitchen is too dark in the mornings," she explained. "But it just looks like a scrap of wood."

He rubbed his stubbled chin, and she caught a whiff of his crisp, woodsy scent. "I could get you a slab of granite countertop if you want."

"Seriously, you'd do that?"

"It's no big deal. You act like I hate you."

Hands on her hips, she said, "Don't you?" They had chemistry, no denying it. But more often than not, it had sparked into disagreements.

"I've kissed you. Twice now, Madelyn." The deep timbre of his voice melted into her, like hot coffee poured over a sugar cube. "I'm not in the habit of kissing women I don't like."

To hide how much his words stirred her, she said, "I told you, we're well past the formal name stage. Maddie works fine."

"I like both, and Madelyn suits you." His lips curved in a smile that sent her heart fluttering. "And much as I like arguing with you, I prefer when we get along."

"Ah, so the granite is bribery for good behavior." She couldn't resist the grin that tugged at her cheeks.

"That, and I love your smile."

She pressed her lips together, trying not to grin, but it was impossible.

"And your dimples."

She couldn't help noticing that he'd said he'd loved not one but two things about her. Three, technically, if you counted both her dimples. And she loved to get technical. "You've got one, too."

He looked taken aback. "No, I don't."

"Do, too. Here," she said, and without thinking, stepped closer and pressed a thumb to the center of his chin. It was rough with stubble, his skin radiating warmth.

"That's called a cleft chin. Very strong and manly." He lowered his voice when he said it, dropping into a falsely deep register, and Maddie giggled.

"I was going to say adorable. But we'll go with manly."

She dropped her hand, self-conscious, but he caught it, intertwining their fingers. "Adorable, huh? Guess you don't hate me, either."

"I wish I did," she said. "It would make all this—" living under one roof, working with him, quieting town gossip "—easier."

"You don't strike me as someone who prefers life easy. Orderly," he said, glancing at the open planner on her dresser with its color-coded pages. "But not easy."

"Careful, Jake. That sounded awfully close to a compliment."

"You're an impressive woman, Maddie. I never stopped feeling that way, even when we were fighting like cats and dogs."

"If you give me a minute, I'm sure I could think of something to argue about." She squeezed his hand involuntarily, unsteady on her feet.

"I like this better, don't you?" His eyes searched hers, and she nodded, breathless.

"Much." She'd barely gotten the word out before he bent and kissed her. The moment his mouth met hers, all thoughts fled from her mind. His lips were unspeakably soft, his beard a delicious scrape along her chin.

He kissed her like they'd been together for years, like he knew her, inside and out. Like he knew how to unravel her. She let him, melting at his touch. His hands slid around her waist, drawing her closer, and she arched up against him. But instead of meeting the solid warmth of his chest, something sharp dug into her breastbone, and she jerked away, the weight hanging around her shoulders reminding her. The camera.

She was tempted to yank the strap off over her head and get back to where they were, but caught the sound of the screen door hinges creaking open.

He mouthed the words, "Expecting someone?"

She nodded and said aloud, "Tash, that you?"

From the hallway, Tasha's voice called, "Who else would it be?"

Jake's eyes went wide. He stepped out of the way, and Maddie hurried into the living room, gesturing him to follow. She shut her bedroom door, but somehow that seemed more incriminating.

Wiping her hands down her pants, she glanced at Jake on her way to the front door. He was standing in the middle of the living room, arms stiff and hands balled by his sides, as rigid as a toy soldier.

"Relax," she whispered. "You look suspicious."

"I'm trying," he whispered back.

"Try harder," she hissed, and he narrowed his eyes in a glare.

A knock rattled the door again. "Hurry, my hands are full."

Any longer, and Tasha was going to sense something was up. With a sigh, Maddie opened the door. Tasha held a paper sack and had a canvas tote slung over one arm.

"Let me take that for you." Peering inside, Maddie saw what looked to be wigs and a makeup case. "Um…"

Tasha slipped off her fuchsia flats. "I'll explain, but only once I'm caffeinated." She must've caught sight of Jake because her eyes widened. "Oh, hi. Didn't see you there."

Maddie turned and saw he'd taken her advice to act relaxed. Or was trying to. He was on the couch, but instead of sitting naturally, he was half reclining, a throw pillow wedged under his elbow and his boots hanging off the edge. He looked all kinds of uncomfortable.

"You good, Jake?" Tasha asked pointedly, brows raised.

He nodded and fixed his hat, which had been knocked askew.

"Mmm-hmm," Tasha said, as if she wasn't convinced. "Maddie, maybe we should go to my place. I've got a sensitive matter to discuss."

Jake cleared his throat. "Does it have to do with everyone in town thinking she and I are a couple?"

So it wasn't just people in Tasha and Celeste's circle that had found out. Maddie's heart sank.

"As a matter of fact," Tasha said, "it does."

"How did you know?" Maddie asked Jake.

"That's what I came to tell you," he said. "Before we…" He trailed off, and a blaze of heat spread along Maddie's cheekbones.

"Before what?" Tasha asked.

"Before we were interrupted," he said smoothly. "By someone pounding on the door."

"You try growing up with four siblings. Noisiness is in my DNA."

Maddie knew Tasha adored her family, but had confessed on more than one occasion to feeling like they were always lumped together. That was part of why she'd left town, to carve out her own place in the world. But she'd ultimately decided to come back home, missing the comfort of being near everyone she loved most.

"Nosiness, too," Tasha added. "My grandma plays bunco with Miss Geraldine and called me today telling me how sweet it was that you'd moved halfway across the state to be near your boyfriend."

"What?" How had they gone from a kiss to people thinking they were in a long-distance relationship? It was like a grown-up game of telephone, but with way higher stakes.

"Yup." Tasha took off her fringed suede jacket, hanging it on the coat rack they'd assembled the other night. "Better make it a double shot of espresso."

Jake watched Maddie brew espresso using the fancy chrome machine. He hadn't drunk many lattes in his life. Come to think of it, this might be his first. The Harbor Bridge Café had a whole menu of fancy drinks, but when he stopped in for a pastry he stuck to simple drip coffee. Most days he just grabbed a cup of black coffee from the gas station on the way to work. They brewed it strong, and if his former classmate Clyde was working, he'd get a free donut out of it.

Not that he needed extra caffeine this morning. His system was already buzzing with awareness from the kiss they'd just shared. This was the first time he'd seen Maddie dressed casually in leggings and a loose tank top. She'd felt soft and warm in his arms, her mouth tasting of honey.

She asked how he took his coffee, and he told her he was craving something sweet. That earned him a sidelong look from Tasha. Dang it. How could he have forgotten how easily she caught on to things? He and her brothers had never been able to sneak anything by her when they were kids. They finally quit trying and let her in on their shenanigans, knowing they were less likely to get caught with Tasha masterminding the plans.

Maddie held up a glass bottle with a stopper, full of amber liquid. "Will vanilla syrup do?"

"Homemade?"

"Our girl is a chef," Tasha said. "Of course it's homemade."

Maddie finished her magic with the coffeemaker, then came over to the table with two mugs and set them in front of him and Tasha. "I'll stick with water," she said. "I'm nervous enough to hear this news without adding caffeine to the mix."

She pulled out a chair and sat down, crossing her arms. Her hair was held back by a thick headband, tendrils of curls at her cheeks. Her face was flushed and shiny, probably from the steam, but it made her glow. Even though he knew from their encounters that she could hold her own in any argument, he couldn't help but feel like she looked angelic.

Tasha blew on her drink before taking a sip. "Sounds like you already know that word around town is that you and Jake are a couple and have been one for a while." She glared at him, like he was to blame for the misinformation.

He held up his hands. "We tried to explain things to Miss Geraldine, but she was having none of it."

Tasha let out a harrumph. "The way I see it, you have two options." She set aside her coffee and bent to retrieve something. "Option one." She placed a bag on the table. "Disguise your identity. Pretend that your twin sister was impersonating the real Maddie and the real you wants nothing to do with him. You can tell everyone you sent her packing and are here to take charge of the catering business."

She pulled out two wigs, one blond and curly, the other brown and straight. "You'd have to commit to it until your hair grows out, but I could help you trim these up, and they're really comfortable—"

"Tasha. No." Maddie covered her mouth, but a giggle escaped, and Jake found himself smiling at the sound. "This is extreme, even for you."

Even though Tasha had lived out of state for almost a decade, it was clear she hadn't changed. Wild schemes, shenanigans. This had Tasha Grant written all over it.

"What's worse? Faking a sibling or calling Miss Geraldine, paragon of the community, leader of the church choir and the annual bake and craft show, a liar?"

Maddie sank low in her chair. "This is a nightmare."

"Hey, it wouldn't have happened if you two had been able to behave." But Jake could tell by her twinkling eyes that Tasha was joking. Mostly.

"Don't blame her," Jake said. "It was my fault." He was used to being the talk of the town. But he had a feeling this was Maddie's first experience with it.

"Not entirely your fault," Maddie said. "I wanted to kiss you again."

Hearing that gave him a rush of pleasure, which was cut short by Tasha clearing her throat. A much-needed reminder they weren't alone.

"Which brings me to option two," Tasha said. "Since you two clearly like each other, why don't you just make the rumors true?"

"That would still be a lie." Maddie frowned. "And I certainly didn't move here for him."

Tasha waved her hand. "Obviously, and I told my grandma that. Both of us will do our part to clear things up. But rumors are always going to spread. If you want to avoid making a big deal of this, all that really matters is that you are together, not how long it's been."

"You're saying we've been taking the wrong approach?" Maddie looked skeptical. "Instead of lying low, we should go out and be seen together?"

Tasha nodded, and Jake wanted to kick himself for things going down this way. He didn't want Maddie to feel like she had to go out with him to save her reputation. Especially when it might have the opposite effect in the long run.

She shook her head. "I want to build trust with people here, not start off with a lie."

Jake agreed and didn't want to pull her into a relationship—for show or otherwise—unless it was something she genuinely wanted. "Nice of you to try to help us out," he told Tasha. "But I think we can handle things on our own." He didn't want to ruin the chance of something real between them with an act.

Letting out a sigh, she said, "I was just offering a rational solution, but I get it."

"Rational?" Maddie crossed her arms. "Your ideas were to wear a wig or fake affection to get off the town's gossip mill."

"Who said anything about faking?" Tasha asked, a glint in her light brown eyes.

"And that's your cue to go," Maddie said.

"Okay, okay." Tasha stuffed the wigs back into the tote. "It makes sense you two would need some time to talk this out. But remember, my offer to forge a new identity still stands."

Maddie smirked. "Why do I feel like you came up with that idea just to get experience styling those new lace-front wigs?"

"That's a side benefit. Helping you would be the real reward."

Maddie didn't look like she bought that for a second, but she gave Tasha a quick hug. "Thanks for the advice." She wrinkled her nose. "Can we call it advice?" She shrugged. "Either way, it's good to know you're in my corner."

Jake raised his mug in farewell. "Bye, Tasha. Good to see you haven't changed."

"Did you think a few years in Chicago would change me? You know better, Jake." She grinned. "Be kind to my girl, or you'll hear it from me."

He gave her a serious nod. Whatever happened, he didn't want to waste any more time fighting with Madelyn Briar.

Chapter Twelve

After Tasha left, Maddie asked Jake if he wanted to finish drinking his coffee out on the front porch. Why waste a warm spring day by hiding inside if the whole town thought they were a couple anyway?

She took a seat on the steps, letting the sunshine soak into her skin. She squinted up at the tree branches, covered in pink and white blossoms. "What are we going to do?"

He sat down next to her and rested one elbow on the step behind him. "No offense to Tasha, but I wish she hadn't shown up when she did. And not just because she interrupted us," he said, brows tugging inward in a frown that Maddie couldn't help smiling at. "But because I wanted to be the one to break the news to you and see if you were okay with me telling everyone the truth—that we're not together and never were—instead of waiting for things to quiet down. I know you want to focus on work, and this can't be helping."

"Oh." She was touched by his thoughtfulness.

"But…" He trailed off, and she glanced at him. "That was before you kissed me the minute I arrived."

"Pretty sure we both had a part in that." Her skin tingled at the memory.

"Which brings me to the other reason I regret not getting a chance to talk to you before Tasha came." Shadowed by the brim of his cap, his face was so serious that Maddie's stomach flipped. What could be worse than town gossip? "I think it's high time we stop acting like we hate each other."

Her heart, already racing, kicked up at his words. "But we're so good at it."

"I think there are other things we could be even better at." His eyes had darkened to a deep amber. "Even though it's probably wiser to stay away, playing it safe has never been my strong suit."

She'd played it safe for years, but since day one being near Jake made her throw caution to the wind. "Keeping our distance didn't work out," she said. "Maybe it's time to stop fighting our attraction and see where this goes."

"Yeah?" His face broke out into a wide smile, and in answer, she leaned close and kissed his cheek.

"Careful," he said. "Someone might see."

"Let them," she said, heart in her throat but confident that she wanted this. Wanted *him*.

A spark lit Jake's eyes. Setting down his coffee, he pulled her close and claimed her mouth with his own.

The moment their lips touched, she felt so light she could've floated away like a blossom on the wind. The caress of his mouth melted away all her worries, and the morning sun filtered through her closed eyes, making everything feel dreamy. Or maybe that was Jake's doing. Craving more of him, her hand cupped his cheek, the scrape of stubble rough against her palm, and she dissolved in a flurry of sensations as his tongue stroked hers.

The stair creaked underneath them as he tugged her closer, and this time there was no camera to come between them. A moan of pleasure escaped her as he deepened the kiss, but all too quickly he pulled away, a smile slanting his lips.

"What I wouldn't give to throw caution to the wind," he said, "but I'd rather kiss you like this when there's no chance we'll get interrupted." He slid an arm around her waist, nestling her close. "Much as I wish the incident with Miss Geraldine was a one-off, I've lived in Orchard Harbor too long to count on it."

Maddie couldn't help but agree. With their luck, one of his parents would drive by next and catch them. Come to think of it, while she knew he'd grown up in Orchard Harbor and had a brother in town, she didn't know much about his family. It was time to remedy that.

"Want to meet me for a picnic tomorrow? The weather is still chilly enough that I bet we'd have the whole beach to ourselves." She'd never asked a guy out before, but her move to Orchard Harbor was all about trying new things and going after what she wanted.

And she was tired of acting like spending time with Jake wasn't high on the list of things she craved.

Maddie scowled at the rolling waves and storm-dark sky. She'd hoped to find a secluded, romantic spot in the dunes for their picnic, but by the look of the clouds, Mother Nature had other ideas. Jake stood beside her, shielding her from the worst of the wind, but sand pelted her bare ankles, gusts turning the soft grains into a menace that would give new meaning to the term "sandwiches."

Clutching the picnic basket tight against her chest, she said, "Guess I should've checked the forecast for this evening."

Jake shrugged. "Might not have mattered. Sometimes these storms pop up out of nowhere. Spring weather is unpredictable. Sunny and sixties in the morning, winter temps by afternoon."

Maddie shivered and adjusted the strap of the folding picnic blanket on her shoulder. She'd also brought a woolen blanket, but even that would be no match for rain. Her plans to prove herself were falling short on all counts.

She raised her voice to be heard over the wind. “Maybe we should head back to the house.” It wouldn’t be as special, but all that really mattered was spending time together.

“We could.” He frowned at the waves crashing on the shore. “Or…” he said, bending so that his mouth was near her ear. She knew it was only so she could hear him, but the nearness of his lips sent a different kind of shiver along her shoulder. “I know of somewhere more sheltered that will still have a great view.”

Of course he did. He’d grown up here. He’d know all the good spots. The realization might’ve set off her competitive drive a few weeks ago, but now she was just grateful their date wouldn’t be ruined.

“That sounds fabulous,” she said, smiling up at him. “Lead the way.”

She’d come to the beach on foot, using the walk to calm her nerves, but Jake had driven. They climbed into his truck, and he turned onto a tree-lined road that housed lakeside cottages and mansions. A few minutes later, he pulled into the half circle driveway of a cabin with weathered siding.

“Wow.” Maddie peered through the windshield at the charming house. “This is yours?” Why the heck was he living in a run-down apartment in town when he owned a place like this?

He chuckled. “In my dreams. A friend of mine recently purchased it and hired us to handle the renovation. It’s in rough shape on the inside, so don’t get too excited,” he warned, leading her around to the back of the house.

“Do you bring dates to your projects all the time?” she asked, remembering how they’d hidden away in the newly built home after the kiss debacle.

He smiled, flipping through his key ring before sliding one into the lock. “This is a first. But my buddy won’t mind.” He swung the door open to reveal a rustic main room with a towering stone fireplace. The back wall was almost entirely glass, with windows reaching all the way to the vaulted ceiling.

Outside was a breathtaking view of the whitecapped lake and overhanging trees, their leaves flashing silver in the wind. Awestruck, she stepped inside and was greeted by the homey scents of pine and cedar. A loft extended overhead, reachable by a curving metal staircase. To the left, she glimpsed a kitchen with knotty pine cabinets and a shellacked wood counter.

"Sorry, maybe this was a bad idea." Jake stood by the door, looking uncertain.

"Are you kidding?" He'd clearly misinterpreted her silence. "This is incredible. I grew up in a subdivision and used to dream of owning a rustic cabin in the woods. This is way better." She swept an arm toward the windows. "Check out this view."

From this vantage point, the lake looked boundless. The steely blue water was an echo of the billowing clouds. The energy in the air from the oncoming storm was electric, and this sheltered spot was the perfect place to experience it.

Still, enjoying a picnic in someone else's home felt off-limits to rule-abiding Maddie. "Are you sure your friend doesn't mind?"

Jake smiled. "He'd be happy we're putting it to use. Tom and I have known each other our whole lives. He actually owns the house you and I live in."

"Wait, the owner is our landlord? He could have us evicted for this." Maddie suddenly thought this was a very bad idea, but Jake chuckled.

"He's my best friend. Trust me, he won't mind at all." There he went again, asking her to trust him. She had to make a choice—keep second-guessing him, which meant walking out the door and going back to a strictly professional relationship, or stay and start letting him earn her trust.

"Okay," she said. "But only because I might not get a better view for dinner ever." She smiled at him to let him know that wasn't the only reason she wanted to be here, and Jake seemed to relax.

He carried the picnic basket over to the open space by the windows and set it down. "We had someone come clean out the fireplace last week. I'm going to go see if I can find some firewood." Pulling his hood up, he went back outside, and Maddie took the chance to explore.

The house smelled musty, like it hadn't been used in a while, but the kitchen had the bright scent of lemon cleaner, and she could picture it being used to prepare food for the grill on summer evenings or trays of cookies for the holidays. Though the space was small, she could envision the potential. Move the sink to the island and create a long prep counter under the window. Cabinets that went to the ceiling for storing serving dishes for hosting. This kitchen would be big enough to cook for a party with the right configuration.

Her mind was spinning with the possibilities, and she didn't notice Jake had come back in until he said, "All the wood is soaked through, so no fire for us."

"It's okay," she said. "You caught me daydreaming."

"Daydreaming?"

"I see a kitchen, and my mind goes a little wild."

Smiling, he asked, "What's a little wild for Maddie Briar?"

"Oh, you know." She waved a hand. "A large prep sink. A magnet bar for knives. Pot filler. Fixing this place up so that I could cook for a crowd." She went over and opened up the picnic basket, and the sight of the flameless candles she'd packed gave her an idea. "During my years working at a catering company, we did a lot of events in homes. You'd be surprised how well a small space can work if you know what you're doing." She clicked on the flameless candles and arranged them on the hearth, creating a cheery glow.

"You obviously do," he said, eyeing the flickering candles. His praise warmed her heart more than any fire ever could. "How would you feel about consulting for the kitchen design? We'd compensate you for your time."

She couldn't conceal her surprise. "This from the man who told me I needed to rethink my own kitchen layout?"

He ducked his head, looking embarrassed, but then met her eyes. "I really didn't mean it to come out that way during the walk-through. It's just that I've done a lot of renovations, and there's been a handful of times clients have had us come back a few years later to redo a layout similar to yours. But I don't have the cooking experience you do, so if you want me to drop it, I'll drop it."

The day of the walk-through, she'd been defensive and expecting the worst, but she did truly value his input. "I'm willing to hear you out. I want to make the wisest choices for my business, and believe it or not, I'm usually not so stubborn."

"Oh yeah?" He unzipped the picnic blanket she'd brought and spread it on the carpet in front of the windows. "I like seeing you that way."

"What way?"

"Ornery, stubborn," he said, grinning. Then his face turned thoughtful. "Decisive. Strong."

No one had ever called her strong. And decisive? It had taken her years to make this leap. But she had known since she was a teenager that she wanted to move to Orchard Harbor, and she'd made it happen. That was pretty tenacious. "Most of those I'll take. But ornery? Have you checked the mirror?"

"I try not to," he said, and she couldn't help a grin. "I

was serious, though. About your input on the design for this kitchen."

"Wright Construction has an in-house designer for that." She'd worked with the design team on her own reno, and they'd contributed great ideas.

"Yeah, but this is for my best friend. I want to make sure everything is perfect."

She was honored he valued her opinion so much. "All right. As long as your friend agrees, I'm on board."

"I know he'd value your contributions, and he's not the only one."

That piqued her interest. "Oh?"

"Have you heard about the Orchard Blossom Fest?"

Maddie listened as he explained how the artist guild organized an art festival every spring with arts and crafts, food and entertainment.

"The guild has a booth for members, which allows local artists of all ranges of experience to show off their work. It's actually what gave me the idea of opening a gallery." He paused, probably realizing the gallery was a sore subject. "At the last meeting, they asked me to reach out and see if you'd be interested in being a food vendor at this year's event."

She was momentarily speechless. All along, she thought they must resent her. But maybe Jake was the only one who was upset, since he'd been the one who was handling the renovation. Or maybe this was their way of offering an olive branch.

Either way, she was thrilled at the chance to take part. "I definitely would," she said. "As long as it doesn't bother you to have me involved."

He shook his head. "I couldn't imagine anything I'd like more. I've felt that way from the start, even when I was too grumpy to show it."

To hide how flattered she was, she began to unpack the basket. It was specially designed to look like a classic wicker picnic basket, but had two insulated compartments, one for keeping food hot and another with pockets for ice packs to keep cold food chilled. The lid stored plates and cutlery, and a slot in the bottom held a custom wooden serving platter that she'd commissioned from an artisan she'd met at the farmer's market.

After checking with Jake about any dietary restrictions or allergies, she'd curated a picnic spread with him in mind. She'd packed smoked cheddar and herbed goat cheese, along with thin slices of prosciutto, Spanish chorizo and salami.

She set out a dish of hot honey and a ceramic container of flaked sea salt. She'd made a dip out of roasted veggies to serve with homemade pita chips and buttery crackers she'd baked the night before. Alongside that was hummus…topped with pine nuts, not garlic, since this was a date.

The realization sparked a sudden awareness in her. Things with Jake had felt so comfortable over the last hour that she hadn't felt the usual first-date awkwardness. She looked up from laying out the food to find his amber eyes on her, lips curved in a gentle smile. He had one knee to his chest, his arm wrapped around it.

For the first time since they met, he looked entirely laid-back. If he liked seeing her stubborn, then she liked seeing him this way, with his walls down, completely himself. She'd thought besting Jake would give her satisfaction, but this was so much better.

Chapter Thirteen

Maybe coming here wasn't the best idea. It was good to get out of the elements, and the view couldn't be beat, but the cozy setting made Jake feel far too comfortable. Next thing you know, he'd let his guard down and tell Maddie everything, and then she'd be gone.

He used to date girls who liked his bad boy status, back before he got his act together. The few women he'd gone out with since had ghosted him once they found out he hadn't always been a hardworking guy with a good reputation.

But Maddie had already had a glimpse of his past, and she hadn't run yet. The selfish part of him wanted a few more minutes of enjoying her company. Even though she knew about his bad track record at Atlas, he owed her the whole story. He would tell her, but first, he wanted to know more about the gorgeous woman sitting across from him.

"So you grew up in the suburbs but always dreamed of small-town life?" He handed her a plate, then began filling his own.

"Yes," she said, following suit. "Our family visited Lake Michigan every summer, but it wasn't until our trip to Orchard Harbor in high school that I felt a pull to a particular town. This felt like a place I didn't want to leave."

"Seems pretty easy for a lot of people to go back to their normal life after visiting," he said, trying to keep the bitterness out of his voice. It wasn't that tourists bothered him. He appreciated the boost they gave to the local shops and businesses, and without the vacation homes to build and renovate, he'd be out of a job.

But he didn't like the idea that most people saw Orchard Harbor as a stopping point, a break from their real lives, when to him, it was everything.

Maddie took out napkins and handed him one. "Maybe for some of them it is. But many are probably like me and wish they could turn their vacations into a long-term stay. It's just not always an option."

He understood that. Much as he loved the town, it wasn't exactly brimming with industry and job opportunities. "But you made it happen."

"Not until years after I planned to. I had a big setback." Her eyes shifted away, like she was reliving a sad memory. "I was able to save money by living with my parents and relying on public transit. Didn't take any big vacations and worked as a caterer in addition to my freelance jobs. Even with all that, there were times I doubted I'd get here, and not everyone is as lucky as me."

"It's not just luck, though. It's hard work and dedication."

"Something you know a little about." She raised her brows, eyeing his scraped knuckles.

He had a feeling she'd given him an opening to talk about himself on purpose, but he wasn't ready. Glancing at his full plate, he said, "I can't believe you made all this. It looks almost too good to eat."

"Dig in," she said. "I love the artistry of food styling, but my true passion is feeding people. Food can be enjoyed with the eyes, but feasting is the real goal." She scooped up the creamy dip with a piece of flatbread, and he did the same, then knocked it against hers in a toast.

"To feasting," he said.

"To feasting," she echoed and took a bite, chewing slowly.

He was mesmerized by her red lips, unable to take his eyes away. "You're beautiful." He'd been holding the words in for so long that they tumbled out.

Her eyes, rimmed by dark lashes, went wide. Dabbing a napkin to her lips, she swallowed and said, "No one looks pretty when they're eating."

His gaze swept over her face, from her expressive brows to her wide, full mouth. The white sweater she was wearing had slipped off one shoulder, revealing smooth brown skin, glowing in the candlelight. "You're always gorgeous."

"Even when I'm arguing with you?"

"Especially then," he said, thinking of her blazing eyes and the electricity between them during a standoff. She grinned but glanced away shyly, and he decided to move the conversation back to neutral territory. "You mentioned you're an only child, right?"

With a nod, she said, "That's the reason I made friends with Tasha and Celeste. We came here for vacation when I was seventeen, and I begged my parents to let a friend come along, but they said it was supposed to be family time. Then they wound up spending all day reading or dozing on the beach, and I got bored. I mean, I loved lying in the sun and swimming as much as the next girl, but I wanted someone to hang out with. Tasha saw me pacing the shoreline and basically dragged me into their game of beach volleyball." She chuckled.

"They invited me out for ice cream afterward," she said. "And that was it. We exchanged phone numbers and kept in touch. I visited every summer in college and made it my goal to move here someday." She leaned on one arm, looking over at him. "What about you? Is Andy your only sibling?"

He plucked out an olive and put it on his plate. "He's married, so I have a sister-in-law as well, Carmen. They live in the country a few miles outside town with their daughter, and they're expecting another kid. A boy this time."

"Cute," Maddie said. "How old is your niece?"

"Katie is four and half. She's trouble but the best kind."

She smiled. "Must be nice having your family close."

"Most of them, yeah." The time had come. He couldn't put it off any longer. "My mom lives in town, but she's in Virginia right now, helping my grandparents move into their new condo. My dad…" He stabbed his fork through the olive. "He's out of the picture."

Not completely. There was no telling when he'd pop up. But he wasn't an active participant in Jake's life anymore.

Concern filled Maddie's eyes. "I'm so sorry, Jake."

"Don't be," he said. "He has a gambling problem. Andy and I had no idea until our parents' house went into foreclosure." His mom had shielded the truth from them.

"That must've been terrible."

It had felt like the end of the world. "We had to sell our car, and my mom wanted to move us to Virginia with my grandparents. Andy was willing to go, but I refused. He was a senior, and I was a sophomore, so she let us stay here with our friend's family."

"She left you?"

He shrugged. "It was more complicated than that. I was stubborn, and she knew Andy would look after me. She was trying to put her life back together. Find a way to provide for us."

"And your dad?"

"She gave him an ultimatum. Don't bother coming back till he could pay his debts." He sniffed. "He took a job as a long-range trucker, promising he'd save. But I think he's still gambling. We haven't seen a cent, even though he comes through town every once in a while."

Not that Jake ever saw him. He visited Andy and their mom, Donna, from time to time, but they'd long since stopped telling him about Chuck's visits. He wasn't welcome in Jake's life, and everyone knew it.

Maddie put a hand over his. "I'm so sorry, Jake. No wonder you had a rough few years."

"How I handled things was on me, though. Mom moved back a few years later, but I made her life miserable trying to punish her for leaving us. Figured I was someone people gave up on, so why try anyway?" He was embarrassed, thinking back on his self-destructive behavior.

Maddie squeezed his hand. "That situation would be hard for an adult to handle, let alone a kid."

"My older brother did just fine, though. Graduated with honors, got scholarships to a community college, and after getting his business degree, he started managing a retail chain. Meanwhile, I got up to trouble, bouncing between jobs and making a mess of things. Because he had to be responsible and look after me, it wasn't until recently that he was able to pursue his goal of working at a vineyard."

He turned his hand palm up and squeezed her fingers. "I don't make excuses for myself, but I have come a long way. Partly because my mom didn't give up on me. She came back and stayed. Gave us a home to come back to. And Reese saw potential in me. Didn't take it easy on me, but gave me second chances when I screwed stuff up. Some people in town still aren't convinced I've changed, but I won't let that stop me from doing my best."

"Thank you for sharing this with me," she said. "I'm sorry I repeated some of the gossip I heard about you. I knew in my bones it wasn't right."

Hearing her say that meant the world. But even though she didn't believe the worst of him, that didn't mean she would want to be with someone who had a reputation like his. "I appreciate that. I thought you should know, in case it changed things. If you want to pack up and go, I'd understand."

Maddie couldn't believe Jake thought learning about his past would dampen her feelings for him. "You're giving up on us already?"

"There's an us?" He sounded surprised, and Maddie summoned her courage.

"I'd like there to be," she said. "I trusted the wrong person once, and I let fear of making that mistake again keep me captive for way too long. But I came here to start taking chances again. To let life be messy. Neither of us is perfect. I don't expect you to be, and I hope you'll give me the chance to mess up, too. But I like you, Jake Winn."

He smiled at her, the corners of his eyes crinkling. "I like you, too, Maddie. A whole lot."

"I know we're just getting to know each other, but I'm so proud of you," she said. "You endured an awful situation and didn't let it ruin you. You could've stayed in that dark place, but you chose to find a way out."

"You don't have to say that. I'm sure you never would've gone down that path."

She let out a huff. "I didn't lash out, but I did choose to hide away for years." She looked out at the storm-tossed waves. "Years ago, fresh out of culinary school, I was working at a restaurant and became friends with a coworker who started not long after I did. We spent a lot of time hanging out, and she seemed great. When she mentioned she needed a new roommate, it seemed like the perfect setup."

Seated across from her, Jake stiffened, and she wondered

if he knew where the story was going. If only she'd had the same intuition back then. "I'd been living with my parents since high school and was ready to move out, and the price was way cheaper than any apartments I'd been looking at. She emailed the paperwork, which didn't even require my parents to cosign. I filled it out but decided not to share the news until I got the confirmation email. I waited weeks but never received one, so I finally asked my parents how I should handle it.

"My mom started asking all sorts of questions. My dad wanted to read the lease, and when he did, I'll never forget the look on his face. He immediately called the apartment complex, but they said it was a fraudulent email. The address listed wasn't even real."

Jake set his food aside, giving her his whole attention, but she couldn't meet his eyes.

"She'd stolen my identity. By the time we caught it, she'd drained my savings and maxed out several credit cards. She tanked my credit, and it took years to sort everything out." Taking a deep breath, she said, "I ended up never moving out until now." She shrugged. "So yeah, I did the opposite of you, but I still made mistakes."

He scooted closer and wrapped an arm around her. "You didn't make a mistake, someone else took advantage of you."

"But I should've been more careful. And I chose to let what happened scare me away from going after my dreams." She heaved a big breath. "I was so scared of losing everything again that I didn't want to try."

"Yet you're here now. Do you know how many people I've met who moved to a new town and started a new business, all at once? Only one." He rubbed her shoulder. "You. So give yourself some credit."

"That's one thing I finally do have," Maddie said, gratified when Jake chuckled. He made no move to pull away, and she let him hold her, taking comfort in being wrapped up this way. But a moment later, his stomach rumbled.

She shifted to smile up at him. "Guess that's our cue to dig in."

"Sorry. If you hadn't made such delicious-looking food, my mouth wouldn't be watering right now."

"You're telling me it's my fault?"

He took a bite of cracker topped with cheese and nodded. "You're definitely responsible for how happy my taste buds are," he said. "These crackers are so buttery. Where do you get them from? I could eat a Costco-size pack all by myself."

"They're homemade."

He coughed, like he might be choking, and she sat up, but he waved a hand, coughing into his elbow. Once he'd taken a drink, he said, "You made crackers from scratch? I didn't know such a thing was possible."

His praise sank right into her bones. "I made everything except the raspberry jam. That, I found at the farmers market, and once the farm stands open for the summer, all the produce I serve will be locally sourced." Michigan had a rich agricultural backbone, and she couldn't wait to prepare dishes using fresh sweet corn, ripe tomatoes and juicy blueberries from the countless farms and orchards that dotted the landscape.

"You should talk to Malcom Rhodes," Jake said. "He owns a fruit farm a few miles from here, and I bet he could give you a great deal. He's also part of the art guild." He paused, eyes flicking to hers, as if he felt guilty for bringing it up.

But she'd forgiven him and wasn't going to bring their past arguments into the present. "It must be great to have their support."

"It is," he said. "And I'm literally eating my words, because your food is art. You'd definitely have a place in the guild if you wanted to join."

The idea of being welcomed by them sounded too good to be true. Jake wanted her there, but his fellow members might not. "I'll think about it, thanks."

He swept his hand over the food arranged between them. "When I think of a picnic, I imagine peanut butter and jelly sandwiches with a bag of chips. This looks like something out of a luxury magazine. You're talented, Maddie." He met her eyes. "It can't be easy to make food that looks and tastes this good. I grew up on casseroles and slow-cooker meals. No shade to my mom's cooking. It's tasty but sometimes looks predigested."

Maddie couldn't help making a face, and he laughed, then said, "Even though it's a picnic, it's the nicest meal anyone's ever served me."

Her eyes teared up, and she looked out at the stormy sky, trying to contain her emotions. It was silly to get so wrung out over a compliment, but she was overwhelmed. In a new town. Starting a venture that could very well crash and burn. And dealing with a kind of attraction she'd never experienced before. Maybe it wasn't wise to get into a relationship right now. But taking a leap of faith had landed her here, in Orchard Harbor. It was time to stop worrying about what might go wrong and live in the now.

She turned to him, ready to embrace the moment, but his attention was focused on the ceiling. "Did you feel that drip?"

Suppressing a reflexive shudder, she forced herself to check the ceiling, but there was no telltale water stain. "Probably just bad memories from the pipe bursting." The cabin was old but seemed well-built, though outside, the storm was gaining intensity.

He groaned. "Don't remind me."

The wind had picked up, whipping the trees into a frenzy and splattering the windows with rain, but she felt cozy and protected with Jake. They finished their meal, and Maddie had just unpacked the cherry tartlets when a drop of water splashed into the container of homemade whipped cream.

She scooted it out of the way, but another drop fell, splattering on the cherry glaze. "At least we made it to dessert."

Jake started putting containers into the basket. "The roof's not in great shape, but we thought it would hold up. We're waiting on shingles."

Another drop left a big splotch on the stone hearth, and she rushed to pack up the candles. "Not in great shape might be an understatement."

"Yeah, I'm getting that impression."

Maddie dug into the cooler for one of the empty food containers and put it under the drip. "Won't hold much, but maybe the storm will blow over?" Lightning streaked across the sky over the lake, and thunder rumbled overhead. *Then again, maybe not.*

Jake cast another glance at the roof, brow furrowed. "I've got some buckets in the truck. Are you cool to wait here?"

"As long as the roof holds, yeah." She attempted a grin, but she couldn't shake the memory of the ceiling at the apartment bursting open with a deluge of water. She wasn't keen to repeat the experience.

A branch broke free from one of the overhanging trees and hurled itself against the window with a resounding *smack.* Maddie jolted, and Jake's mouth pulled into a grim line. "On second thought, come with me."

Jake hustled Maddie out to the truck, holding his coat over her head to protect her from the downpour. He took spare buckets from his truck bed and went back in the house to set them under the worst of the leaks, then ran back outside to the truck.

Maddie was huddled in the passenger seat, her curls speckled with glistening droplets, the shoulders of her jacket dark with water.

He cranked up the heat, but he still felt terrible. He should've taken them somewhere less picturesque and more, well, sturdy.

But Maddie surprised him by smiling. "I'm starting to think I should carry an umbrella whenever you're around."

He was just happy she wanted to spend more time with him. "Might not be the worst idea." But when she shrugged out of her wet jacket, he saw goose bumps on her arms. "You're soaked through. Here." He reached into the back and settled the blanket she'd packed around her shoulders.

"Thank you." She palmed his cheek with cool fingers, pulling him in for a kiss. Her mouth opened under his, and he couldn't help a rough groan of pleasure at the teasing stroke of her tongue. This woman. She'd come to town and turned his whole life upside down. Spoke to the deepest parts of his soul. He felt all his worries fade away in the pure delight of kissing her.

Long moments later, they pulled apart, and he smiled at her. "Thank *you*."

"For what?"

"For not running when you heard about my past," he said. "It wouldn't be the first time."

"I have no intention of running, Jake Winn. Or hiding. Not anymore." She tucked the blanket tighter around herself, and he turned out onto the road.

"Bad luck aside," she said, squinting through the windshield at the downpour. "I had a wonderful time with you."

He navigated around a downed branch, kicking the windshield wipers up a notch. "I don't put much stock in luck." His dad used to blame bad luck for everything from flat tires to lost keys. Chuck seemed to think his choices were in the hands of fate, and he refused to take responsibility for the damage he caused by chasing the odds. "But I had a great time today, too."

Neither the leaky roof nor his confession had scared her off, but he wanted to make sure the rest of their date went perfectly. He was about to tell her that he'd take her home so she could change into dry clothes while he bought a pint of ice cream to go with the delicious tarts she'd made, but the sight of fire trucks parked downtown made his blood run cold.

Next to him, Maddie let out a horrified gasp. "My shop!"

Chapter Fourteen

Maddie's teeth wouldn't stop chattering, more from shock than cold. They stood outside the shop, talking with the firefighters who'd just given the all clear. The ancient wiring in the building wasn't up to code. It was on the renovation to-do list, and in the meantime, they'd been careful not to overload the system and only ran appliances when someone was on-site.

But Neil had left an industrial fan running when he went on break. The outlet sparked, causing the framing to catch fire.

"Luckily, the clerk in the clothing store next door saw the smoke," the firefighter in front of Maddie said.

Luck. She'd just learned how Jake felt about that word and was starting to agree with him. Even though the fire hadn't spread, it had charred a whole wall of framing. She shuddered to think what would've happened if someone had gotten trapped inside. Jake's preoccupation with safety at the jobsite suddenly seemed a lot more justified.

"We're going to have to put everything on hold until the electricians come update the wiring," Jake said. "I should've done that first thing, but they told me they couldn't get anyone out here until next week."

"It's not your fault," Maddie said. "It was an accident."

"Carelessness. On both my part and Neil's."

Maddie glanced over to where the young man was standing off to the side, his head hanging low, hands in his pockets.

Rain was still drizzling down, and it was hard to imagine that all her hopes had been so close to going up in smoke.

"I'm just glad it was put out in time, and no one was injured," she said.

"The Orchard Harbor Fire Department is the best around," said one of the firefighters, an older gentleman with close-cropped gray hair who'd introduced himself as Francisco. "Anton told me you're opening up a catering business?"

Anton was Tasha's brother and a volunteer firefighter. He was chatting with the business owner who'd called in the fire, but when he saw her looking, he lifted his chin in acknowledgment.

"Um, yeah," Maddie said, too shell-shocked to say much more, but Francisco seemed to understand. He was probably used to dealing with people in the aftermath of fires.

"Glad to have someone renovating this place." Francisco's reassuring tone helped calm her. "Having everything up to code will go a long way toward keeping this whole block safe." He gave her a brief smile, then circled a finger in the air. "Clear out, everyone."

The firefighters shouldered their equipment, heading back to the truck.

Anton stopped and gave Maddie a hug. "Call Tasha," he said, stepping back. "You shouldn't be alone after something like this." Then his gaze drifted over her shoulder, and his cheeks dimpled with the cocky smile she remembered from all her visits here. "Then again, maybe you're not."

She didn't have to turn around to know he was looking at Jake. His lighthearted teasing helped bring a sense of normalcy to what felt like an overwhelming situation. She had a feeling he'd done it on purpose to brighten her mood. "I'll call her, don't worry."

"Good." His expression turned serious. "Be safe, Maddie."

She gave him a salute, since it seemed appropriate with his firefighter gear, and he grinned again.

"See you around." He walked off, and she saw that most of the men were already in the trucks.

One was talking to Jake, though, a scowl on his face. In the quiet, she caught a snippet of the conversation.

"Might want to have a chat with your guys about standards," the firefighter said, an edge to his voice. "Last thing you want is for people to lose confidence in another Winn." She saw Jake stiffen, hurt flashing in his eyes. "Then again, maybe it wasn't the kid's fault. Heard you had a plumbing disaster out at the house you're fixing up for Tom."

Jake's jaw tensed, and Maddie's heart sank. Everything she knew about him pointed to his integrity. He was a man who cared deeply about the work he did and the people in this town.

She stepped up next to him, hoping he could feel her support. "I'm very confident that the crew will be able to finish the project with no more accidents," she said. "Jake prioritizes safety and good workmanship."

The firefighter gave a small snort. "Really? From where I stand, it looks like the apple didn't fall far from the tree."

A sharp whistle cut through the air, and Maddie looked up to see Anton in the driver's seat of the fire truck, scowling. "Yo, Chase. Let's go."

"Sounds like you've got somewhere to be," Maddie said, hands on her hips.

With one last glare at Jake, the firefighter walked away.

From the fire truck, Anton called, "Hey, Jake. A bunch of us are going to Driftwood Tavern tomorrow night. You in?"

The other firefighter looked at Anton in surprise, but Jake straightened up. "I'll be there."

"Awesome. You, too, Maddie," Anton said. "There'll be a group of us."

She had a hard time imagining drinks with Anton and his friends; he was three years younger, and she'd always viewed him as Tasha's baby brother. But his invitation was a show of support with Jake, and she was grateful. "Sounds good."

The slam of the fire truck door showed Chase's opinion on the matter, but Maddie couldn't care less what he thought. She only hoped Jake could ignore him just as easily.

The fire trucks drove off, and Maddie found herself alone on the sidewalk with Jake. "That guy seems great," she said sarcastically.

Jake blew out a breath. "My dad borrowed money from his and never repaid it. Lied and said he needed to make a house payment to keep the bank from foreclosing. That was true, but he spent it on bets, not the mortgage."

"But that's not your fault."

"No, but my dad's not around. I'm an easy target for Chase's anger."

"That's not okay."

He shrugged. "That's small-town life," he said. "He knows how to get under my skin, but normally it wouldn't matter. I just..." He trailed off and raked his fingers through his hair. "I was enjoying myself without a care in the world while your building was burning down."

"Hey, don't say that. It's still standing. And this is not your fault. Accidents happen."

"But Neil is new. I shouldn't have taken today off with him on the schedule."

"You can't always be here. You have to trust your guys to a point."

He didn't answer, just walked to the back door.

She joined him, peering inside, and let out a gasp. It was worse than she'd imagined. Smoke charred the walls and ceiling like a piece of well-done steak. The burnt timbers were splintered, and the acrid scent of smoke churned her stomach.

"I suppose a kitchen fire isn't that out of the ordinary in this business, but you'd figure it would happen after the grand opening, not before," she said in a half-hearted attempt at a joke.

Jake put an arm around her shoulder and pulled her close. Letting his embrace steady her, she surveyed the soot-covered walls.

Another delay. Yet all she felt was grateful. Grateful no one was hurt. Grateful she'd filled out all the insurance paperwork. Grateful that she'd gone through enough hardship to know she wouldn't let a setback stop her this time.

"I'm going to make this right," Jake promised.

"I have total faith in you," she replied, realizing it was true. Somewhere along the way she'd come to trust Jake wholeheartedly. "What's the plan?"

He rubbed a hand over his head. "We need to hold off until we can get the electrical taken care of. It'll mean we'll have to work faster to meet the timeline, but I think we can manage."

"If we don't meet the deadline, I can take on more freelance food-styling gigs," Maddie said. "The important thing is that everyone stays safe."

"Thank you for being so understanding," Jake said.

"These things happen. Don't listen to what that guy said. You're nothing like your dad."

"You've only known me a month."

"Doesn't make me wrong." She pulled away enough to look up and meet his eyes. "The first thing you did was check on your crew. The next thing you did was reassure me. Those aren't the actions of someone who puts themself ahead of others. I'm confident your good reputation will only continue to grow."

"I've never seen Francisco be so nice to a stranger, so I'm pretty sure you're well on your way to winning over the town's surliest residents and building a great reputation of your own."

"Are you including yourself in those surly residents?" She grinned up at him.

"Nah. The tough guy thing is an act."

"Too bad. I kind of liked it," she said.

In answer, he bent and kissed her. She wrapped her arms around his neck, loving the feel of his touch. This was so much better than arguing.

Trusting Jake felt so natural that it was hard to believe there'd been a time she'd doubted his every word. When they broke apart, she said, "Everything's going to be fine. I believe in you."

She believed in herself, too. She'd made it this far; there was no going back to the fearful person she'd been for far too long.

Maddie's words from yesterday were still ringing in his ears when Jake claimed one of the long tables on the rooftop seating area at the Driftwood Tavern. If it weren't for her, he would've stayed home tonight. He couldn't shake the feeling that he'd failed her right when she'd started to put her trust in him, but he also remembered how hearing about his past hadn't fazed her.

She'd been out when he left, but he'd texted to see if she still wanted to meet him and the firefighters at the bar and received a thumbs-up emoji. This definitely didn't count as a date, but here he was, ordering every appetizer on the menu in an attempt to impress her.

Anton showed up with a few people Jake recognized from the firehouse, though to his relief Chase wasn't among them. The firefighters' eyes widened when they saw the food. "Wow, man, you didn't have to do this, but thanks."

They grabbed plates and made quick work of the appetizers. In minutes, all that was left was a lone mozzarella stick. He'd have to order another round of everything. He was calculating the hit to his wallet when he caught sight of Maddie coming toward them.

He wasn't sure whether she'd appreciate a kiss hello, so he restrained himself to a hug, but the way she held him tight for a moment before letting go eased his nerves. Between their date being cut short and the fire, they hadn't exactly had time to define their relationship, but Maddie had told him she wanted to keep spending time with him, and that was enough for tonight.

Anton gave her a hug as well, pulling her into conversation. It was hard not to be jealous of Tasha's brother, with his good looks and heroic job. His dark brown curls were cut short at the sides, and he wore a polo and nice jeans. Jake suddenly regretted his unbuttoned flannel and T-shirt. He'd showered and changed after work, but did it look like he hadn't made an effort?

He smoothed a hand over his shirt and tried to look natural as Anton and Maddie caught up, chatting about life since her last visit before she moved to town. Jake was just about to place another order of food when a server brought over a heaping platter of nachos.

Anton leaned over from the other end of the table. "Consider this our contribution after eating all the apps." He handed Maddie a plate. "Better go first. Once the others dig in, there'll be nothing left."

Having seen that firsthand, Jake was glad to see Maddie take a hefty serving.

"This is amazing," she said after her first bite. "I didn't have time for lunch today. I spent forever on the phone with the insurance company. I need to get an appraiser to come out while things are stalled so we don't lose more time."

Jake was impressed by what she'd managed to do already, though not the least bit surprised.

She turned to Anton. "Thanks again for putting out the fire."

He waved a hand. "That's our job. Did Jake tell you he used to volunteer with us?"

"He did not." Maddie turned to Jake with her brows raised.

"Yep. He's done pretty much every job you can think of. Waited tables, worked at the coffee shop. He even bartended here for a summer."

Jake ducked his head. Anton was making him sound hard-working, but the truth was he'd quit or been fired from most of those jobs. But he'd turned things around, he reminded himself. And he'd worked his way up to a foreman position.

"Sounds like I don't need to bother with the drink menu," she said. "What would you recommend?"

"I can do one better than a recommendation." He jumped at the chance to do something special for her and walked over to where the bartender, Emily, was pouring shots and pulling pints. "Mind if I mix something up real quick?"

"Go ahead. Let me guess, you're trying to impress that pretty woman at your table?"

"She impresses me on the daily. I'm renovating her catering business, and you should taste her food. It's incredible," he said as he washed his hands.

"Oh, that must be your girlfriend, right? I heard you were dating someone new in town."

He hesitated, knowing Maddie liked privacy despite deciding to stop hiding their relationship.

Emily laughed. "Don't worry, I won't tell anyone. But you must be smitten to risk Steve catching you behind the bar." The owner of the bar hadn't been too thrilled with Jake walking out on his shift one busy summer night after one too many tourists had spilled beer on him. It had been years ago, but then again, Steve had a long memory, like a lot of locals.

Jake remembered Maddie had preferred sweet, fruity wines at the tasting room and used vanilla syrup in her coffee, so he went to work on a strawberry mojito for her. The firefighters had all been drinking beer, so Jake also pulled a pitcher of the local brewery's seasonal spring brew, a rhubarb-infused sour beer.

"Nice pour," Emily said. "Don't look now, but I think your plan might've backfired. You sure leaving her alone at the table with Anton was a good idea?"

Jake jerked his head around and found Maddie bent toward Anton, looking down at something on his phone. A knot of jealousy formed in his belly, but he refused to be that guy. Maddie had kissed him yesterday, and she didn't seem like the type of person to turn around and flirt with another man.

Still, he quickly finished garnishing the mojito and lifted the tray with the ease of muscle memory.

"Sure you remember how to do that?" Emily joked.

"One way to find out." He carried the drinks to the table and set them down.

"That was fast," Maddie said, and he blushed. Did she know he'd hustled back here? "Anton was just showing me some photos of you from back in high school."

"You have those on your phone?"

"Say what you will about social media, but it's great for preserving embarrassing moments for all eternity." Anton turned the phone and showed the picture on the screen.

Jake expected an awkward selfie or photo of him with the scrunched-eye smile his mom insisted was adorable, but instead he saw his football teammates hoisting him on their shoulders after they'd won the state championship sophomore year, just a few weeks before he'd found out about his dad's gambling problem.

Anton grinned. "I had you going for a minute, huh?"

Jake's heart was still racing. Sooner or later, he feared Maddie would discover one of his mistakes that would be a deal-breaker.

"I'll save the embarrassing stories for next time." Anton pocketed his phone and slid the drink closer to himself. "Since you've treated us to the entire menu and drinks…on the house," he added, more loudly.

From the bar, Emily called, "Just because Jake made those doesn't mean they're free. In fact, I might add an amateur-hour surcharge."

They all laughed, and Jake felt some of the tension leave his body as Maddie joined in. He reminded himself she wasn't like the other women he'd dated. She knew his whole story and still thought he was a good person, capable of being the man he'd set out to become.

She took a sip of her drink and sighed appreciatively. "This is amazing. What is it?"

"A strawberry mojito. I noticed you're drawn to sweet things."

"Sweet and a little sour." She gave him a pointed once-over. "Like someone I know."

He pretended to scowl. "I am not sour."

"Nah, you're more like butterscotch. Sweet, but with depth and dimension." Her expression turned playful. "Or maybe salted caramel."

"Who are you calling salty?"

She wiggled her brows and took a saucy sip of her drink. "Considering how you've been glowering at Anton, I think we both know who."

Feeling guilty, he looked down, but Maddie leaned over

and squeezed his hand. "Anton's like a brother to me. And even if he weren't, I'm here to support you. I'm *with* you," she said meaningfully.

His whole body relaxed. What had he done to deserve this wonderful woman?

They settled into conversation, talking about their interests and upbringing. He was glad now that the reno had given them a reason to stay connected, but equally grateful they'd found common ground outside of it.

About an hour later, they'd finished their food, and Maddie had gotten pulled into a conversation with the firefighters. Jake leaned back, enjoying being near her and surrounded by friends. He was happy to see how welcoming everyone was, knowing how much she craved community.

Glancing toward the entrance, he saw a familiar face and waved, beckoning over his friend from the guild.

Garrett changed course and came up to their table, pulling up an empty chair. "Didn't expect to see you out tonight. Figured you'd be burning the midnight oil on your piece for the showcase."

"Honestly, man, I'm ahead of schedule." Jake was feeling more inspired than he had in months, even though restoring Maddie's business in time for her grand opening took priority. That reminded him; he needed to tell the guild Maddie was on board to work with them.

But she was deep in conversation, and he wanted to wait until she could take part, so he asked Garrett, "Is your entry finished?"

"I've made a few pieces, but none of them feel quite right." Garrett's glass designs were elaborate, and he set a high bar for himself.

There was a lull in the conversation, and he turned to find

Maddie listening in with a polite smile. "Hi, I'm Maddie. Are you a friend of Jake's?"

Garrett nodded. "*The* Maddie?"

Her eyes flicked to Jake's, and he knew what she must be thinking. That word had spread about her and possibly him. Together. She seemed bothered by the idea. "Um, yes?"

"The caterer?"

"That's me," she said, looking even more worried. But why?

"Please tell me you're considering setting up a booth the festival."

Her face showed relief. She must've been wondering if news of the caterer dating the contractor was spreading. He understood, even though he was a little disappointed that she still didn't feel comfortable with people knowing.

"You're really offering the gig without tasting my food?" she asked.

"I mean, we wouldn't be opposed to tasting it," Garrett said with a smile. "But your reputation precedes you, plus Jake vouched for you."

"He did?" Her eyes flicked to Jake's, and guilt laced through him again that she thought he'd do otherwise, especially since for a fleeting moment he'd considered not speaking up at the meeting. He was so grateful he had. She deserved this opportunity, and he wanted everyone else to see how incredibly talented she was.

"Don't look so surprised," Garrett said. "Jake was singing your praises from the moment he was assigned your renovation. We were actually hoping we could hire you to cater snacks for the upcoming meeting. Elise usually provides treats, but she's been short-staffed lately."

"I heard," Maddie said sympathetically. "I hope she finds a new employee soon, because I recently tried one of her pastries, and they're to die for. In the meantime, I'd love to help out. Especially because my renovation recently suffered a setback, and we won't be open for business as soon as I'd hoped."

She explained the fire, and Garrett offered his condolences.

"Seems like you've got your hands full. I don't want to put more on your plate, and I know it might be a long shot with your timeline, but we'd still love to have you be a vendor at the Orchard Blossom Fest. If there's anything we can do to help, let us know. Between all our members, we have quite the range of skills and connections."

Maddie smiled at him. "I might take you up on that, thank you."

"Please do. And I understand if you're too busy to stay after dropping off the food, but feel free to stay for this weekend's meeting. There's no cost to sit in on your first three, and we offer a lot of benefits for members, not the least cf which is catching up on news around town."

"He means gossip," Jake said, and Garrett shrugged good-naturedly.

Maddie frowned. "But I'm not an artist."

Jake opened his mouth to disagree, but Garrett beat him to it. "Jake mentioned you were a food stylist."

"Well, yes, but—"

"No buts about it. I looked at your portfolio. Incredible stuff."

Jake couldn't agree more. From what he'd learned of Maddie, she was a multitalented woman. He watched as they exchanged emails and Garrett passed on the information about the guild website, then said goodbye and headed off toward the friends he was meeting.

"I meant to give you that information the other day," Jake said.

"No worries," Maddie said. "I'm just shocked he was so welcoming."

"Why wouldn't he be?" Jake's heart sank as he realized the real reason she'd seemed wary of Garrett knowing who she was. "Because of me." He took her hand. "If I could go back and change how I reacted that first morning, I would. But I was the one who bid on that space, on my own. It was meant to be a gift, to prove how far I've come. That's why I got so upset, but none of it was ever your fault. It was a foolish plan in the first place."

Realization slipped onto her face. "All this time, I thought everyone was upset with me."

He squeezed her hand. "It's me who screwed up by making you feel unwelcome. The art guild will welcome you with open arms."

Maddie blinked fast, squeezing his hand. "Sorry, it's just..." She dabbed a knuckle at the corner of her eye. "I just really needed to hear that. I know you mentioned it on our date, but I wasn't sure if it was just you being nice."

"Oh, Mads." He looped an arm around her shoulder and pulled her close. "I'd never lie to you about something like that. They jumped at the idea of having your food at the festival, and Garrett is right. The guild would be honored to have you as a member. You belong here in Orchard Harbor."

She sighed against his chest, then gently pulled away, sending a wobbly smile his way. "It's starting to feel that way."

He hated that he'd ever made her feel less than welcome, but he'd take every chance he got to keep showing her how much he wanted her here. They sat hand in hand while she finished her drink.

A chime came from her phone, and she checked it.

"It's my mom calling," she said. "My parents are night owls, and I forgot I'd promised to chat tonight." She gave his hand a squeeze and raised her phone to her ear. "Hi, Mom. Yeah, I'm out with some friends, and it's noisy. I'll call you back in a few."

She hung up, and the others looked their way when she stood. “Great to meet all of you. Thanks for inviting me to come out tonight, Anton.” She pulled her jacket off her chair, and Jake stood to help slip it over her shoulders.

He bent to speak low in her ear, loving the warm, vanilla scent of her. “Can I walk you home?” The house was only a few blocks from here, but he still wanted to see her home safe and, selfishly, spend more time with her.

She shook her head. “Stay and enjoy yourself. I’m going to call Mom back on the walk home.”

“All right.” He stepped away to fight the urge to press a kiss to her neck, but the look she sent over her shoulder made him think he wasn’t the only one battling temptation.

“See you tomorrow,” she said, her voice husky, and he almost said, *Tonight would be better.* Instead, he managed a quick nod.

“Have a good night.”

Once Maddie was gone, he turned and found the whole table of people watching him. One of the firefighters, Nicole, leaned in. “Something going on with the two of you?”

“Definitely,” Anton said. “He even made her a drink after he promised never to step behind the bar again.”

“I made everyone a drink,” Jake protested.

“Did you also smell everyone’s hair?” Anton smirked.

“I did not smell her hair.”

“Sure looked like it to me,” he said. “Nicole?”

“I mean, there was a definite lean. Did you see a lean, Ronnie?”

The bearded man nodded. “Oh yeah. And the way you two were in your own bubble at the end of the table all night? Very sweet.”

Jake crossed his arms. “Glad to know you’re all good at minding your own business.”

“Where’s the fun in that?” Anton looped an arm around Jake’s shoulder, not seeming bothered when he kept his arms crossed. “But seriously, man, we’re happy for you. She seems really into you.”

Despite himself, Jake relaxed a little. “I almost ruined things with her. I’m just amazed she’s even talking to me now, let alone—” His phone buzzed in his pocket. He pulled it out and saw a text from Maddie.

Maddie: Help, I’ve got a possum emergency!

He blinked at the screen, wondering if that was some sort of code. A moment later a photo appeared, and Jake zoomed in, trying to make out the blurry image. It was a small blob of white on a dark background.

Maddie: It staked a claim on our porch and won’t let me in.

Our porch. He liked the sound of that. Biting back a smile at the mental image of Maddie in a standoff with a possum, he texted that he was on his way, then took out his wallet. He had zero clue what to do about a renegade possum, but Maddie had called for his help, and he wasn’t going to let her down this time.

He tossed down enough cash to cover the appetizers and drinks, which earned him good-natured whistles and back slaps from the crew.

Anton looked at him with a gleam in his eye. “Headed out already?”

“Maddie needs help. There’s a possum on the porch.”

With a slow blink, Anton said, “That’s one I haven’t heard.”

Jake gave him a good-natured shove. “I’m serious.” He showed him the photo.

"That's one kind of emergency I wasn't trained in," Anton said. "Good luck. And remember, no matter what people say, you deserve to be happy, man. Don't doubt your worth."

He nodded, grateful for Anton's vote of confidence, then hurried down the stairs to the street, brightly lit by wrought-iron streetlamps. When he rounded the last corner, he saw Maddie standing on the sidewalk in front of the house.

"Are you okay?" he called. She looked his way and nodded. He hurried over to her and peered into the darkness. "Where is it?"

She pointed. "There. In the middle of the porch."

"I can't see," a disembodied voice said.

Startled, Jake glanced around for the source, only to realize that Maddie was on a video call.

"I called Tasha, but she was too scared to come help."

"So I was your second call?"

"Third," Maddie admitted. "Celeste was next, but she was out for dinner."

That was a small hit to his ego, but he was glad she had a strong support system. Besides, now was not the time to worry about his ranking on her contact list. He had a possum to catch. Shoo? He wasn't sure, but he rolled up his sleeves.

A car screeched to a halt on the curb, and they both turned around. Celeste climbed out of the driver side, but didn't come any closer. "Where's the possum?" She darted a glance toward the porch as if it would leap out of the shadows. "And what's *he* doing here?" Her tone made Jake wonder how much of their history Maddie had shared. Probably all of it, from the sounds of it.

"Helping," he said, even though he had no idea how to budge an angry possum.

Maddie frowned at her friend. "You weren't supposed to leave your date."

"Trust me, I'm not missing anything. I don't know why I even bothered to try. I'm happy on my own." Celeste had been divorced for over a year, and from gossip around town, he knew enough to say her husband hadn't done right by her.

She looked over and seemed to remember he was there. "I called animal control, but apparently they're not open at this time of night," she said, shifting her tone to be more business-like. "As if animal emergencies only happen from nine to five."

From the phone, Tasha said, "I Googled what to do, and I think we need to buy a trap."

"A trap?" Maddie frowned toward the porch, where the white-gray animal was barely visible in the shadows. "That seems extreme."

"I agree," Jake said. "It'll probably go away on its own."

"That's where you're wrong. It's making a stand."

He tried not to laugh at Maddie's serious tone. It was a wild animal. All they had to do was get closer, and it would probably run off. Jake took a few steps toward the porch, and the possum hissed.

He jumped back. "Why is it hissing?"

"I don't know," Maddie shrieked. "See what I mean?"

He eyed the animal uneasily. "Does it have rabies?"

"Highly unlikely," Celeste said, and Jake turned to see her scrolling on her phone. "Apparently it's rare in possums since their body temperature is low."

"Don't get close." He held out an arm to stop Maddie. "Just in case." He took a step toward the animal, but it didn't move. "Easy, big guy."

"What are you doing?" she whispered.

"I'm going to gently shoo it off the porch," he whispered back.

"It's not a dog," Tasha's voice came from the phone.

He didn't bother to reply, just kept his eyes on the possum. It had its mouth open, fangs bared. "Sure looks like it has rabies."

"That's because it's scared." Celeste was scrolling on her phone. "This article says hissing is its defense."

"I'm not going to hurt you, bud." He took another step. "Mads just needs to get inside."

"Mads?" Celeste sounded amused, and he scrunched his eyes shut. He hadn't meant to say the nickname in front of her friend. But he glanced at Maddie and saw a tiny smile on her lips. It gave him a quivery feeling in his stomach and the urge to pull her close for a kiss.

Celeste cleared her throat, and he straightened up. *Right.* He was supposed to be dealing with the possum, not gazing into Maddie's beautiful brown eyes.

He reached the porch steps, and the possum immediately fell on its side, lying stiff and still. "Um. Is it playing dead?"

Celeste was reading off her phone. "Sounds like that's another way possums defend themselves."

"Not the best strategy," he said.

"This is so much worse." Maddie's arms were crossed over her stomach, and she looked totally defeated. "With it lying in front of the door, we're really stuck now."

"I'm sure it will give up in a few minutes," he said. "Maybe we should just back off for a while, let it do its thing."

Maddie's face crumpled. "But I really need to go to the bathroom."

The corners of his mouth twitched. He fought against it, but she had an adorable pout on her face. A smile broke out, and then he chuckled.

"Are you laughing at our girl?" He'd forgotten Tasha was still on the phone.

"Not at her. The whole situation." This was a problem he

could solve. The possum, not so much. He reached for Maddie's hand. "C'mon, I know somewhere we can go."

Celeste crossed her arms. "Where? Back to the bar? Everywhere else is closed."

"My studio is never closed." Squeezing Maddie's hand, he looked down at her. "If that's okay with you? You can use the bathroom without rodent interference."

"It's a marsupial," Celeste piped up.

"Either way." Jake kept his focus on Maddie. "You good with that?"

"I've been wanting to see more of your art." She winced. "But I don't want to inconvenience you. I can go back with Celeste."

"You're never an inconvenience." He let go of her hand to open the passenger door of his truck for her.

"Even when I'm using up all the hot water in this old house?"

"I like cold showers anyway," he said as she climbed in.

A loud *aww* came from the phone, where Tasha must still be on the other end of the line, and Maddie raised it to her face. "Good night, Tash." She ended the call and turned to Celeste. "Sorry you rushed over for nothing."

Celeste waved her hand in a dismissive gesture. "Like I said, I was glad to skip out early."

"You, too, Jake. I didn't mean to cut your night short."

"There's nowhere else I'd rather be," he said honestly, though his heart rate sped up at the thought of showing her his art. Tonight he'd realized that Maddie was quickly becoming a huge part of his world.

Chapter Fifteen

Maddie had been overwhelmed when she left the bar. Finding out that no one at the guild resented her had seemed too good to be true, but tonight Garrett's welcoming attitude confirmed it. And she'd been shocked to discover Jake had placed his own bid on the space, but it made sense, given his huge heart for the town.

She glanced over at him in the darkened interior of the truck. Their bond had deepened beyond attraction. The more she found out about him, the more Jake seemed reliable, caring and honest. Exactly the kind of person she might be able to trust with her heart.

They'd left town behind, the sky outside her window bursting with stars, so many more than she was used to. It made her think of possibilities. Of a new life here and a future with the man next to her.

Up ahead, a house came into view, light pouring from the windows, and Jake slowed down. He turned into a long driveway sheltered by overhanging branches and parked near a red pole barn.

She wasted no time in jumping out, and he ushered her in through a sliding door. She hurried to the bathroom, expecting something rustic. But a copper vessel sink sat atop a beautiful wooden vanity. Textured wallpaper added an elegant touch, and the artisan soap smelled heavenly. Even the towel bar looked custom.

"That might be the most beautiful bathroom I've ever seen," she said when she came out.

Jake grinned. "Thanks. It was one of the first remodels I did on my own. Carmen makes the soap in there. She'd tell me not to mention it, but she sells it if you're interested."

"Definitely." The faint smell of lilac lingered, and her hands felt moisturized. "I wasn't expecting something so luxurious in a barn."

"Hey now," he said with mock offense. "It's not just a barn, it's my studio."

She looked around at everything she'd been in too much of a rush to notice. Scraps of metal were piled in one corner, and rows of shelving held everything from wire to porcelain vases to antique lamps. But what caught her attention was a huge mural covering one wall.

"The lighthouse," she said.

He palmed the back of his neck. "Yep. I finished that one during the winter. Business was slow, and I had a lot of time to create."

She stepped closer, and as she neared the piece of art, she realized what she'd assumed was paint was actually bits of glass, plastic and rusted metal layered to form the picturesque lighthouse amid turbulent waves. "I couldn't even see these individual pieces from over there," she said. "It's stunning."

"It's trash," he said, and she whipped her head around, but he held up his hands. "Literally. I found all the objects by the lake and on the side of the road. Lots of visitors come to enjoy the beach but don't give a second thought to littering in the natural landscape, so I wanted to at least make something meaningful out of it."

"What you've created is stunning." Every time she looked at it, she spotted something new, yet from farther away, it looked seamless. "You really don't want to sell your creations?"

"When I did, it took away the joy. I want to be able to use art to express myself and for the joy of creating. When I designed pieces to sell, I was worried about how they would be perceived. I still gift the pieces sometimes, but there's no outside pressure to create something that will appeal to someone else."

She could understand that, though she felt differently. She liked to cook for others and to see clients' faces light up when she captured their vision for a magazine spread. Even though she and Jake both used art as an outlet, they had different goals, and she was starting to understand the value in looking at life from different perspectives. They complemented one another.

"What you've made is incredible." She slowly strolled around the room, noting the pieces in various stages of completion: a small freeform sculpture out of driftwood and wire, a bike wheel with yarn looped around the spokes, and an end table inlaid with a mirrored mosaic.

A huge frame lay against one wall, covered by a sheet. "A secret project?"

He'd been hanging back, giving her space to take everything in, but stepped up by her side. "It's the piece I'm working on for the festival. I don't usually mind people seeing my works in progress, but this one is special."

There was a twinkle in his eye that she attributed to the fun in keeping her in suspense, and even though she was eager to see the hidden creation, she didn't want to spoil his fun.

The way he spoke about his art was different than the way he talked about construction. With the renovation, his passion was evident, but it was layered with responsibility and seriousness. Surrounded by his art, he was fully relaxed.

Affection tugged at her heart. "Thank you for bringing me here." She was honored to be trusted with this side of him, especially given their rocky start.

He pulled her close and pressed a kiss to her temple. Leaning into the comfort of his embrace, she was startled when the back porch light flicked on, and a moment later, a girl with light brown pigtails came running in.

"Uncle Jake!" She stopped short when she saw he wasn't alone, and Maddie stepped back, breaking their embrace.

"Hey, Katie." Jake swung the girl up into his arms, and she giggled. "Maddie, this is my niece."

She waved at the little girl. "Is that your bike I saw outside?"

"It's a tricycle. If I practice enough, Mom says I can get a big-girl bike when the baby comes." She leaned her head into Jake's shoulder and pouted. "Why didn't you say hello?"

"I was showing my friend the studio." He shot Maddie a sly glance, hinting that the label didn't quite fit their situation anymore, and butterflies flitted in her stomach.

"Did you show her my creation?"

Jake set his niece down gently. "Why don't you go ahead?"

Katie ran over to a rack and lifted off what looked like a wind chime. She brought it over, and Maddie saw it was smooth pieces of beach glass and driftwood strung on fishing line. "I made this for Mom to hang on the porch. Uncle Jake tied the knots, but I chose all the pieces by myself."

"It's beautiful," Maddie told her. "I bet she'll love it."

"I want to make something for Grandpa next," she said. "Can I, Uncle Jake?"

Jake didn't answer, and Maddie turned to find his face had lost the happiness from a moment ago. Was Katie talking about Jake's father? From what he'd said, his dad didn't visit often and wasn't welcome when he did.

Silence stretched, and Maddie wasn't sure what to do. Before she could make up her mind, a man's voice called, "Katie?"

"She's out here," Jake called back.

Andy walked up and smiled when he saw Maddie. "Hello again. I see you've met my daughter." He put his hands on his hips. "I told her not to bother Uncle Jake and his…friend." There was a slight question in the word.

Maddie's stomach dipped with nerves. He'd been there the night they met. Almost caught them kissing. Of all the people in Orchard Harbor, he must know there was something going on, and she wanted to make a good impression.

"It's fine." Jake didn't sound ruffled in the slightest. "I was just showing her the studio, and Katie's project is the best work out here."

"Both of you make amazing art," Andy said, ruffling his daughter's hair and smiling at Jake. "But she's supposed to be getting ready for bed."

Katie gave her uncle a hug. "'Night. See you soon!" She dashed off toward the house.

"Hope we didn't disrupt your evening," Maddie said.

"We aren't staying long," Jake added. "We had a little situation at the house."

Andy's eyebrows rose. "Not the plumbing again."

"Nope. A possum problem."

His brother blinked. "Did you say 'possum problem'?"

Maddie giggled. "Weird, I know. But a possum was camped out on our front porch. Jake brought me here in hopes it would leave before we got back."

Katie reappeared at the back door of the house and called, "Dad, guess what?"

"I thought I told you to get ready for bed," Andy said.

"I will. But, Dad," she said, bouncing on her toes, "Grandpa's here."

Across the workbench from Maddie, Jake went pale, eyes wide. This couldn't be good.

Why tonight, of all nights? *Bad luck*, his dad would say. But Jake didn't believe in luck, just bad timing. He couldn't deal with his father right now. Not tonight, when things were going so well.

There was no doubt in Jake's mind who Katie was talking about, but it was confirmed when Andy asked, "Grandpa Chuck?"

Katie nodded. "He brought me a present, but Mom told me I should come tell you he's here before I open it."

Jake's eyes pinched shut. He'd had a wonderful evening with Maddie. Brought her to his studio and had been on the verge of confessing his growing feelings, but now his dad was back. Not for good. He never was. Just long enough to mess things up.

He opened his eyes to find Maddie's worried gaze on him, and he almost wished he hadn't told her. Then maybe she wouldn't notice how the situation with his dad continued to affect him, years later. "Ready to go?"

"We don't have to." She glanced between him and his brother, hesitating. "I can find another ride."

Jake shook his head. "I'm leaving anyway."

Andy grabbed his sleeve as he walked past. "Jake..."

He pulled away. "I can't." He saw the sadness in Andy's eyes. His dad and brother had reconciled, but Jake didn't plan on doing that anytime soon. Chuck was all empty promises, and Jake was a man of action. If his father really wanted another chance, he'd have to prove he'd changed. But that hadn't happened, and Jake doubted it ever would. Leaving now was the best way to keep from getting his hopes up.

You're a grown man, and you're running away.

The thought came with a sudden urgency, but he didn't slow. Yes, he was grown, and no, he wasn't going to stick around. The only way to get through this situation without falling to pieces was to get out of here now. Hopefully, his dad wouldn't stay long, but if he did, that would be a problem for tomorrow.

Jake opened the truck door for Maddie, then climbed in. He cranked the key in the ignition and backed down the driveway, maneuvering around a vehicle he remembered all too well. The same beat-up car his dad had when he'd left. So his luck hadn't turned.

Jake couldn't shake the feeling that his own luck had run out.

Next to him, Maddie was quiet on the ride home. He'd expected her to ask questions or try to reassure him. He was prepared to tell her he was fine, just tired. But she stayed quiet, and it left him too much space to think and feel, when all he wanted was to push down his emotions. Finally, it got to be too much.

"I don't normally—" He stopped himself, unsure of what it was he didn't normally do. Run away? "I wasn't expecting him."

"He didn't tell you he was coming?" she said, her voice soft.

"Never does." His fingers tightened on the steering wheel as he pulled to a stop at a red light. "My brother puts up with his surprise visits. God knows why."

Maddie looked like she wanted to say something but held back, and Jake felt the need to explain. "He knows he's not welcome here. That's probably why he doesn't announce when he's coming."

"How does he know he's not welcome?" Maddie's question came as a surprise, and his eyes flicked to hers.

"He hasn't paid his debts, for one." The light turned green, and he eased onto the gas pedal, driving with extra caution to combat his restless mood. "Everyone in town hates him, for another."

"Everyone?"

His mind flashed to his niece, all smiles at the arrival of her grandpa. She didn't hate him. But she was a kid and didn't know better. Andy? Well, he'd always been a forgiving person. Jake was still working on forgiving himself. Hadn't gotten around to forgiving his dad.

"He made a lot of promises he didn't keep. It wasn't just money he gambled with. It was friendships. Our family." A stack of IOUs that still weighed on Jake.

"And he hasn't made amends?"

Jake shrugged. "I make it my business to stay out of his. Better that way."

Maddie made a noncommittal noise.

They arrived at the house, and he walked her inside, carefully checking for the possum.

Outside her door, she took his hand. "It's not my place to judge. I've never been in your shoes. But I have been betrayed by someone close to me, and I know how hard it is to recover from that kind of hurt. I just hope you're not letting the pain your father caused you in the past impact your future. I did that for a long time. Until finally I realized I was only holding myself back by holding on to it." She rose on tiptoes to kiss his cheek, then unlocked her door and went inside.

More than anything, he wanted to stay with her longer. To invite her upstairs and let her presence soothe the ache in his chest.

But he owed her more than that. He wanted her for far more than company, or a sympathetic shoulder. He wanted all of Maddie, and being with her the right way meant being honest with himself first.

Even though she longed to go upstairs and knock on his door the next morning, Maddie knew Jake needed space to process his dad's unexpected arrival.

Instead, she got in touch with Garrett to find out more information about the Orchard Blossom Fest. She confirmed she would supply snacks for their meeting that weekend as an informal tasting. After discussing menu ideas and pricing, he asked her to send over the invoice so the treasurer could submit payment.

The chance to scale up some of the recipes she'd been testing and earn a little extra money was just the mood boost she'd needed. Knowing no one resented her was a huge relief, and now she couldn't wait to meet the group of people who were so important to Jake.

Oh, how things had changed since that first day they'd faced off in her shop, and she couldn't be happier.

After the productive phone call, Maddie's mind was spinning with all the prep work she'd need to do for the meeting, but first she needed to finish up a freelance photoshoot. She tried to focus on work rather than worry over Jake, who must've left the house earlier than usual, judging from the silence overhead.

A day spent working indoors left Maddie in need of some fresh air, and she headed to the beach on foot after dinner. The sun was dipping toward the horizon when she reached the lake. Low waves lapped at the shoreline, and the sand was empty except for a few seagulls. Perfect for decompressing after an emotional roller coaster of a few days.

Just as she bent to slip off her shoes, her phone rang. She pulled it out, hoping to see Jake's contact, but it was her mom calling. Their conversation last night had been cut short because of the possum situation. Now she'd have to update her parents on the fire, which was bound to be a rough call.

But finding out what Jake had gone through with his dad made her realize how much her family supported her, even if they were overprotective at times, and she answered after only a slight hesitation.

"Hi, Mom. How are you?" She made her way to a bench on the pier, knowing cell service would be spotty farther down the beach.

"Good, sweetie. Your dad's cooking dinner, and I just finished another chapter in that charming book you sent. I can't believe you're friends with the author."

Maddie had gone to the bookstore party for Crystal's new mystery novel last week with Celeste and bought an extra signed copy for her mom. "I'm not sure if we're friends yet, but she's been so kind and welcoming. Pretty much everyone here has been."

"Except for that no-good contractor of yours."

Maddie winced. She really wished she hadn't vented to her mother about Jake early on. Even though she'd told her things had gotten better between them, her mom was Team Maddie and much less quick to forgive. "I told you, Jake's a good guy. It was just a misunderstanding."

Her mom let out a little huff.

"Really, Mom. He's done an amazing job with the renovation."

"As long as he doesn't flood the building like he did your home, I guess that's something."

"Nope, no floods." Maddie grimaced. "There was a fire, though. Not Jake's fault," she rushed to add. "No one's fault, really. Just old wiring."

But her mom was already shouting for her dad to come to the phone. "A fire? Are you okay? I'm putting you on speaker." She spoke so quickly that Maddie wasn't able to get a word in.

"What's this about a fire?" Her dad's voice this time. "Are you hurt?"

"No," Maddie said. "I mean, yes, there was a fire at my

shop, but no one was hurt, and the firefighters put it out quickly."

"Didn't I tell you not to rent an old building?" Her mom let out a sigh.

"The building has a lot of character."

"What's left of it maybe," her mom said.

"It's what I could afford."

"You could've stayed here longer and saved up," her dad said. "There was no rush."

"No rush?" Feeling her temperature rise, Maddie focused on the rolling waves, letting the rhythm settle her mind. "I waited years for this move. I planned and prepared and saved up. I have insurance, and I can keep doing freelance work as long as it takes to finish the renovation. What I need most is for you both to stop acting like I'm one mishap away from moving back home."

There was silence, and she squeezed her eyes shut. She didn't want to sound ungrateful for their support, but she desperately wanted them to see she was capable and didn't need coddling.

"You're right, sweetie." Her mom's voice was quiet, but she didn't sound upset, just remorseful. "We're your parents, and we're always going to worry about you, but it's time we start trusting you to take care of yourself."

"We'll always want to keep you safe," her dad added. "But we don't want to keep you stuck. I promise you that we're thrilled to see you living the life you've dreamed of. It's hard to show we're here for you without making it sound like we expect you to come home, but believe me, I've got big plans for your old room."

She let out a laugh. "Oh yeah?"

"I'm talking movie projector, stadium chairs—"

"In your dreams, honey," her mom chimed in. "What about a Pilates studio?"

"You don't even do Pilates."

"I might start."

Maddie smiled as her parents bickered good-naturedly over the transformation of her room. She knew they'd probably always keep it open for her, but she also knew in her heart that they did believe in her. Just like her friends, new and old, and a certain contractor by day, artist by night.

She just hoped whatever Jake decided to do about his dad's unexpected arrival would bring him the same peace she'd found by sharing her feelings with her family.

Jake poured himself into work in the days after Chuck's arrival, which he was still processing. He'd wanted to do more with Maddie's reno, but things were at a standstill until the insurance appraisal was finished.

The guild meeting was coming up that weekend, and he really needed to put the finishing touches on the piece he'd kept hidden from Maddie. Hearing her plans for an accent wall had inspired him to create a mosaic just for her, and he wanted to keep it a surprise until it was unveiled at the festival. Time was running out to complete it, but he didn't want to go to his studio for fear of running into his dad.

The moments he'd spent with Maddie in the evenings had been his lifeline. They'd run into each other in the entryway of their home midweek, and she'd invited him for dinner. She had found out he'd never seen a cooking competition show and decided to introduce him to her favorite one, but they'd quickly lost interest in the show while cuddling on the couch. Their lingering kisses were interspersed with conversation, though both had avoided any mention of his dad. As midnight had approached, Jake had pulled himself away with a promise to bring her favorite croissants from the café in the morning.

Even though he longed to do more than kiss her, Jake didn't want to take things further until his mind was clear. He wanted to offer all of himself to Maddie, and right now, he felt torn and a little lost.

The morning of the meeting arrived, and Jake gave Maddie a ride to the hall an hour early to set up, then helped her carry in the food. Only then did he remember he'd promised to bring the patio table he'd made as a housewarming gift for Gloria's niece.

He felt bad leaving to go grab it, but she shooed him out of the meeting hall's kitchen, telling him there wasn't much left to do. As long as he hurried, he'd be back long before other people started showing up.

His nerves grew the closer he got to Andy and Carmen's house, but he told himself chances of seeing his dad—if Chuck was even still in town—were slim. In and out; he wouldn't linger.

But when he pulled into the driveway, seeing his dad's car parked between Andy's and Carmen's vehicles jostled something loose in his chest. He'd truly expected his dad to be gone already. Instead, here he was, right in the thick of things with the rest of Jake's family.

He cut the engine and climbed out, his steps turning toward the house instead of the studio. Dread mingled with anticipation in his stomach, making him queasy, but he didn't turn around. It was time to face his dad and the lost years he'd rather forget.

Jake knocked on the front door. His sister-in-law answered, wearing leggings and a long cardigan that draped around her pregnant belly, her wavy black hair in a loose bun. Carmen smiled when she saw him, then darted a look behind herself, toward the kitchen, where he heard the clatter of silverware and conversation.

"It's okay," Jake said. "I know he's here. I was hoping to talk to him."

She pulled her cardigan tighter against the chilly evening air. "Are you sure? I know you weren't expecting him. I keep telling Andy we should let you know when Chuck's planning a visit, but—"

"He tells you in advance?" Jake didn't mean to interrupt, but he was shocked by the news.

She looked puzzled. "Always has, ever since he got into therapy."

Therapy? Jake's confusion must've shown on his face, because Carmen pulled the door wider, beckoning him inside.

"Sounds like you really do need to talk. Why don't you help yourself to dinner? Andy and I can take Katie to grab pizza in town."

"I don't want to interrupt." He was actually glad for the excuse to leave. What had he been thinking? He should prepare for a conversation like this. "I can come back another time."

"You sure?" At his nod, she gave him a quick hug. "I hope you will. But no matter what you decide, we love you, Jake."

That nearly brought tears to his eyes. His emotions were all over the place, confronted by the reality of almost talking to his dad after years of avoidance. He took a deep breath, knowing he'd need a few minutes in the barn to collect himself.

But he'd barely made it inside his studio when he heard the screen door at the back of the house bang shut. Faulty hinges he kept meaning to fix. Right now he was thankful he hadn't because knowing someone was coming gave him a moment to compose himself.

A moment was all he had. A shadow fell across the open

barn door. Jake looked up, bracing himself to face the person he'd avoided for years.

Seeing his dad still came as a shock, especially when Chuck's heavily lined face broke out into a smile. He was wearing a button-down and slacks, his gray hair neatly combed. He took a step forward, then stopped. "Didn't expect to see you today."

"Didn't plan to come," Jake said honestly. "Don't skip dinner on my account."

Chuck sniffed. "Dinner can wait. I didn't want to miss this opportunity."

He sounded worried that Jake wouldn't come back, and he was probably right. Trying once had been hard enough.

"This is the first time I've been out here," his dad continued when Jake stayed quiet. "Didn't want to come uninvited." He looked around the barn. "These all your projects?"

"Works in progress." Jake was surprised his dad had respected his space by staying out. "But the wind chime is Katie's. Secret project for her mom."

Chuck smiled, the lines in his cheeks deepening, and Jake was struck by how much older he looked than the last time he spoke with him. How long had it been? Three years? Five?

"She brought it up to the house the other day to show me. Swore me to secrecy."

"Guess she must have a lot of faith in you," Jake said, failing to keep the edge from his tone.

Chuck sighed. "I've done my best to earn her trust, but haven't always done the same with you. I should've tried harder to make amends, but you told me you weren't interested in seeing me. I didn't want to disrupt your peace."

"You did apologize. So you can rest easy on that account."

His dad shook his head. "But I didn't make things right. Words are no good without action behind them." Exactly why the apology all those years ago had felt hollow. "For far too long, I was stuck in self-pity. Wanting your mother to take me back without any real change. Feeling abandoned."

"You're the one who abandoned us," Jake said.

"She told me to go," his dad countered. "But yes, I could've found another place in town and stayed in your and Andy's lives. Instead, I ran away. Didn't change my habits. Thought I could win back what I lost in the casinos if I kept playing." He leaned against the sliding door. "It's no excuse, but I struggle with compulsive gambling. You're actually the reason I started seeking help."

Jake's mouth fell open. "But we haven't talked in years."

"Your mom kept me updated. She told me how you'd fallen into self-destructive behavior, and I blamed myself. Instead of working to be a better dad, I let it fuel my negative impulses. But then, a few years later, I got word you'd turned things around. You found a steady job. You made amends. I thought, wow, my son, barely an adult, is making changes that I've failed to do for decades. That's the moment I realized I wasn't powerless like I'd let myself to believe."

His dad met his eyes. "I made an appointment with a therapist that day and went to my first compulsive gambling support group meeting that night. It hasn't been an easy road, and I've had some setbacks, but I haven't placed a single bet or set foot in a casino since before Katie was born."

Jake could hardly believe it. But he knew Andy and Carmen wouldn't let someone untrustworthy around their daughter. "If that's true, why not move back to Orchard Harbor?"

"My job has kept me on the road most of the year, but I'm ready to find something closer to home now. That's why I'm here, to look for work nearby. I've been saving up and started to settle my debts."

"When you decided to get help, why not tell me?"

"Because I'd hurt you enough. And there's always a possibility I may fall back into old habits. I'm doing my best to stay away from gambling with strategies and my support system, but it's important you know that this will always be something I struggle with. I violated your trust, and I didn't want to come to you until I felt I was strong enough to earn it back."

Jake swallowed, his throat thick with emotion. "But that's something you want? To earn my trust? To make a home here again?"

"Very much, son." Chuck sniffed, eyes shiny. "Not sure I'll ever be the father you deserve, which is why I decided to let you come to me when you were ready."

Was he ready? Jake wasn't sure. It was a lot to digest. "I appreciate you telling me," he said, the words feelings stiff and formal. He was afraid to say more for fear of breaking into tears.

His dad seemed to sense he needed space and moved toward the door. "Thank you for listening," his dad said, voice hitching. "I love you, Jake." He scrubbed a hand under his nose, blinking fast, then left Jake standing alone in his studio with more questions than answers.

He remembered the good times. How his dad had taught him to throw a football. How to test the ice on the pond for skating. How to use a level and hammer a nail. But he remembered how it had ended, too. With him hurting and his dad's promises broken.

He'd finally dug himself out of the mess he'd made after his dad left, and he was afraid of going back there. But for the first time, hope was tipping the balance away from fear and toward a reconciliation he hadn't dared dream of.

His phone buzzed, and he took it out of his pocket to see a text from Maddie asking if he was okay. The meeting was starting in a few minutes, and he'd totally lost track of time.

He'd wanted to be there to introduce her to everyone and make sure she felt comfortable. He knew she was more than capable of befriending strangers; she'd been doing it since she arrived. But he'd wanted to be there to show his support, and he'd blown it.

He loaded the end table into his truck bed as quickly and carefully as he could, then rushed to the guild meeting, hoping his lateness wouldn't make Maddie feel like she wasn't a priority. She was a bright spot in his life, and his feelings toward her were growing stronger by the day.

Chapter Sixteen

Members of the art guild had started to trickle into the meeting hall ten minutes ago, and while Maddie had put off conversation with a friendly wave before disappearing back into the kitchen to put the finishing touches on the food, the time had come to go out and mingle. Checking her phone, she felt a rush of relief from reading Jake's reply saying he'd lost track of time and was on his way. Since his dad was staying with Andy, she'd worried he'd gotten pulled into a confrontation, but hopefully all was well.

She picked up the last platter of food, an array of desserts, and carried it out into the main room. She'd brought an assortment of bite-size items from her future menu, a big bowl of spicy-sweet snack mix and a carafe of homemade lavender lemonade, inspired by the lavender-matcha latte from the café.

She set the tray of desserts on the table, and a woman nearby turned to her. "You must be the famous chef."

Maddie grinned. "How'd you guess?"

"Just a hunch," the woman said, smiling. "I would've come help, but I know what it's like when there's too many cooks in the kitchen. I banished my parents to the living room the first time I hosted Easter dinner and decided that would be our new tradition." Blue eyes sparkling with mischief, she held out a hand. "I'm Laurel, by the way."

Maddie shook it, grateful for Laurel's warm welcome.

Garrett walked over and eyed the assortment of food. "Thanks for making this happen on such short notice." He wore a graphic T-shirt like the first time she'd met him, his dark hair piled in a messy bun.

"It was my pleasure. I've been working on these recipes for months, so I'd love to have everyone's feedback on how they taste." Each platter was labeled, and she'd indicated which dishes contained common allergens. Cheese was featured in many of her menu items, but she'd also prepared a few vegan treats and hoped everyone could find something to enjoy. If not, she had vouchers ready to hand out for custom snack boxes.

A woman with beautiful gray hair cut in a chin-length bob started filling her plate with desserts. Maddie recognized her from the website as the president of the guild, Gloria Torres. "This is quite the treat," she said, helping herself to a strawberry-lemon eclair. "I always like to start with dessert."

"It's even more indulgent to bookend dessert. You could have some to start and end your meal," Maddie said.

Gloria's eyes lit up. "Now there's an idea. Jake has been telling us you're a food genius, and I never doubted it."

Maddie's cheeks warmed at the praise. "Thank you. To be honest, I've been so nervous to meet all of you, so when I found out it was only Jake who was upset about losing the gallery space, it was a huge relief."

Gloria set the down the tongs she'd been using. "Which gallery? My art is in several."

Maddie noticed a few people had started listening to their conversation, and her heart sank. "Not yours personally," she said. "I'm referring to the place Jake wanted to renovate for the guild. I thought you might all resent me for leasing it out from under you. Which would've been understandable," she added.

"Sorry, dear." Gloria's dark brown eyes were sympathetic behind her glasses. "I'm not following."

"The downtown gallery idea?" A bearded man seated at a nearby table spoke up. "Didn't we decide that was a waste of time?"

"Who told you about that?" The question came from a slender, balding man who held a plate piled high with snacks.

Uh-oh. Maddie was starting to wish she hadn't spoken up. Jake hadn't mentioned the plan was a secret. But how could it be? With everyone staring at her, she couldn't come up with any answer other than the truth. "Jake told me it was something he'd wanted to do for the guild."

A murmur went through the group.

"It sure was," said the man at the snack table.

"Jake came up with the idea of a gallery for guild members," Gloria said in a regretful tone. "It can be intimidating to approach galleries, and he wanted to provide a way for artists who were starting out to be able to showcase their work without pressure."

A cheerful-looking woman with short gray hair chimed in, "The profit from the pieces sold would've gone toward the rent."

But the guy near the snack table rolled his eyes. "Provided they sold at all. Orchard Harbor is a ghost town once the summer crowds leave."

"Not anymore," Gloria countered. "The fall festival has really grown in years past, and we're starting to see the same with the Orchard Blossom Fest."

"Still, November, December, and January… Where are the tourists then? Not here." He popped a piece of cheese in his mouth as if that settled things.

Next to her, Garrett murmured, "This is what happened each time Jake brought it up."

"You can see why we decided not to move forward with the gallery idea." Gloria raised her voice to be heard above the commotion. "It had its merits, but we couldn't reach a consensus."

"But Jake did place a bid." Maddie blinked, trying to make sense of it all.

"That's not true. Or at least it better not be," said the man at the table.

Maddie had a flashback to what Jake had told her about his father. Gambling. Borrowing money without repayment. People losing faith in him. Had Jake gambled the guild's funds and lost?

"Maddie?" A voice came from near the entrance. Even though she couldn't see the source because of all the people crowded around her, she'd know that voice anywhere.

Jake was here. And it turned out she wasn't the only one who had some explaining to do.

Jake had driven over as fast as he safely could, but the lot was full by the time he arrived, ten minutes after the meeting was set to start. He regretted not being there to make introductions and set Maddie at ease. But he felt she'd understand once he explained he'd gotten caught up talking with his dad.

He expected to walk into a room full of cheerful conversation. Meetings tended to start late because people got caught up chatting—good-natured gossip, mostly. He wasn't surprised to see Maddie at the center of the crowd. What he didn't expect was for all talk to cease the moment he walked in.

"Um, hi, everyone." He stopped at the threshold, the familiar sights of his friends' faces at odds with the suspicious glint in many of their eyes. Including Maddie's. That hit him the hardest. It was a look she hadn't used on him since their truce, and completely different than the sweet smile she'd given him after kissing him goodbye an hour ago.

What had happened? She looked like she'd discovered something unpleasant about him, the way a lot of people in town had looked at him after the truth came out about his dad. The kind of look that used to make him want to go ahead and sink down to the level the naysayers expected of him.

But that was before. He'd changed and grown, and he wouldn't let anyone's opinion of him hurt. Then again, Maddie wasn't just anyone.

The room was silent, but then Walter Hewitt spoke up. Of course it would be Walter. "This little lady—"

"Madelyn," she said, interrupting him, and Jake felt a surge of happiness at how quick she was to stand up for herself. "My name is Madelyn Briar."

"Ms. Briar," Walter said, and Maddie gave a curt nod. "She's under the impression that we'd planned to rent a building downtown for a gallery."

Oh no. His secret was out.

"Apparently," Walter went on, "you placed a bid on the building she's leasing. Which is odd, because we never voted to use our funds to bid in the first place."

Everyone's eyes were on him now, and all he could think of was his father, mortgaging their family's house to fund his gambling habit. But Jake had used his own money, not the guild's. Still, he'd been afraid to tell anyone about this plan, just like his dad had been too scared to approach him about the changes he'd made. Maybe they weren't so different after all.

"The offer was made with my own funds," he said. "I planned to renovate it myself, too."

Gloria cleared her throat. "So this was an act now, ask forgiveness later situation?"

He felt embarrassed under her glare but kept his head up.

"It was more about me having the time and means to remodel the building as proof that it would be a good option."

"It sounds to me like you were trying to go over our heads." Jen, a potter who'd been against the idea from the start, spoke up from the back. "To prove yourself right."

"I was, at first. But losing the bid made me realize that doing it on my own was the wrong plan."

Walter scoffed. "Even if you pulled it off and we agreed to the idea, you'd expect to be reimbursed, I'm guessing. With the money from our dues?"

Jake shook his head. "The only money the guild would pay would be toward rent if the majority voted to move forward with the idea, not a penny to me." Jake had raised his voice to make sure everyone could hear him.

"So why hide it?" The question came from Maddie, and his stomach dipped.

But he'd never lied to her and wouldn't start now. He'd own up to this mistake, just like all his others. "Once I realized I messed up, I was embarrassed to tell everyone. I figured no harm, no foul, but it really came down to protecting my image."

Gloria stepped forward, her expression a mix of concern and disappointment. "Why would you put that much of your own money on the line?"

He felt the weight of everyone's eyes on him. "I wanted people to see me as more than Chuck Winn's kid. It feels like they're always waiting for me to mess up again." And he had.

"I wanted to prove I had turned my life around. But I went about it the wrong way. You don't build community by going behind your friends' backs, even if it's with good intentions. I understand if you'd like me to resign from the board. And Maddie..." He gave her all his focus. "What I'm most sorry for is ever making you feel unwelcome. You belong here in

Orchard Harbor, and my life is so much better with you in it. I learned a long time ago that I can't go back and fix any of my mistakes, but if I could go back in time, I'd throw you a welcome party that first day instead of accusing you of stealing my spot. You're a light, and I'm sorry for how my impulsive decision affected you."

Everyone's heads swiveled toward Maddie, and shoot, he hadn't meant to force the attention back onto her.

But she didn't shrink away. If anything, she stood taller. "All I wanted since I've arrived was to be a part of this wonderful community." She met his eyes. The judgmental look was gone, replaced with something softer, more understanding. "It sounds like that's what Jake wanted, too." After the whole mess, she was defending him? "I hope you all enjoy the food. But since I'm not an official member, it's probably best I sit this meeting out."

Head held high, she walked through the crowd, right past him, and out the door.

Once again, he was the object of distrustful glares, but this time, he only had himself to blame. This time, he'd lost far more than the town's regard. He'd lost the trust of the woman he was falling in love with.

Chapter Seventeen

Jake had never felt more alone than when he stood in front of his fellow guild members—friends, neighbors and mentors—whom he'd let down.

Gloria was the first to speak up. "You put an offer on the space downtown, *after* you lost the vote?"

The idea got voted down by those who thought it would be too costly and time-consuming. When he'd seen a retail location go on the market for a steal of a price, he couldn't resist placing a bid of his own. When he didn't get the building, his instinct was to keep it quiet so it wouldn't be added to his list of mistakes.

But Maddie had helped him realize that even though he'd made a mistake, he *had* changed. He would never be perfect, but he wasn't the reckless, stubborn person he'd once been. He could admit to his mistakes, apologize and do better. He wanted to run after her and explain, but he had a feeling she'd understand he needed to stay and work things out here first.

Addressing Gloria's question, he said, "After the vote, a great property went on the market. I applied for a loan and placed my own offer. I knew it was a long shot, but given how poor shape the property was in, I thought I might have a chance."

Walter brandished a stalk of celery like a gavel. "What

would you have done with the property if we didn't decide to use it as a gallery after the renovation?"

"I would've sublet the building. Downtown spaces are never empty for long."

"Sometimes they are," Walter said, bringing to mind the former mini golf course that had sat unused for years before it was demolished for condos.

Honestly, Jake hadn't thought that far ahead, which made him feel even more foolish. "I didn't think it through. I wanted to help, and I was worried—" He stopped himself. Saying it aloud would be confessing his biggest fear, but he could do this. "I was worried people hadn't voted in favor of it because it was my idea. I thought you didn't trust me after what my father did."

"Your father?" This time it was Gloria who spoke. "What's he got to do with this?"

"My dad left a legacy of theft and broken trust. That's why I wanted to prove I care about people. That I'm not him."

"Well, that's obvious," Walter said, surprising Jake. "He would never have stood here facing the music like you are. He would've hightailed it out of here, then acted like nothing happened next time I saw him at the grocery store. No offense," he added, like he felt he might've crossed a line.

Laurel spoke up. "Why would you think you need to prove anything? Have people been talking?"

Gloria sighed. "Of course people have been talking. They always talk. The problem is, Jake's been listening to the wrong ones." She gave him one of her teacherly looks, the kind that was half sympathy and half frustration. "One of these days you're going to have to learn that some people are mean. Some people are rude, and some are just plain tactless. But their opinion of you doesn't hold water unless it's true."

A murmur of agreement came from the others.

"We didn't vote against you because we don't trust you," she said. "We needed time to draw up a budget, scout properties and clarify how it would operate. It wasn't a matter of you being wrong, it was about following a process to ensure success."

Jake felt himself shrinking under the weight of her words, but she was right. "I shouldn't have taken it so personally. It's just that when people talk, it's hard not to listen."

"Is it?" Gloria tilted her head. "Because it seems like you haven't had any trouble ignoring all the good things people say about you."

He thought about how Maddie told him she was proud to know him. About the clients who'd asked for him specifically. About all his friends and family who'd encouraged him throughout the years. Even his dad, who made a huge change in his life because of Jake's example. He'd tuned them all out, choosing instead to listen to the naysayers.

"We love you, Jake," Garrett called out, hands cupped around his mouth, and everyone laughed. "But why are you standing here talking to us when you should be catching up to Madelyn?"

Every time he thought today couldn't be more embarrassing, he reached a new low. "Don't worry, I will. But I didn't want to hide from my responsibility."

"That's exactly what we've come to expect from you," Laurel said. "Which is why you shouldn't be so hard on yourself."

"Wait, so the rumors about you and Maddie are true?" Jen leaned forward with interest.

He rubbed the back of his neck, wondering if he should've escaped when he had the chance. "Sort of."

"That's the real mistake," Bob, one of the guild's most senior members, said from his seat in the back. "I'll never understand your generation and making things complicated.

When I was young, if a man took a woman out, you were going steady. That simple."

"That why you've been married three times, Bob?" Laurel asked, brows raised.

He let out a harrumph and settled deeper into his chair.

Arnold, the guild secretary, said, "Go tell that woman we're glad she outbid you. Better yet, give her one of these." He pulled a membership application off the stack of printouts he always brought, even though there was an online form on their website. "Tell her the membership fee is waived the first year. Sounds like you put this poor woman through a lot over that darn building, and it's the least we can do."

From over by the snack table, their treasurer, Arnold's younger brother, spoke up. "You don't have that authority."

"I'll pay the fee myself, penny pincher," he shot back, and waved the application at Jake, who took it. Anything to get out of here faster.

He had a feeling making things right with Maddie might not be as easy as fixing things with his friends, but he had to try.

Maddie hadn't waited around to see if Jake would follow her. She wasn't ready to hear his explanation until she thought things through. They'd reached a place where they shared their secrets, but all along, he'd been keeping a huge one from his friends at the guild.

He hadn't wronged anyone, but going behind their backs didn't sit right with her. She needed space to process, and that meant finding clarity in the place she felt most at home: the kitchen.

She put on her monogrammed apron—a gift from her dad when she graduated culinary school—turned on the vent hood for white noise to drown out her thoughts and started chopping. She never liked to use earbuds while cooking because her ears were a helpful tool, alerting her to when the oil was sizzling or the pot boiling. The rhythm of the knife hitting the chopping block in steady strokes settled her mind.

She decided on a spring soup. Fresh peas and mint, accompanied by a hearty loaf of sourdough she'd made using the carefully tended starter she'd brought from home. A fruit salad to remind her of the sweetness of life, even when moments like this left a bitter taste in her mouth. Jake hadn't lied to her, but he'd hidden his actions from some of his closest friends. Even with good motives, his omission of the truth made her wonder what else he'd be comfortable hiding.

She wanted to believe she'd never trust the wrong person again. But now she wondered if she'd gone and done exactly that.

Tears welled, but she blamed them on the onions. She scrubbed the well-oiled cutting board until the sting went away, wiped her face and got on with it. Shelling peas came next, then she added them to the simmering broth.

Once the peas were cooked, she used her immersion blender to puree the soup to silky smoothness. The loaf she'd set to rise last night was in the oven, emitting a warm yeasty smell, and the fruit salad was chilling in the fridge, when someone knocked at the door.

She hadn't texted Celeste and Tasha yet to invite them over, but maybe they'd been drawn by some sort of best friend telepathy. Or more likely, the Orchard Harbor gossip mill was going in full force. She swung the door open without thinking.

Not her friends. Jake.

Eyes wide, she shut the door on reflex. A moment later, her phone rang with a call from him. She answered and said, "You don't owe me an explanation, Jake."

"It's not an explanation, it's a realization." That caught her attention, and she leaned her forehead against the door, listening intently.

"I came to tell you that I realized I was trying win over the group by proving how far I'd come, but really, I was stuck in the past." His voice was husky with emotion. "I couldn't let go of the version of me I was back then, and as a result, I thought everyone else saw me that way, too."

"I didn't," she said.

"I know." His sigh was audible through the sturdy door. "That's what kills me. You saw the good I'd done and believed I'd changed. Then I went and showed you I'm still very capable of screwing things up."

"I'm not upset about that," she said into the phone. "It's that you hid it. Going behind your friends' backs to prove yourself right makes me wonder what else you'd be willing to cover up. And I know it might not be fair, but it's really hard for me to trust people after what happened to me."

"I get it," he said. "I thought I could never speak to my father again after what he did. But I talked to him today."

Her mouth fell open. "When?"

"That's why I was late. I'd planned to avoid the house and just pick up the table from my studio but…" He cleared his throat. "It felt like time."

She wanted to open the door and pull him into a hug, but she needed to keep a clear head. "And was it?"

"Past time," he said. "Turns out he's in recovery for compulsive gambling. He's been paying his debts and wants to move back to Orchard Harbor. Carmen and Andy trust him to be around Katie, and that says more than words ever could."

"Oh, Jake," she said. "That's huge. But do you trust him?"

He gave a small laugh. "That's the thing. I walked away from our conversation wondering how I could. Thinking he could never change was keeping me from believing I'd changed."

Was that what she was doing? Holding herself back because she thought she was the same person who'd been easily taken advantage of?

"But he has," Jake said. "And I have, too. Doesn't mean I have to forget what he did, but it's my choice to see him as he is now or hold tight to how I remember him."

The door squeaked on its hinges, as if he, too, was leaning against it, and she rested her palm on the smooth surface, craving the comfort of his touch. "I saw renovating that property for my friends as my ticket back into the town's good graces. And then I got outbid, and I was mad at whoever stole that chance from me."

He paused, and she heard a shuffle. Imagined his forehead tipped against the door, hand pressed to the frame, as close as he could get. "But then I found out that person was you. The gorgeous, smart, inspiring woman I'd had an instant connection with, and my emotions went haywire. By the time we were finally on good terms again, I was already halfway in love with you."

Maddie's heart leaped. Had he said love?

"By then I was even more scared, not of failing my friends, but of failing you. I wanted to be the man you seemed certain I was. Someone who didn't come up with reckless, half-baked ideas. But everyone makes mistakes. The difference is what comes next. So I came to tell you my mistakes aren't just in the past… There will be more in the future. And if that's not something you can sign on for, I understand. But I don't want my biggest mistake to be not telling you how I feel."

She couldn't let him say any more. Not when she'd made up her mind. She ended the call and pulled open the door.

Jake was standing on the other side of it in his rumpled denim jacket, wavy hair falling over his forehead.

"I know your heart was in the right place, but what I need most in a partner right now is honesty. I want to believe you'd never lie to me, but I'm not sure anymore. I just don't trust you, and I wish I did because…" She stopped herself. She wouldn't say she loved him. Not when she was saying goodbye. "I think it's best we don't see each other anymore outside work."

"Mads," he said, but she shook her head.

"I can't, I'm sorry."

She couldn't bring herself to close the door until he'd turned away. She wanted desperately to run upstairs after him and tell him she'd changed her mind, but she'd promised herself she'd never again give her trust to someone who might break it. She needed to protect her heart.

Chapter Eighteen

Jake missed Maddie fiercely. But he was committed to respecting her boundaries and keeping his distance. He valued honesty, too, and he'd promised it to Maddie. He couldn't fix their relationship, but there was one relationship that might be able to be salvaged.

The next day, he texted his brother to see if they could talk, and Andy told him to meet him at the winery. The tasting room wouldn't open for another hour, but his brother opened the door when he walked up, latching it behind them.

He was holding a clipboard and had a pencil behind his ear, probably for taking inventory on the sales racks. "Guessing you're here to talk about Dad."

"Did he tell you about our chat?"

"Only that you had one." Finding out that his dad hadn't shared their private talk was another sign that he might be someone Jake could learn to trust again. "I can't wrap my head around all the changes he's made."

"It's been hard not to tell you." Andy set down his clipboard and leaned against the gleaming bar. "But that's what he wanted."

"I called Mom on the drive over, and she told me the same thing. At first, I wanted to be mad at all of you for not saying something, but you were respecting my wishes. I shouldn't have been so stubborn. I've needed so many second chances, and I refused to give him one."

"There's still time."

Jake leaned on one of the empty barstools. "I'm going to talk to him. It won't be easy, but if he's following through, I want to give him a chance. Part of forgiving him was forgiving myself. I thought I'd come a long way, but the guild found out about my failed gallery bid. Talking through the situation with them made me realize I have work to do on accepting my past."

"You messed up, no denying that. But your heart was in the right place. I know it must've been hard to stand in front of your friends and tell the truth, but you did. I'm proud of the man you've become, Jake."

He let the words sink in, grateful even though his heart ached. "I know my friends will forgive me, but I've lost my chance with Maddie."

"Don't say that. I'm sure she'll understand."

"That's the thing. She does understand, but I lost her trust. There's no winning it back. She wants nothing to do with me."

His brother squeezed his shoulder. "In that case, I'd offer you a glass of wine, but I know that's not your drink of choice. Sit down, and I'll see what ale we have behind the bar."

Jake shook his head. "Thanks, but I'm headed to the studio. I'm finishing up my entry for the festival, and I want to show Dad some of my pieces." Maddie probably wouldn't appreciate the gift now, but he wanted to finish nonetheless.

His brother's face lit up. "Yeah?"

Jake nodded. Art had healed him in the past. Sharing it with his dad might help build a bridge between them, even if it didn't help him get over his feelings for Maddie. He was pretty sure nothing would.

Maddie's friends had shown up the next afternoon when she'd ignored one too many texts. She didn't have the energy to cook, but the stress-induced meal she'd made yesterday made good leftovers, and she heated it up while she explained everything that had happened.

"This looks like spring in a bowl," Celeste said when Maddie served them the mint pea soup.

Tasha took a hesitant slurp, but immediately went back for a bigger spoonful. "Okay, this is seriously delicious. That crème fraîche takes it over the top."

"Amazing," Celeste agreed. "You spoil us."

"Yeah, you're the one who's hurting. We should be spoiling you with ice cream and good wine."

"Maybe later," Maddie said. Comforting as that sounded, right now her stomach was too tense to eat. "I don't have an appetite."

Tasha speared a section of orange from the fruit salad. "I understand why his friends are upset, but he told you it was just him who bid, so why are you?"

"Isn't it obvious?" Celeste said. "If he hid things from the guild, what's to stop him from hiding things from Maddie?"

"But he didn't hide *things*," Tasha said. "He hid one thing. A very big, potentially embarrassing thing. Doesn't that count for something?"

"I'm not saying it's not understandable." Maddie stirred her untouched soup. "But I need someone I can count on. I don't want him to feel bad for his decision or the motivation behind it. But I have the right to set boundaries for the type of relationship I want, and that includes openness and honesty."

Celeste pointed her fork at Maddie. "Yes, you do."

Tasha held up her hands. "Absolutely. I'm just bummed for y'all. I had such high hopes." She sounded truly regretful, and Maddie appreciated that she'd come around to her dating Jake. Too late, though. "What are you going to do now?"

"I can't imagine running into him at this point. Any chance you're open to a roomie?"

Tasha made a face. “You’re always welcome, but that’s not exactly a long-term solution.”

“Just kidding. But I don’t know what I’ll do when I see him again. He pretty much told me he loved me.”

Tasha’s spoon hit her empty bowl with a clatter. “And you let him walk away?”

“Tasha,” Celeste scolded.

“Sorry. But the man confessed love. That’s new information.”

“The worst part is, I was starting to feel the same way.”

Celeste rubbed her arm. “I know I warned you to be careful, but I’ve seen the two of you. That kind of connection is real. Are you sure you can’t make it work?”

“It’s not him I don’t trust as much as my own judgment,” Maddie said. “What if I’m just blinded by how I feel for him?”

“I think that’s called love,” Tasha said, but Maddie shook her head.

“I want to have my eyes open when I fall in love. To know exactly what I’m getting into and who I’m falling in love with. And after what happened, I’m not one hundred percent sure about Jake.” Tears threatened to break out, and she sniffed.

“I hope this isn’t another instance of you playing things too safe,” Tasha said. “But I trust your judgment, and I’m proud of you for setting boundaries.”

Both her friends came over and wrapped her in a hug. After a few minutes, Tasha pulled away and looked at the meal. “Girl, this soup is not bad for being healthy, but couldn’t you bake a breakup dessert like a normal person?”

“I’ll get right on that.” Maddie smiled through her tears. Things weren’t meant to be with Jake, but she was here with her best friends, making a fresh start. That would have to be enough.

Later that night while she was eating the pint of ice cream

her friends had insisted was better fuel for a breakup and crying through episodes of her favorite cooking show, a piece of paper slipped under the door.

She picked it up and unfolded it to see an application for the Orchard Harbor Art Guild. Scrawled at the top in pencil, she read:

> The guild wanted me to pass this along. You can fill it out online, but Arnold insists on printing some out for each meeting. They want you to know your dues are waived because of what I put you through with the bidding argument.
>
> I know we don't have a future together, but you have a future here. This town will be your home, just like it has been for me, and you are going to shine.
>
> —Jake

She swallowed hard, but the emotion welled up anyway. Tears ran down her cheeks and dropped off her chin, hitting the paper. She wiped it, but the ink smudged. Darn it. At least he'd said there was an online application. The thought made her grin, in spite of the tears. It was exactly the kind of comment Jake would've made.

Maybe in the future they could be friends, but right now, her heart was broken.

Jake tried to keep his mind off losing Maddie by putting in extra hours to finish the showcase project on time. After the fire damage was cleared, the flooring had arrived while the electrical was being updated, and now the project was proceeding with only the usual minor hiccups. He'd focused the rest of his attention on making time to reconnect with his dad. Today he'd met his brother, niece and father at the beach.

"Where's your friend?" Katie took a messy bite of the ice cream cone her grandpa had bought her in celebration of the first truly hot day of the year. "I liked her."

"Maddie?"

Katie nodded, blue moon ice cream dripping down her chin.

"I haven't seen her in a while."

"Why not?"

"I'm not sure we're friends anymore." True, and all a child needed to know of the situation, but his brother was watching him with a look that said that wouldn't be enough to satisfy his curiosity.

When Katie ran ahead to search for stones along the shore with her grandpa, Andy said, "Still no word from Maddie?"

"She made it clear she's not going to forgive me, and I'm not going to pester her."

Andy bent to pick up a flat rock "Okay, but all you've done is apologize."

"And?" He resettled his hat against the wind.

His brother leveled a look. "You haven't done anything to show her how much she means to you."

"I told her how I felt." He remembered how much it hurt to say the words through a door. To not be able to see her face or hold her. He'd put it all on the line, and it wasn't enough.

"Words are cheap." With the flip of his wrist, Andy sent the stone sailing toward the water.

Jake watched the rock skip along the flat surface of the lake before sinking. "What can I do, though? She doesn't want to see me."

"I dunno, that's on you. But if you want her to see how you feel, you can't just tell her, not after how you lowered the value of your word. You have to show her. Then maybe she'll listen." Andy checked his phone. "Shoot, I've got to get to work. Dad's watching Katie, so if you don't want to stay—"

"I'll stay," Jake said.

Happiness shone on his face. "Things are going well?"

With his dad, yes. With Maddie? Never worse.

As his brother headed back toward town, Jake made his way along the shore toward where Chuck was showing Katie how to skip rocks. He thought about what Andy had told him. How could he show her how he felt when she didn't want to see him? He'd never go against her wishes and seek her out.

An idea started to form. What had she said she wanted more than a renovated shop? A welcome party.

Well, he'd give her both.

Chapter Nineteen

Maddie had been receiving updates from Jake about the renovation, and she couldn't believe how well things were progressing, despite the delays. She'd walked through the empty space with Terrence and settled on a layout, and while she hadn't been able to afford all the high-end appliances she'd wanted, she had been able to get new windows and tile. Maybe with the savings on utilities, she could upgrade down the line.

Over a month had passed and today was the final walk-through. She braced herself to see Jake again for the first time since the disastrous guild meeting. She'd run into him in the hallway a few times and caught sight of him around town. But he never tried to talk to her, just gave her a polite smile in passing. It tore her heart out, but she kept telling herself it was for the best. Letting someone untrustworthy into her life would only be a recipe for disappointment.

Today would be a good test run to see if she could be around Jake without crumbling, because their paths were bound to cross again in the future. She only had to keep it together for an hour, tops.

She'd tried to park out front, but the street was full. Warmer weather had brought an influx of tourists on the weekends, but that didn't explain why they were all in front of her shop. She circled the block and finally parallel parked a few streets away. Hurrying so she wouldn't be late, Maddie rushed into the back door and was met with a loud cheer.

"Surprise!" A sea of friendly faces greeted her. She recognized Crystal and Britta, Shreya and even the grumpy barista; her best friends; Garrett, Laurel, Gloria; and at least another dozen people from the art guild, all cheering and clapping. Above the front windows hung a banner that read Welcome to Orchard Harbor, Maddie.

Before she could take it all in, Maddie was swallowed up in hugs and well-wishes. A few minutes later, Celeste and Tasha made their way over, beaming.

"What going on?" Maddie said under her breath, overwhelmed in the best way.

"Can't you tell?" Tasha swept out her arms. "It's a welcome home party."

"But the shop isn't even open for business."

"It's not a grand opening," Celeste said. "We can help you plan one of those, but this is a welcome home party."

A welcome home party. Silly as it was, she'd wanted one. When she'd tried to move out the first time, she'd had her identity stolen and stayed put for years. This was her first chance at making a home of her own, and she was thrilled to celebrate it. "Thank you both, so much," she said, beaming.

"This wasn't us." Tasha glanced at Celeste, who nodded. "We're just guests."

"Then who arranged it?"

"The only person in town who isn't here," Tasha said with a mischievous glint in her eyes.

Maddie glanced around. Her shop wouldn't fit everyone in town, not even close. But she did recognize dozens of residents, from the firefighters to the owner of Wright Construction. She even caught sight of Jake's brother, Andy, and his family. But wait… Jake. The one person she'd expected to meet up with today wasn't here.

"Jake did this?"

Her friends nodded.

Not sure what to think, Maddie said, "You knew and didn't tell me?"

Celeste shook her head. "We only got the invitation this morning, and he wanted it to be a surprise."

"And you listened to him?"

"You wouldn't have come if we told you who was behind it, but he told us he wouldn't even be here," Tasha said, linking her arm through Maddie's. "Regardless of who did it, this is an amazing celebration for someone we care about very much. We thought you deserved to enjoy it."

"Why would he do this?"

"Didn't you tell us he loved you?"

"Well, yeah. Right before I told him it was over." The memory still ached.

"And he's stayed away. But feelings don't just disappear overnight."

She knew that from personal experience. She'd lain awake for weeks on end, listening to his footsteps above her and balling her fists in the sheets against the urge to go talk to him. "Where is he, then?"

"Don't know," Tasha said. "But Orchard Harbor isn't exactly a big place. You know where he lives, after all."

She did, all too well. She was aware of his comings and goings. Knew when he was using the hot water to wash dishes from the way the pipes rattled. Heard the muffled sound of lyrics from his speakers. Knowing he was so close but out of reach had been awful.

"You know, I've been thinking," Celeste said, sharing a

conspiratorial look with Tasha. "Didn't you keep something from us recently?"

Maddie thought back. "I don't think so, why?"

"I'm pretty sure she did. For a few weeks," Tasha told Celeste, like Maddie hadn't answered. "Something potentially embarrassing."

"Oh yeah, that's right," Celeste said. "She failed to mention that she'd kissed the man she kept asking for advice about."

"But we didn't hold it against her." Tasha's eyes glimmered with mischief.

Celeste shook her head. "Nope. Because she's an amazing person, and she was just trying to save face."

Maddie narrowed her eyes, catching on. "I know what you're doing."

"What?" Her friends spoke in unison.

"Keeping the kiss a secret isn't the same. It didn't affect anyone but me."

"Not quite true," Celeste said. "It could've had a huge impact on the people Jake worked with, if your rivalry would've pushed you to find another contractor."

She'd never thought about it that way. "Why didn't you try to point that out before?"

Tasha threaded her arm through Maddie's. "For one thing, we thought Jake had given up too easily. But a grand gesture shows commitment."

Celeste took a bite of one of the croissants Jake had ordered for the party. "Also, we wanted to give you time to see the parallel for yourself."

"Well, next time, feel free to not withhold information." Maddie tried to sound stern, but she couldn't quite hold in a smile. She might have a future with Jake after all.

"Do you think you could give him another chance?" Tasha was watching her closely.

Could she? Yes, he'd hidden his plans from the guild, but that was because he'd been embarrassed about a good deed he hadn't thought through. Plus he'd done all this for her, even after she'd turned him down.

"I've been longing to let him into my life again," she confessed. "I just wasn't sure it was the right choice. But I realize now there's no guarantee I won't be hurt again. What matters is I open myself to people who care about me and want what's best for me." She looked around at the room full of people he'd invited to welcome her home. "And I think it's pretty clear Jake Winn is one of them."

So while everyone was busy enjoying pastries from the Harbor Bridge Café and soup and sandwiches from the Gull and Loon, she sneaked out the back door into the warm afternoon air. She'd had plenty of practice leaving parties early. In fact, she was kind of an expert at it. Celeste and Tasha would run interference, and no one would be the wiser for her absence until she slipped back inside.

She encountered her first problem when she got to her car. She'd left her keys in her purse in the kitchen. If she went back in, she'd risk getting pulled into another conversation, and she couldn't bear to wait a second longer.

One positive thing to be said for surprise parties: she wasn't dressed up. She glanced down at her sneakers and jeans. Better than a skirt and heels. She decided to put her years spent on the cross-country team to good use and run to the house. But she'd only gone a few blocks when a car did a U-turn and pulled up to the curb beside her.

"Miss Briar, are you running away from your own party?"

She slowed to a stop and looked over to find none other than Miss Geraldine in the passenger seat, her window rolled down. Leaning over, she saw a man with short locs in the seat beside her. "I don't think you've met my grandson. Wade, this is Madelyn."

He gave her a nod. "Sorry to bother you, but my grandmother was worried when she saw you running."

Maddie was breathing hard, her hands on her hips. "It's fine. I was just, uh—" She tried to concoct an excuse, but none came to mind. Then she realized Miss Geraldine's version of the truth would do just fine. "Jake and I broke up, and he thinks I don't want him at the party, but I do."

"You were going to run all the way back to the house?'

"It's not that far."

"It's far enough," the older woman said. "Wade, get the door."

"Ma'am?"

"We're going to take her there. Can't let the guest of honor stay away longer than necessary. Hop in," she told Maddie.

Knowing there'd be no point in arguing, she climbed in just as the rumble of a diesel engine cut through the air and a fire truck pulled to a stop across the street.

Anton leaned out of the driver's side window. "Heard you might be in need of an escort,"

"Oh, and who told you that?" His sister, no doubt.

He just grinned and turned on the lights. "Hurry up, your guests are already asking where you went."

They were? She was either losing her edge or people cared about her more than she realized. And she had Jake to thank for it.

Wade pulled out into traffic, following the fire truck. The old Maddie would've felt mortified to accept a ride from Miss Geraldine on a mission to find the man she loved, but as she watched the flashing lights of the fire truck, all she felt was giddy. Filled with excitement and joy and hope that she had a future here. Might have a future with Jake.

Either way, she was going to tell him how she felt, just in case the emergency vehicle escort didn't show him.

They reached her apartment in probably the same amount of time it would've taken to run there, given all the delays, but the ride saved her from arriving a sweaty mess. Not that she thought sweat would deter him, but if she was going to admit that she'd been the one to make a mistake this time, at least she could do it without raccoon eyes and sweated-out curls.

The fire engine crunched to a halt, and Miss Geraldine's grandson pulled to a stop behind it. Maddie leaned forward between the seats. "Thank you, Wade, Miss Geraldine. You're sweet to do this, but why don't you head back to the party? Don't want the food to get cold, and Jake can give me a ride back."

She didn't mention the other possibility: that he would turn her down. In that case, a walk of shame back to the party would be preferable to confessing the bad news to a waiting Miss Geraldine and her grandson.

"You sure?"

Maddie nodded. "Thank you, though. Truly." She squeezed the older woman's small shoulder, and Miss Geraldine patted her hand.

"All right then. Get out there, we'll see you back at the party."

Maddie took a deep breath and stepped out onto the sidewalk. She waved at Anton in the truck, hoping he'd take the hint and follow them back to the party. He waved back cheerily, looking like he was enjoying the diversion and in no hurry to leave, so she unlocked the door and stepped inside.

It was quiet, no hammering or telltale whir of a drill. Jake's boss and coworkers were at the party, so she couldn't imagine him being at work. She took the stairs two at a time and knocked on his door before thinking through what she might say. All she knew was that she wanted to see him.

When he didn't answer, she tried again, even though her heart was sinking. There was the possibility that he was there and ignoring the knock, but that didn't sound like the Jake she'd come to know. He was impulsive and tenderhearted and quick to jump to conclusions, but he'd arranged the party. He wouldn't keep her waiting.

A thought occurred to her, and she thundered back downstairs to see if she could catch Wade before he drove away, but she discovered the fire truck had turned around and was idling by the curb, with Francisco in the passenger seat. She hadn't realized he was there, too. He smiled kindly from the open passenger window. "Not there?"

She shook her head. "No, but I have an idea where he might be."

"His studio?" Anton asked, leaning forward.

"Maybe. But I want to try somewhere else first. Any chance civilians can ride in those?"

Anton flashed a wide smile, a match for his sister's. "I thought you'd never ask."

Maddie hurried over. How was this her life? A few months ago, she'd never even jaywalked, and now she was about to ride in a fire engine to go tell a man she'd met only a couple months ago that she was in love with him?

Yeah, she was.

She realized that she didn't know the first thing about how to get into a fire truck, but luckily, Francisco hopped out and opened the door for her. He gestured her to take the front seat, but she balked. "I don't want to take your spot."

"Nonsense. I insist. It's quite the experience to ride up front." She was about to protest again, but he said, "You need to give Anton directions, right?"

"Right." She accepted his hand and clambered into the truck, grateful once again for her jeans and sneakers. Once she'd settled in and buckled her seat belt, she pointed toward the vast expanse of Lake Michigan, visible through the rows of buildings in town. "Head toward the lake on Dune Trail. I don't have an address, but I'll know the cross street when I see it."

"Yes, ma'am," Anton said, clearly enjoying himself.

Maddie's heart sped up as he accelerated onto the road. The wind rushed in through the open windows, kicking her curls up into a tangled frenzy, but she smiled in exhilaration. She hadn't had this much fun in years, and in a roundabout way, she had Jake to thank for it. She definitely had him to thank for the party, and she would, very soon, from the way Anton was driving.

The fire truck careened around corners, then slowed as it entered the residential streets of vacation houses on the road leading toward the lake. She spotted a familiar cottage built out of large stones. "This is the road—turn right."

"You're the boss," Anton said.

From the back, Francisco piped up, "Hey, I'm the still the chief."

Maddie cringed. She'd forgotten he was here. She turned in her seat to apologize, but found him grinning.

"Most fun I've had in this truck ever. I love the job, but we're usually racing toward tragedy, not reunions."

"It might be a tragedy yet."

He waved a hand. "Nah. That kid threw a party for you and invited the whole town."

"Everyone but himself."

"Maybe he wasn't sure he'd be welcome."

She remembered the echo of Jake's words through her door. The confession of love she'd left unanswered. Jake didn't think he was welcome, that was certain. But what if the party was just his way of making things up to her? He might've stayed away because he was merely paying a debt and wasn't interested in being with her again.

"This is so rash," she groaned, looking at the bright green buds on the trees they passed. "What have I done?"

"This new for you?" Anton asked.

"Um, riding in a fire truck to tell a man I'm in love with him? Definitely."

"Glad to be your first," he said.

"None of that, young man," Francisco grumbled. "Apologize to the lady."

"No worries," Maddie said, chuckling. "I'm used to this kid."

"Kid? I'm twenty-five."

"And you'll always be Tasha's baby brother to me." He scowled, looking so much like the teenage version of himself that she'd first met that she laughed. "Thank you for this, Anton. Seriously. I owe you. First y'all save my shop from burning down, now this."

"Always happy to do our best for Orchard Harbor residents. All part of the—"

Maddie pointed out the window. "Stop, that's it!" The cottage was partially hidden by a front hedge, but she saw Jake's truck parked in the driveway and knew they'd found the right place.

Anton frowned at the ramshackle cottage. "How'd you know he'd be here?"

"Just a hunch. You can let me out here. I don't think you'd make it out of the driveway."

"Want us to wait?"

She shook her head. Walk of shame or no, she'd asked enough of them. "Whatever happens, I'll deal with the fallout myself."

"Good luck," Francisco said from the back, his voice an encouraging rumble.

She hopped out of the truck and jogged up the driveway. She lifted the worn knocker and let it fall, a timid knock to match her bubbling nerves. No answer, so she tried again, more decisive this time. Nothing.

She turned around and called, "You can go, I'm sure he's here somewhere."

"We're not leaving you stranded," Anton said.

A moment later, Francisco leaned out the door with a megaphone. He turned it on, and at the resounding screech, Maddie covered her ears. "Jacob Winn," Francisco said into the speaker.

"What are you doing?" Maddie called.

He lowered the bullhorn. "Helping. It's what we do in Orchard Harbor."

"You use fire department property to summon civilians?"

"If the occasion arises."

From the window above him, Anton grinned. "Let the old man have his fun."

Francisco turned the megaphone toward Anton. "Look who's volunteered to wash the engine when we get back."

"Aw, c'mon. I was just teasing."

Grinning, Francisco said into the mic, "What's that? I couldn't hear ya. Want to give it a go?" He hoisted up the bullhorn, then yanked it back when Anton reached for it. "Ha. Nice try, youngster."

Maddie watched all this play out with the growing sense that this was her life now. Whether or not things worked out with Jake, she'd be happy here. Happy in her new home, with the support of the community she'd made her own.

The fire chief raised the bullhorn to his mouth again, but the bewildered voice she heard came from behind her. "What's going on out here?'

Jake. She spun around, taking in the sight of him in a blue

flannel shirt, sawdust covering his chest and shoulders. Ear protectors were around his neck, and he wore a look of puzzlement, then he caught sight of the truck and his eyes went wide. "Is the house on fire?" He grabbed her hand and tugged her away from the door, craning his neck to check the structure.

"Nothing's on fire," she said, squeezing his hand. "They just gave me a ride."

"A ride? Are you hurt?" His perusal switched from the house to her face before drifting down the length of her body.

She stepped closer. "I'm good. Safe. I just needed to see you, and I was kind of in a hurry, so..."

He looked back at the fire truck, understanding finally dawning on his face. "You left the party."

She smiled. "I did."

"You didn't like it." He sounded resigned, and she rushed to assure him.

"No, I did."

"But you're here."

"You weren't there."

His brows pulled together. "You left because of me?"

She seemed to have lost the ability to form coherent sentences. "I was *there* because of you. Because you invited an entire townful of people to a welcome home party for me."

"Not the whole town," Jake protested. "Just the kind, uplifting people."

"About that..." She trailed off, looking into his eyes. "You missed one of the good ones."

"Who?"

"Yourself."

His throat bobbed in a swallow. "You said you didn't want to see me."

"The truth is, I wanted to see you so badly that I didn't trust the urge. I thought it would make me do something I'd regret.

But the only regret I have is not letting you in that night and telling you how I really felt."

"How exactly do you feel?" His eyes held a glimmer of hope, and she was done making him wait.

"I want to be with you, Jake. We haven't known each other very long, but I've never felt the way I do when I'm with you. You make me feisty and bold and ready to embrace whatever life throws at me. I risked the embarrassment of explaining to half the town that I put it all on the line for love just to get to you, and I'd do it again in a heartbeat because I don't want to celebrate without you. You bring the kind of joy I never knew I was missing. You're kind and loyal and generous. And I'm falling in love with you."

In answer, he bent down and kissed her. His lips were sweet and soft, and she caught a fistful of his shirt for support, the buttons digging into her palm as she tugged him closer. He slanted his mouth, deepening the kiss, and she arched up, letting her love for him consume her.

Kissing Jake was the purest pleasure, pushing aside all her doubts and worries. This was even better than the new life she'd dreamed of. This was love unlike any she'd ever known. Unexpected and overwhelming and perfectly off course.

She lost all sense of time in kissing him, forgetting about the party guests or that they might have an audience. When they broke apart, long moments later, her senses came rushing back and she looked over her shoulder, but the fire truck was gone. Anton had given them privacy, after all.

Her phone dinged with a message.

Tasha: Where are you? Did you find Jake?

She'd found him all right. And she didn't plan on losing him again.

Epilogue

Maddie walked hand in hand with Jake through the newly renovated tasting room. She'd decided against a wooden accent wall because Jake had gifted her with something far better—a huge mosaic wave created from beach glass, pieces of plates and teacups, antique silverware, and stones he'd picked up along the shore.

The present had been a huge surprise, even more so when she found out this was what had been hidden under the sheet in his studio on the night of his dad's unexpected arrival. But this was the kind of secret she didn't mind. In fact, she was starting to learn that she really enjoyed the good kind of surprises, maybe because she'd spent so long being worried that bad news was around the corner.

The design was a permanent reminder of the step she'd taken into love and trust. How she could be flexible and strong, like the waves that buffeted the shore.

The wall was empty for now because the mosaic was in the tent reserved for showcase entries along with pieces from the other guild members. Jake had already received several offers, despite the placard stating it wasn't for sale. He told everyone who was interested that they should come to the grand opening of Maddie's shop the next weekend if they wanted to see it again.

Maddie looked around the tasting room. "I can't believe all this is mine."

"You deserve every bit of it." Jake squeezed her shoulder. "I'm just glad you didn't let that grumpy contractor chase you off."

"Nah. I hear he's really a sweetheart, once you get to know him." She stood on tiptoes and patted his cheek.

"Oh yeah?" He bent his head for a kiss.

"Yeah," she said against his lips, then wrapped her arms around his neck, deciding some things were better than arguing. His kisses, for one.

All too soon, he pulled away. "I'll let you get to work." He kissed her temple. "Sure you don't need any extra hands in the kitchen?"

"No offense, but I think your hands will be better put to use setting up tables and tents."

"Is that a dig on my cooking skills?" he asked in mock-offense.

"What cooking skills?" She grinned. "Now shoo before I get too distracted and miss the oven timer." Still, she gave him one more lingering kiss, then watched him walk out the door, taking a piece of her heart with him.

How she'd fallen for a man she'd known such a short while would forever be a mystery, but she was done second-guessing love.

Pulling her mind from Jake, she got to work on picnic orders. She'd opened up for online business once the kitchen was finished, and next week she would officially open the tasting room for walk-ins. But for now she was getting the hang of things without the surprise of day-of orders.

She carefully packaged the items and placed everything, including flameless candles and locally sourced flowers, into the baskets. Since she was just starting out, she included a handwritten note. Someday she'd be too busy—she hoped—to personally write each one, but now she had time and it brought her joy.

Soon all the baskets had been picked up, and she switched gears to prep for the Orchard Blossom Fest. The guild was counting on her, and she intended to wow them. She'd hired Britta to be her assistant for the weekend, knowing she'd need help to feed the size of crowd they were expecting.

The Harbor Bridge Café would have a booth at the event, too. Elise had finally found full-time help—Chuck. Jake's dad didn't have experience in food service, but he was eager to find a steady job in town. He'd even started to get involved in the baking process, which meant they'd be serving their signature pastries at the festival. Several other local restaurants would be in attendance, including the pizza parlor, which was using the photos Maddie had styled on its mobile menu board.

Jake's relationship with his dad had continued to improve, and family dinners at Andy's house had become a weekly occurrence. Carmen and Maddie had become good friends, and she was teaching Katie how to make simple recipes. She missed her parents, but was excited to introduce them to all the amazing people she'd met when they came for the grand opening.

Once prep was finished, there was nothing left to do until the festival tomorrow. Maddie locked up the shop and walked the few blocks to the house. The lights in Jake's apartment were on, so she hurried to get cleaned up. She took off the scarf she'd worn over her hair and fluffed her curls, then changed into a tank top and linen shorts.

She went upstairs and knocked on Jake's door. When he stepped out onto the landing, she took in the sight of him wearing a short-sleeve button-down with jeans and canvas slip-ons. "You're all dressed up. Maybe I should change."

“You look gorgeous,” he said. “But you might want to grab a sweater in case the weather turns.”

“Where are we headed?”

“It’s a surprise,” he said.

“Not to you, hopefully,” she teased.

He pulled her in for a kiss. “Sassy.”

“You can never be too careful.” She grabbed her cardigan from the coat rack.

“You mean *you* can never be too careful,” he said, opening the front door for her. “Me? I like living on the edge.”

“That’s why you have me around. To keep you grounded.”

“Oh, is that why?”

“Mmm-hmm.” She felt his arms come around her waist.

Nuzzling her neck, he asked, “And why do you keep me around?”

“To keep things interesting, of course,” she said, melting at his touch. “That, and you’re handy with a drill.”

“A drill, huh?”

She rolled her eyes and linked her fingers through his, tugging him down the front steps. Anyone might walk by and see them, laughing together, hand in hand, and maybe they’d wonder how a newcomer fell head over heels for the first man she met in town.

But when they arrived at the beach, and Jake led her to a picnic blanket laid out in the sand among the dunes, under a sky rosy with the setting sun, she knew following her heart was the right choice.

* * * * *